THE KINSMEN
BOOK 4
THE EDGE OF
REALITY

Pete Cruickshank

First published in the UK in 2021 by Pete
Cruickshank

ISBN 978-0-9927964-6-4

British Library Cataloguing in Publication Data.
A catalogue record for this book is available from
the British Library.

www.thekinsmen.co.uk

DEDICATION

For Heather
You can be whatever you want

CONTENTS

ACKNOWLEDGMENTS

I would like to thank
Steff Madawi, my first port of call for editing.
Steph Dagg, my main editor.
My wife Catherine for the final proofread.

PREFACE

A cast of characters can be found at the back of the book.

This is the final book in The Kinsmen series, which consists of 'The Kinsmen Prelude: Between Gods and Mortals', 'The Kinsmen: The Infinite Darkness', and 'The Kinsmen: Fall of Heaven'.

My primary reason for writing this story was because the idea of The Kinsmen, the concept of who and what they are, has been with me now since I was fifteen years old. By the time I was in my thirties, the evolution of that idea needed an outlet. I am now in my forties at the time of writing this and the sun is setting on this part of my life. In the beginning, I realised that my first novel was a more of a prelude, set apart from the others and that while writing the third book in the series, 'Fall of Heaven', it became apparent that the perfect number of books to tell this story would be four. Yet four is such an odd number (a contradiction in terms, I realise) when science-fiction and fantasy quite often give us serials in trilogies. It now seems obvious that the way to present The Kinsmen series is as a prelude and then a trilogy.

I always try and present my books in a manner I would like to read them. If a book involves many characters then include a cast of characters. If it involves a great many locales, include a map. And why not? Not all readers can keep track of all these things, even if the author can. As soon as it becomes hard work for the reader then the author isn't doing their job.

Another problem that may arise when reading a series of novels such as these is the time interval between reading each one. If you simply read one after another, the story is fresh in your mind. However, if this is not the case, a reader can forget who did what, where and when. Readers have often said to me that they have to go back to a previous novel to remind themselves of what happened. So why not make it easy for the reader and supply them with 'the story so far'? The main purpose of these reading aids is to provide options. If you don't require them, skip them, and jump straight in. However, we shouldn't take such things away from those who may welcome or need them.

With this in mind, here is a quick recap.

The Kinsmen Prelude: Between Gods and Mortals

The story of The Kinsmen begins with a man called Jonas, born in Syria in the year 327BC. Jonas meets a woman called Garianne who asks him to help the Galacien, a conglomerate of alien worlds, to fight against the Nacuerian invasion of the galaxy. Jonas is what the Galacien refer to as a super-sentient: a person with incredible abilities. Jonas has many, but most prominent is his ability to learn and evolve at an augmented rate. With Garianne's comrades, Min and Davern, the four leave Earth for Galacien Prime, the centre of this galactic civilisation.

Jonas learns a great many things while onboard the sentient starship known as Lom. He is also able to deduce that the Nacuerians intend to hit Galacien Prime much sooner than anyone anticipated. In the Amelerian system there is a confrontation with the Nacuerians. Jonas allows himself to be captured in an attempt to learn more about the Nacuerians and to find a way to defeat them.

Whilst onboard one of their vessels, he encounters an entity in one of their computer systems. The entity identifies itself as The Kinsmen, and Jonas believes that only their great power can save the rest of the galaxy from the Nacuerians. Jonas tells the others that the living machine race known as the Phalinon may possess knowledge of The Kinsmen. They travel to one of the Phalinon's archives yet are betrayed when Jonas attempts to interface with their system. The Phalinon are in league with the Nacuerians, believing that, in return for their help, they will be spared the impending galactic genocide. With help from Garianne, Jonas breaks through his mental limitations and is able to save Lom and his comrades, destroying the archive and enabling their escape.

Jonas then travels to Galacien Prime in his ethereal form, or what super-sentients call the metaphysical self, to warn Garianne's trusted friend, Nemulous, of the Phalinon traitors, and that they will be fighting a battle from outside and within. Lom enters the Galacien solar system with the invading Nacuerian armada not far behind. Garianne and Jonas are able to utilise a device that can disrupt all Phalinon in the Galacien system, yet it is only temporary, and it is not long until chaos ensues with the Galacien fighting their once-trusted allies. Lom is disabled and his crew are teleported to the surface of the old Galacien homeworld. Jonas looks up into the night sky to see the stars blotted out by the vast number of Nacuerian vessels in the Galacien system. Garianne tells him he is all that stands between the Nacuerians and the death of all sentient life in the galaxy.

Jonas pushes far beyond his limits once more and destroys the Phalinon. He then confronts the Nacuerians, discovering the terrible truth: the Nacuerians were once the most peaceful and noble race he could imagine. They were changed into destructive creatures by a mysterious god-like entity known as The Adversary. The Nacuerians are on the verge of destroying everyone in the Galacien system. Having no time to undo what has been done, Jonas has no choice but to destroy them.

Praised as the saviour of the galaxy, Jonas is granted his wish to be left alone. He is given an entire planet of his own, Terra, of which he is the only inhabitant. Before Garianne and Min depart, leaving him to his life of solitude, Jonas confronts Garianne. He has deduced that each of the crises that he overcame was of her design. Min is outraged by such a statement, yet Garianne admits it is true; she always knew there was no way to stop the Nacuerians unless Jonas was pushed beyond what was deemed acceptable by the Galacien. Garianne orchestrated events, where Jonas would have to evolve and save them. Min leaves in disgust. However, Jonas knows that even though it is his name the universe shouts in gratitude, it should truly be Garianne's. Jonas knows that The Adversary will come, and he decides to devote his long life to trying to figure out a way to stop it.

The Kinsmen Book 1: The Infinite Darkness

Over two thousand years later, Lytpniuph and his crew travel to Terra to contact Jonas. Lytpniuph tells Jonas that the Galacien require his presence on Galacien Prime: an asteroid the Galacien have dubbed Sol 9173 is on a collision course with Earth obliterating all life on the planet. This is humanity's test. If they work together, they will be deemed a mature species by the Galacien and will warrant their help. However, the Galacien don't believe this will happen and must allow the asteroid to proceed. They want Jonas' assurance that he will not interfere. Jonas tries to convince them that he won't, but the Galacien can't be sure of his intentions and attempt to subdue him. After a short battle, Jonas escapes.

On Earth, Alicia Elde, a new and unknown super-sentient, travels in her metaphysical form to observe Alex Lethbridge. Alex is a student at university. It is late and the campus is all but deserted. Alex is somehow able to sense invisible beings who appear to be intent on doing him harm. After a short confrontation where Alex exhibits other unnatural abilities, such as teleportation and the projection of force-fields, he is saved by a man called James.

James tells Alex that all his questions will be answered if he goes to meet Garianne the next day at the Galacien Institute for Technological Advancement. Alex does so and is told that GITA is a front for the Galacien Observation Agency for Earth, that they have been watching every inch of Earth for thousands of years and that Alex is super-sentient. They also tell Alex of the impending arrival of Sol 9173.

Alicia believed she was invisible in her metaphysical form whilst she accompanied Alex's visit to GITA. However, the mysterious woman called Garianne looks straight at her. Anxious, Alicia leaves her home. On a secluded street, she is confronted by Garianne, who tells her she may have more potential than any other super-sentient who ever lived. However, she must remain hidden from friend and foe alike, for, if they fail, then at least Alicia will remain and perhaps stand a chance of finding a way to defeat The Adversary. Garianne tells Alicia she must lose herself in the multiverse where no-one can find her.

Min and her partner Kallon are attacked in their home on Galacien Prime by Galacien citizens possessed by The Adversary. Jonas is able to rescue them both and explains who the Nacuerians were and that The Adversary is already here, subverting those around them to do its bidding. Jonas still believes that The Kinsmen may be able to help them. He has discovered an ancient artefact built by the super-sentients of the past called the Entrophier. It is located in the distant galaxy of Antlia Dwarf. The Entrophier allows the user to view the past. Although almost prevented by a fleet of attacking Galacien vessels, Jonas is able to use a new starship engine, which he invented, to make the first intergalactic jump.

Jonas confesses to Min that Kallon is, in fact, a copy of Jonas himself, downloaded into another body. It was his way of making sure she was safe. Min is horrified and Kallon is upset that he may have to give up the life he is accustomed to.

Whilst searching for the Entrophier on the dead planet of Tren-dos, they discover a great number of Nacuerians in hibernation. The proximity of other life-forms wakes them from their slumber. Jonas convinces Min and Kallon that he must try and save the Nacuerians this time. Kallon understands what this means to Jonas, for they were once the same being, and in the end, Jonas is able to transform the Nacuerians back to their original forms.

Back on Earth, Alex tells his sister Theresa about his abilities, and after demonstrating them to her, he adds that he may not see her for a little while. He explains that he has 'business' to attend to and that if she meets a man named Nemulous then she must trust him implicitly.

Later that night Alex falls asleep and abruptly awakes to find himself on an alternative Earth. This Earth is reminiscent of Victorian England, where an attack from Mars is threatening the human race's existence. Queen Marina and young Princess Victoria ask for Alex's help. Ruth, Alex's implant, is able to help him realise that time on this Earth runs significantly slower than back on his Earth. Alex decides to help the people of this Earth and in a matter of months, their time, Alex and Ruth are able to put an end to the Martian invasion.

Garianne appears before Alex as a quasi-sentient hologram, explaining that, back home, the Galacien are coming for him and that it was she who was able to manipulate his powers and teleport him to another universe. Alex agrees to Garianne's proposition: to help other Earths in dire need, while the current crisis on his Earth passes.

Back in Alex's home universe the Galacien are indeed coming. General Krrikant and his crew are under the influence of The Adversary. The only crew member untouched is James' wife, Korina. After a visit by General Krrikant, she too is possessed by the enemy.

Jonas is able to use the Entrophier to observe what happened over two thousand years ago when he spoke to The Kinsmen. He is then able to detect a trail that leaves his universe for another. Jonas needs a multiversal teleporter to continue his quest.

Nicola is a mercenary with unmatched skills. Her mission is to retrieve Alek, an alternate version of Alex Lethbridge. Before completing her mission, she is teleported away by another Alex and Garianne. Later, Garianne makes Nicola an offer she can't refuse — to act as her bodyguard for a substantial reward.

It is not long until General Krrikant arrives, demanding Garianne hand over the super-sentient Alex. Krrikant is dismissive that Alek is not of their universe and attempts to abduct him. There is a short conflict between Alek, Nicola and Kirkland's forces, from which Krrikant emerges victorious. However, Alex, Ruth and a great number of Alexes from other universes, which Garianne has been gathering to form an army of super-sentients, arrive. Krrikant threatens to destroy the Earth but Jonas arrives and nullifies his threat, sending him on his way.

Garianne gathers all the alternate versions of Alex together to inform them of the threat The Adversary poses to all their native universes, and that it is in their best interests to work together. Jonas will search for the elusive Kinsmen, while Garianne tries to discover a possible strategy for them to finally defeat their enemy.

Later that night, James and Korina share a rare, private moment, away from the prying eyes of the Galacien's Earth observation network, Unfortunately, Korina infects James and now he too is a puppet of The Adversary.

The Kinsmen Book 2: Fall of Heaven

Alex and Ruth return to Earth 3 many years after The Martian War which ravaged their world. They meet with Queen Marina and Princess Victoria, who is no longer a child, but the same age as Alex. Soon after their formal meeting, the princess secretly confesses her affections to Alex. However, the queen steps in, making all parties aware of the difficulties of any kind of relationship since Alex does not age and that he must return to his own Earth at some point. The relative time differences means Victoria will die of old age within weeks of his arrival back home.

While Alex sleeps he dreams. Alicia is training him to develop his abilities. Yet when he wakes he remembers none of this.

On Earth 142, Jonas, General Alexander, Al, Min and Kallon follow the trail of The Kinsmen. While they are there, they discover a woman called Vasha, who turns out to be a super-sentient from their own universe. She was born on Earth many thousands of years ago during the Galacien golden age and trained by the Galacien. Vasha has the ability to control matter and energy. She joins their party hoping to return home. She also queries why Jonas has not evolved as much as those who came before him, over the last two millennia.

On Galacien Prime, Garianne, James, Korina, Nicola and Alek Lethbridge interrupt a council meeting with Captain Dermarlaine. She discusses with them the two recent attempts to abduct super-sentients from Earth. The council claim ignorance. Garianne is convinced there is more going on here than appears but decides to find out for herself. She visits the Galacien memory archives and discovers that all of Galacien society's memory stores have been corrupted. As a result, all Galacien citizens are now mortal.

Dermarlaine is ordered, by the council, to go to the planet Terra and discover its secrets. With her will be another Alex counterpart called Al-X who hails from a universe where it is hundreds of years in the future.

Jonas and company travel to another Earth where they encounter a Jonas counterpart. He is far more powerful than Jonas. He seeks a confrontation with The Adversary. The resulting battle makes Earth's sun go supernovae. Fortunately, they are able to teleport away from this universe moments before Earth is destroyed.

Alex's sister, Theresa, tells him that president Nemulous Handerrel, the president of Lorusia and agent of the Galacien, has given her an implant as well as enhancing her mind and body. She now works for him.

Dermarlaine, Al-X and also the Amelerian, Lytpniuph arrive at Terra. Al-X is able to destroy a key component of the machine that generates the cloaking field around Terra. He and his team then teleport to the surface. They enter Jonas' small, primitive home. Al-X discovers Jonas' account of the Nacuerian/Galacien war, and also a mysterious door which defies his senses. The door opens and pulls him and his troops inside.

Al-X wakes later in darkness and meets the real Jonas. He is the original Jonas, and he created the Jonas who searches for The Kinsmen to act as a decoy while he could find a way to stop The Adversary, unobserved. Meanwhile, in orbit above Terra, hundreds of Nagoad and Fenrari warships emerge from hyperspace. As with all enlightened spacefaring species they are at peace with the rest of the Galacien Conglomerate of worlds yet seem ready to battle for Terra's secrets. Dermarlaine's first officer reveals that he is an agent of Garianne's and that this turn of events is only a distraction; other fleets have been drawn away from Galacien Prime, which is soon to be invaded. Alex and Ruth, speak to Garianne about recent events when Alex suddenly teleports the three of them to the other side of the multiverse, a place where technology doesn't work and a super-sentient's ability is greatly diminished. Alex has also been corrupted by The Adversary and has taken them to a dangerous world where death is almost certain.

Elsewhere Alexander and Al also reveal that they've been corrupted by The Adversary. Jonas and Vasha try to stop them and fail. Even a sliver of The Adversary's power is more than a match for them. Alexander teleports to Earth 3 and kick-starts a second Martian invasion. Al tells Jonas he is to continue his search for The Kinsmen. The Adversary is also interested in finding out who, or what, they are.

Back on Earth Nicola is attacked by Alek, James and Korina. They have also been corrupted by The Adversary. Despite a confrontation against some meta-humans and a multiversal teleporter, she emerges victorious. The Adversary releases James and Korina from its influence and Nicola, begrudgingly, lets them live. They are aware of a planned attack on the Galacien system. They teleport onto the starship Lom and set a course.

In universe 148, the trail of The Kinsmen leads to a mysterious artefact. Within its interior, they discover a perfect simulation of the multiverse, apparently created by The Kinsmen. Min irritates Al, who in turn murders Kallon. Al then continues to follow the trail of The Kinsmen alone.

In the Galacien system, Lytpniuph's first officer, now captain, Chnar, investigates a disturbance in space. James, Korina and Nicola arrive on the starship Lom, warning him of an impending attack. A massive wormhole opens and hundreds of Nacuerian ships come pouring through from the far-off Antilia Dwarf Galaxy.

Jonas follows The Kinsmen trail. He ponders over recent events and deduces that he has not fulfilled his potential, that someone has restricted his abilities. The real Jonas appears before him explaining that he is a mere copy. A decoy for The Adversary. Unfortunately, he is aware of his true origins. The real Jonas must allow the illusion to continue and so, once again, wipes Jonas' memories and sends him on his way.

The Galacien system is under attack from thousands of Nacuerian ships. Dermarlaine's fleet and many others join the fray. However, they are outnumbered. Vasha and Min appear on Galacien Prime. They then teleport on-board Lom. Vasha is able to use the wormhole to demonstrate a level of power unseen before, as she destroys the wormhole and the majority of Galacien vessels. In the aftermath, it is made known that individuals are being controlled by The Adversary at the highest level of Galacien society It is impossible to know who to trust. They have no option but to flee.

Jonas and Al, who is corrupted by The Adversary, reach the end of the trail. They arrive in a pocket universe. Artificially created. The Kinsmen make themselves known; giant figures hidden in darkness. The Adversary battles them and wins. Jonas escapes during the confrontation, hoping The Adversary will believe he was destroyed by the incredible forces unleashed. Returning to Terra, Jonas remembers The Kinsmen telling him to observe. He saw The Adversary stumble. Jonas realizes The Adversary isn't omnipotent. There is hope for defeating it. Jonas leaves, and the real Jonas appears, satisfied that his doppelganger is proving most useful.

At the cost of her own life, Garianne is able to find a way for Alex, who is no longer corrupted by The Adversary, and Ruth to return home. Alex senses Sol 9173 minutes away from impacting Earth. He attempts to teleport the entire asteroid, but just when he's about to achieve his goal, he is knocked unconscious. Sol 9173 impacts Earth. Nothing survives. Alex is left unconscious in space, where he is picked up by Jonas.

In an unknown universe, Alicia and the real Jonas discuss how The Kinsmen were a creation of Alicia to stop The Adversary and anyone else searching for the real Kinsmen. Alicia refuses to tell Jonas who or what The Kinsmen are. They both know that it won't be long until The Adversary realises what's happening, then it will be coming for them. For all of them.

There are many universes
Some are almost identical to your own
Others are completely different

For the most part, they exist as self-contained islands
Never affecting one another
Or aware of each other's existence

Universes are born and die every day, yet the multiverse
continues
However, at some point throughout all of eternity,
Even the multiverse must face a threat

1. FAILURE

If you think you have taken the measure of a Kinsmen, then you are probably wrong.

Principles of The Kinsmen

The Nexus of the multiverse

Jonas, the real Jonas, looked upon a sight not seen by any other sentient, save one. The Nexus of the multiverse. It was a place awash with light, which pulsed out from a singularity. A place so bright, yet it did not blind him or cause him any harm, for he was Jonas and had evolved into a creature of pure energy, only becoming physical when necessary. He felt as if this were his natural habitat, bathing in the tides of energy, the waves of hyperspace and superspace. Under any normal circumstances, he would feel at peace, yet he was not the only one who resided here. There was another.

From a great distance, he sensed the one they called The Adversary on the periphery of the actual singularity. Impossibly unmoved by the incredible forces battering against it.

What was it doing here?

He knew he was taking an awful risk being here, yet he felt events of utmost significance must be taking place.

It was worth such a risk, he told himself.

His luck had held. When entering this realm, he found no elaborate traps or triggers to warn The Adversary of his presence and, for now, its focus was entirely on the singularity itself. But for what reason?

He dare not actively scan the singularity in case The Adversary was to notice. He could only wait in the shadows, as it were, and watch, hoping that any obvious changes in the singularity were possible for him to observe from here, and from that somehow deduce what was happening.

Jonas did not have to wait long.

He was glad when The Adversary finally left the nexus, teleporting to who knows where. He could now actively scan the singularity of the multiverse. What he discovered shocked him to the core.

He instantly teleported.

A fraction of a second later and he would have been killed.

Terra

Jonas appeared in his home, on the planet Terra. Back now in his physical form, he gripped onto the ancient, gnarled wooden mantelpiece. The fire danced shadows across his horrified face. *We must do what we have always done,* he heard Lom's all-too-familiar voice in his head. They had been merged such a long time ago, him and what once had been the sentient starship, that he saw it as just another aspect of himself. *Stay the course, as we have always done, do not despair.*

"I will not," he said out loud. "Yet it has been so long since I've felt afraid, confident that it was only for lesser beings, that I was unprepared for it to come snapping once more at my heels. It is alright. I am recovered and am my old self. My resolve is stronger than ever and I am ready to continue the work."

It is understandable. The revelation — the end of everything — is a shocking one, said Lom.

"I do not understand why The Adversary has done such a

thing. The multiverse is its playground. Why would it destroy it?"

Perhaps it has grown bored with life and seeks to end its existence; it would be in keeping with what we know of it. It merely wants to take the rest of us with it, said Lom.

"I'm not sure we can rely on anything it has said in the past. We have only just discovered it is not truly omnipotent," said Jonas.

Just extraordinarily powerful.

"Yes," said Jonas, knowing that this piece of information came as small comfort, for The Adversary still possessed the ability to somehow significantly disrupt the multiversal singularity thus creating a unique effect across all of reality. The laws of physics would break apart in each universe; matter and energy would crumble.

Quite literally reading Jonas' mind, Lom said, *What exactly is going to happen?*

"It is difficult to say. This scenario, which is now a reality, has never been considered before. I must converse with Alicia once more. She must know. This changes everything," said Jonas.

It was then that he sensed something fundamentally disturbing, a deep foreboding. The room seemed to become darker.

Jonas turned away from the fire, only to come face to face with himself.

It was obvious who this counterpart was. Quelling any panic that threatened to rise to the surface, he reached out and within, using his extraordinary senses. He was being prevented from teleporting. A frontal assault would be useless. From what he knew of The Adversary's encounter with The Kinsmen, he stood little to no chance of surviving a confrontation with what stood before him, despite his considerable might. For this was no possessed lackey of The Adversary, bestowed with a fraction of its power. It was The Adversary itself. For some reason, it had taken his form.

"I, too, would like to converse with this Alicia," said The Adversary in a voice as smooth as silk, and disarmingly calm. It was difficult to believe that this 'person' could destroy the multiverse. "I have a feeling she is the one who has been causing me a few problems of late."

Jonas had anticipated this eventuality. The formidable planetary defences were supposed to self-destruct the planet, destroying him along with it, before The Adversary could glean any information from him. He did not want to die, but it was the only option. The Adversary had interfered with this process, leaving Jonas with only a few options, all which required him to play for time.

"Problems?" said Jonas.

"Yes, I believe that it is she who has been gathering information, looking for a kink in my armour," he said, smiling with amusement, "setting up scenarios across the multiverse in a vain hope of discovering some way to put an end to my existence. For a time, I thought these events were natural. However, it soon became apparent that someone was working behind the scenes, attempting to create something that would stand a chance against me."

"To no avail, it seems," said Jonas.

"Not even close. I admire her, nonetheless. I have never come across a more resourceful being," said The Adversary.

"Hmm. I am curious," said Jonas. "Your speech and mannerisms are very human. Quite different from the entity my counterpart encountered in the void between this galaxy and the Antlia Dwarf galaxy."

"True. It has been some time since I adopted a physical form. So long that it feels quite alien, but I am adapting. It will make for a more enriched experience of what is to come," replied The Adversary with ominous emphasis.

Jonas said nothing.

With what seemed like genuine sadness, The Adversary continued, "I am sorry Jonas because, for you, this is the end. It was a good life. Better than most."

The fire in the room began to wane, the light flickering and fading.

"You should not have come looking for me. Your curiosity,

which has served you so well in the past, has proved your undoing. How ironic. Your part has been of utmost entertainment," The Adversary said.

Jonas' mind raced. His power and ability far exceeded that of his younger counterpart. The one he had created. Yet it was nothing compared to that of The Adversary. He felt The Adversary upon him, like a giant hand holding a tiny doll, and, like the doll, he was unable to move, physically or in his metaphysical form. He saw no way to win and no way to escape. Not even a way to die and deny The Adversary access to his memories. Nevertheless, he continued to try.

"I have already taken your memories," The Adversary informed him.

"Why?"

"They may prove useful. But that's not what you meant, was it? You meant the destruction of the multiverse. You ask why?" said The Adversary, pausing and making a show of thinking. "Because I can. Because I want to. Because I am tired of you lesser beings and your reality. The null wave I have initiated is spreading from the singularity and has already extinguished those universes closest to it. It will spread. Soon it will reach this far out, and then further until it reaches those first universes birthed so long ago, now out there on the outer edges of the multiverse. Then it will be all over. I will move on to pastures new. There is next to nothing here now to hold my curiosity anymore. Except for those two little mysteries I've been keeping back, just to keep things interesting."

"And what might those be?"

"I want to see for myself what kind of super-sentient this Alicia Elde is, and what exactly Nicola is."

Jonas looked confused at this last part.

"Nicola? What is so special about her?" asked Jonas.

"She's an anomaly. I want to know why," said The Adversary.

Jonas had a strange smile on his face, a mix of satisfaction and deep sadness. His last thought before the planet Terra exploded was of Min and what could have been.

Where once the planet Terra had been, now only The Adversary remained. It reflected on the memories it had cleansed from this real Jonas, especially his last one.

Jonas had spent a lot of his time further out from this universe where time moved much slower, elevating his being. He had evolved far beyond any other super-sentient in history, except, perhaps, for this Alicia, always searching for a way to end The Adversary's existence. Secretly collaborating with Garianne and then Alicia. Now his time was at an end.

As all things must end.

The Adversary's thoughts turned to Alicia and Nicola. But first, there were other loose ends to attend to.

2. THE SECOND MARTIAN WAR

It is inconceivable to believe that those who have not lived for thousands of years can become Kinsmen. However, this is not to say lesser beings cannot practice the basic principles. For these are, in their own way, the greatest of rewards for any sentient. The fulfilment of which is far beyond the pursuit of fame, wealth, power or even love.

Principles of The Kinsmen

Windsor Castle, London, Earth 3
Queen Victoria pushed the curtain aside and peered out of her bedroom window into the darkness outside. Far in the distance, she could see a faint orange glow on the horizon, the only indication that her city, the City of London, was on fire. Again, she felt that blow to the pit of her stomach. She couldn't imagine the horror and chaos happening there at this moment. She'd had no choice but to flee, she told herself. The attack had been so sudden. Far quicker than the Martians' first invasion when she was a little girl. That was thirty years ago now, and she was no longer a little girl, yet recent events made her feel like one.

There was a soft knock at the door. "Yes?" she said.

"It's Captain Trent, Your Majesty," came a voice from the other side.

"Enter," instructed Victoria, her gaze never leaving the view in the distance.

She heard him open and close the door behind him. "Your Majesty, perhaps you should close the curtain. It may be unwise for you to be so exposed."

She did not move. "Do you think the Martians know or care who I am, Captain?"

The Captain thought for a moment. "If they do you are in great danger, no doubt. If not, then you are still in danger."

"They are here to eradicate us all." She was surprised at how calmly she said it.

"I know," he replied, looking down at the rug.

She finally pulled the curtain closed and turned to him. "I'm sorry."

"For what, Your Majesty?" he asked, not meeting her eyes.

"This must be hard for you and your men. Facing such an enemy as this. An enemy we cannot hope to defeat," she said, smiling.

"I…" he stammered, looking uncertain.

"It is alright, I am not losing hold of my sanity. If this is indeed to be the end, if we are to fall in this, our final hour, then we won't go down without a fight, will we Captain?" said the Queen.

Captain Trent visibly straightened; his eyes blazed proudly. "Certainly not, your Majesty."

Victoria swallowed hard. Walking to the mirror, she looked herself over in the standard military uniform she now wore. "What do you think?"

Trent approached her. "May I?" he said, raising his hands.

"You may," she acquiesced.

He made adjustments, pulling at the collar, cuffs and the back and front of the tunic. "Perfect," he stated.

She inclined her head in gratitude.

"Shall we?" he said.

They both left the bedroom. The two guards, who had been standing outside the door, fell in behind them as they continued down the corridor, down the stairs and into what had been one of the dining rooms but now a briefing room. The large table in the centre of the room was covered with maps and documents. Several military personnel and a few of the Queen's staff occupied the room.

"Gentlemen. Ladies" said Victoria in greeting as she strode into the room and up to the table.

Captain Trent stood beside her and spoke. "Communications are breaking down throughout the country, throughout the world, although we are still receiving infrequent telegrams. The Martians are hitting every significant populated area. Multiple sightings of the standard war machines we encountered during the first invasion. Also, sightings of air support and… troops."

There were whispers and gasps around the table.

"What do they look like?" asked one of the soldiers curiously.

"Small. About the size of a ten-year-old child. Quick. Wearing a sort of flexible armour. They carry some kind of lethal energy weapon. They kill on sight. That's all we know."

A silence descended upon the room.

Victoria's jaw was set so firm it made her teeth hurt. "We all know what they are. It is time for us to show them, and each other, what we are. Will we cower in the night like frightened beasts, or stand and fight?" she said, her voice rising and falling. One moment it fell almost to a whisper, the next it felt like the force of a thousand cannons. "This may be our final fight," she went on, looking around at them, "but I know which way I would choose. And be under no illusion it is a choice. I know you are afraid. I am afraid. But I refuse," and she hammered her fist onto the table, "to give in to despair, even though I may die." They all looked at her rather stunned, yet she saw in them, to varying degrees, a flicker of pride amongst themselves and defiance for the enemy.

"We're with you, Your Majesty, until the end," said Captain Trent.

"Until the end," she heard another soldier say.

Then it came again and again until it was a chorus around the table.

She reached out and uncharacteristically patted Captain Trent on the shoulder. "Thank you, John," she said.

He nodded, and she noticed the poor man was struggling to hold back the tears in his eyes, for she had uncharacteristically called him by his first name.

They then heard a distant rumble. A moment later a soldier ran into the briefing room with a stricken look on his face.

"Our spotters report three Martian war machines heading this way," he cried.

They all paused for a beat.

"I'll take the Queen to the underground tunnel," Captain Trent told the others.

"We'll cover your escape," said one of the soldiers.

Captain Trent gave him a curt nod. They could see in one another's eyes what this meant. Anyone who stayed was certain to die. However, the more who tried to escape the longer it would take, and the more likely it was that they would be caught in the attempt.

"Majesty, this way quickly," the Captain said, striding from the briefing room.

He signalled for the two guards to accompany them. They moved quickly from one room to another, hearing more noises from outside.

The Captain took them into a room full of weapons.

"Grab what you need, and be quick about it," he instructed the two soldiers.

They efficiently went about arming themselves. After hooking some grenades to his belt, Captain Trent picked up a rather large Vickers machine gun and handed the stand for one of the soldiers to carry.

"Won't that slow us down?" asked Victoria.

"If it hampers our progress too much we can drop it, yet we may find we need it," he replied.

They continued through the castle, the sound of its cannons reverberating throughout the structure. The Martian's energy weapons were relatively silent in comparison, but they could hear the destruction, nonetheless.

Down a corridor, they caught a view out of the window, of a

Martian war machine. Some small shapes dropped gracefully from it to the ground. From a low crouch, they rose and began a quick lope towards the castle.

Victoria gasped in horror. She was barely aware that Captain Trent was dragging her down the corridor, where they turned right into a small, abandoned room. One of the soldiers locked the door as the other helped Captain Trent manipulate a complex mechanism which moved what appeared to be a false wall.

Captain Trent took an oil lamp hanging on the wall, lit it and led them down the dark steps into the tunnel.

Victoria felt marginally safer as every minute passed, taking them further away from the castle and the battle.

"Where does this lead?" she asked.

"To an alehouse cellar about half a mile away, Your Majesty," said Captain Trent.

"A drink now would calm the nerves, don't you think, Captain?" said Victoria.

The two soldiers looked at one another.

"Normally, I would agree" said Captain Trent. "Yet under these circumstances, perhaps not."

She looked at him and laughed. "Captain, I was making a joke."

"Oh, of course," he said. Despite feeling foolish, he could not help but smile.

There was a distant explosion which echoed down the tunnel. They all stopped in their tracks and looked back, their smiles changing to looks of shock.

"That was in the tunnel," said Captain Trent. "Let's move."

They all broke into a run, desperate to reach the end.

"What happens when we reach the alehouse?" said Victoria, not wanting to consider the 'if' they reached the alehouse.

"There is a carriage waiting to take us to a safe house in the country," replied the Captain.

And then what? thought Victoria.

There were unmistakable scurrying noises coming from behind.

"They're coming!" cried one of the soldiers who was struggling with the machine gun stand, trying to keep the panic from his voice. Victoria could not blame him: her heart felt like it was going to burst out of her chest, her own panic threatening to overwhelm her. As they continued down the tunnel the unmistakable sound of their alien pursuers grew closer.

"We're not going to make it," uttered the Captain.

"Give me the gun," said the other soldier without the stand. "We'll buy the Queen the time she needs to escape."

The Captain was about to protest, but he knew that if they didn't do this, they would all die. They had to protect the Queen.

"Go," said the other, as they busied themselves setting up the machine gun. "Go!" he bellowed.

Victoria had no words as she and the Captain sprinted down the tunnel. Just as she saw the ladder, which must lead up to the alehouse, she heard the machine gun open up behind them, lighting up the tunnel in a pandemonium of strobing and deafening noise.

They reached the bottom of the ladder. "Go ahead, the trapdoor will open easily," shouted the Captain.

Victoria scrambled up the ladder, glad to be wearing something as practical as the soldier's uniform. The machine gun fell silent and they heard the unmistakable sound of their men being slaughtered by the Martians.

Victoria grit her teeth as she neared the trapdoor and pushed it open with all her strength. She entered a well-lit cellar. Victoria spun around and saw Captain Trent alight from the ladder. He threw a couple of grenades back down into the tunnel and slammed the trapdoor closed. He took her hand and pulled out his pistol when they heard the grenades go off. They stood there a moment, both breathing heavily. Captain Trent pointed his pistol at the trapdoor.

"Head up the steps," he whispered. "Out through the back of the alehouse, the carriage is waiting."

"Not without you."

"Go!"

The trapdoor burst open and a moment later a Martian, completely covered in dark emerald armour, came through the gaping hole.

Captain Trent fired at it with no effect. The Martian approached them slowly, like an animal ready to pounce.

"Go," he whispered, as he drew out a medieval-looking club with metal studs.

Victoria paused only a moment before bolting up the steps and into the alehouse. Confused for a moment, she looked around before deciding which way led to the back. She'd only taken a few steps when, from nowhere, another Martian appeared a few metres before her. She stared at it in horror, wishing she had some weapon, anything. In a fluid motion, the Martian drew its energy weapon and fired. Victoria turned and shut her eyes. She heard the weapon discharge, but she was still alive. Confused, she opened her eyes to see General Alexander Lethbridge standing between her and the Martian, protecting her with some kind of barrier of his conjuring. He raised his fist and the Martian simply vanished. Two more Martians appeared from the cellar and attacked Alexander. He slammed one against the floor and the other against the wall with such force that chunks of plaster and bricks came loose. They fired their intense energy weapons, yet it didn't even slow him down. Victoria turned away from the terrific heat. Alexander again gestured and the two Martians disappeared. All Victoria could hear was the sound of her breathing as silence descended.

She regarded Alexander with wild eyes.

"You," was all she could say.

He looked at her almost timidly. "Your Majesty, I…"

"You did this," she said, looking at him accusingly.

"Before. That was not me. It was The Adversary."

She looked at him, trying to fight back the tears.

"How can I know for sure?" she asked, remembering the cruel look of malice in his eyes.

"We can never know for certain. But, at some point, we have to trust again. Otherwise, we are lost. It is just another weapon which The Adversary utilises, planting doubts in our minds."

"Alexander?" she said, reaching towards his face.

"It is me. The one you teased as a child. The one who was over-protective when you were a young lady. The one who—"

Victoria flung herself into his arms. "The one who saved me from the Martians," she said as she looked up at him.

He smiled. "Yes."

He didn't seem to have aged a day since she first met him when she was a little girl. Their apparent ages now were pretty much the same.

"How did you escape the enemy's control?"

"Well, I had help," admitted Alexander.

Victoria pulled away suddenly. "Oh no, Captain Trent."

She rushed down the steps to the cellar with Alexander close behind. She stopped abruptly when she saw the Captain's body, face down and unmoving on the floor. Her vision blurred as she wept.

"I'm sorry," said Alexander. "He was a good man."

"He served us well," said the Queen, "but more than that – he was my friend."

"Take my hand, Your Majesty. There is someone you need to meet."

3. ALEX AND RUTH

Perhaps one of the most significant machinations of The Kinsmen is that of deception. A popular mantra of The Kinsmen is: 'Reveal nothing more to your enemy than is necessary, lest they discover and take the measure of your true potential.'

Principles of The Kinsmen

New York, Earth 17

Alex's eyes fluttered open.

He was lying on a soft, well-made bed. A window was open. He could feel a fresh breeze as it caressed his face, hear the faint unmistakable sounds of car horns in the distance from the streets below.

Alex sat up. He could see he was in a large, ornate mid-twentieth-century hotel room. His extra senses now stretched out permeating through solid walls. He could sense the other residents around him on the eighteenth floor, their overlapping conversations. Thoughts and feelings mixed in a confusing concoction. He found it disorientating. Then Alex remembered.

Earth.

What had happened?

He'd teleported onto the asteroid Sol 9173. Alex had put

himself to the task of moving all of that great mass away, in the hope of saving Earth from an impending extinction-level event. Pouring all his will, everything he had, pushing beyond his limits. Alex remembered being on the verge of what he had thought beyond his ability to achieve. He had it. Every inch, every particle of that massive rock.

He had it! Then, here, in this hotel room.

He felt a familiar presence in his mind.

Ruth, are you there? Alex thought.

I am always here, said Ruth.

What happened?

I don't know. Not exactly. I recall we were struck from behind, the teleportation process… incomplete.

No!

I'm… I'm so sorry Alex. He could feel her sadness.

No… He felt as if he was falling in slow motion into a bottomless pit. His mind screamed in despair as each revelation hit him. He knew all too well what the impact of Sol 9173 meant. His friends and family, dead. All of humanity's history, their future, lost.

All of your history is stored in the Galacien archives and there are still the meta-humans on Galacien Prime, said, Ruth.

"What?" cried Alex out loud in frustration. "A memory in some dusty old record? A record no Galacien will regard with any degree of interest or empathy. And the Galacien meta-humans. The self-same ones that tried to abduct me for their own ends. Those ones?"

There was no response from Ruth, but he could feel her withdraw, almost see her head downcast.

Sorry, he thought after only a moment.

He could feel her come closer and, ever so gently, mentally embrace him.

Alex just sat on the bed; alone, yet not alone, for she was with him. In those last moments before Sol's impact on Earth, he'd felt her mind completely open to his. He knew that she felt the same way he did about her. How he'd felt for a long time now.

To begin with, she was merely in his head, a constant friend, as close as any he'd ever had. She constructed a perfect physical body with which to more easily interact with him. At first, he'd thought how he felt was merely down to the fact that Ruth was beautiful. What heterosexual male wouldn't find her attractive? The longer he got to know her, the harder it was to dismiss this as nothing more than simple lust. He loved everything about her. But he was afraid his feelings would not be reciprocated. Ruth had lived multiple lives. Always as an implant. Even for Garianne herself, at one point. He was a mere child of an immature species, and yet…

I believe I made it clear how I feel, he heard Ruth say in his head.

I'm sorry, I just find it hard to believe, said Alex.

You still hold to a human's limited point of view, said Ruth, the *Age difference is not stigmatised in Galacien society, nor are differences in beliefs or species. I love you because I have never felt this way about another sentient before. You're young without being immature. Lacking in knowledge, without being ignorant. I find your outlook on the world fresh and invigorating. You bring out the best in me. I don't know what the future holds for us. I only know I want to continue being with you.*

For Alex, it seemed to be the only light in an otherwise bleak world.

I want that too, said Alex, with a sad smile.

We will find out what happened, said Ruth, *I promise.*

Thank you.

Alex looked around the hotel room saying, *Now, how on Earth, quite literally I might add, did we end up here?*

Firstly, what universe are we in? asked Ruth.

Can't be ours, my Earth is gone, said Alex.

This hotel could easily be replicated by any sufficiently advanced society. Perhaps to help facilitate your recovery from such a recent traumatic ordeal, said Ruth.

Let's find out, thought Alex, as he took the bedside clock in his hand and concentrated. He felt confident enough now to know instantly whether this object was from his universe or not. It wasn't. *We are in a universe much further out from the singularity than our own. Perhaps I teleported subconsciously.*

Here?

I see your point, Alex acknowledged.

Calculating the forces at play, I believe you would have, in fact, slingshot around the Earth and ended up in deep space perpendicular to the solar plane. Since super-sentients can survive in the vacuum of space, you wouldn't have been in danger.

So how did I get here?

Well, if you didn't bring us here, someone else must have, deduced Ruth.

Alex focused his acute senses on their immediate surroundings.

I detect no Galacien micro wormholes watching us, said Alex.

I'm detecting no Galacien signals whatsoever, said Ruth.

It's feasible there is no Galacien in this universe.

There's certainly no presence within the solar system.

I'm not sure whether to be comforted by that or unnerved, said Alex.

What do you mean?

I mean The Adversary infiltrated the Galacien back home, so if the same holds true here, it would already know we were here.

Alex walked over to the window. Down below he could see what looked like an alternate version of the streets of New York City in the 1950s. He recognised the styles of the many cars but not the models. Perhaps designed and manufactured by car companies he'd never heard of before. The people wore fashions reminiscent of the mid-twentieth-century, and even though some forms of attire were exactly as he'd seen portrayed in the media, others were very different, as if altered by some unseen hand. The architecture seemed familiar enough; however, he was sure that if he asked Ruth, she would reveal the many differences which lay therein. Such details were inconsequential, considering everything they'd lost. It appeared that the Galacien Conglomerate of Worlds was falling apart, Garianne was dead, and his Earth just another casualty of The Adversary's madness. He gripped the open window frame, his knuckles white.

"I don't know what to do, Ruth. I don't understand this thing we're supposed to be fighting, or even how to," said Alex.

"I understand your frustration," came a deep, steady voice from behind them.

Alex spun around, stepping back against the window with a thump, to see Jonas in the room. Alex, his mouth agape, could sense Ruth's surprise as well.

"You did not expect to see me. As for what to do? You should come with me, or I with you, it depends on how you look at it. Together we'll find out who and what The Adversary is, and perhaps if we dare to hope, a way of stopping it."

4. VASHA

It is impossible for others to fully understand and comprehend truly who and what The Kinsmen are.

Principles of The Kinsmen

Space

Vasha Ilsa Nemrod stood alone in one of the ship's many viewing rooms, staring out into the depths of space. The galaxy had changed much since she had left it well over eight thousand years ago. Before the construction of Galacien Prime. Before the Galacien had fully explored every corner of the galaxy. She had consulted her newly installed implant to look up her old friends and acquaintances. Many of them had placed a copy of themselves into storage to be woken every hundred years or so to see if anything significant had changed. They must have thought not, for the amount of time between awakenings had become longer and longer, and time spent living their lives when awoken shorter and shorter. A few had left the galaxy entirely, never to be seen again. And some, like herself, had become stranded on far-off, unreachable worlds whether in this universe or another, when the last of the multiversal teleporters had gone. Were they still alive? Had they survived somehow, as she had? If they could overcome the current crisis then she must try and find them.

Vasha sensed Captain Dermarlaine and her first officer, Hok Neels, heading her way. She felt a pang of regret about how she had commented to Dermarlaine, in front of her crew, on the futility of their situation. She shook her head: even at her age, she had never been very subtle, always preferring the direct approach.

The Adversary had subverted an unknown quantity of the Galacien. They were wanted for insubordination after leaving the Galacien system, against direct orders. Worse than this was the fact now that all the Galacien memory archives had been tampered with. What this meant she did not truly know. The worst-case scenario was that those that were in storage were now lost forever. If all backup copies were gone too then essentially the Galacien were no longer immortal. If any were to die, then they would no longer wake up in a new body with your latest copy imprinted into that body's brain. That would be the end for you. The Galacien were demanding to know how this could have possibly happened. And not just the Galacien. All the different alien species in the galaxy used similar and now corrupt Galacien technology for the same purpose. The dynamic of the galaxy had changed from one of peace and security to one of fear and suspicion.

The recent news about the destruction of her birth world, Earth, was deeply disturbing. She had been well aware of the threat Sol 9173 posed. She found herself torn between accepting the Galacien's stance of non-interference on the barbaric backward world, and siding with her recent comrade's point of view. The starship Lom and its crew were unsuccessful in destroying the asteroid. She had not heard from them since. She hoped they were alright. Min and Jonas, wherever he was, were the only two people she knew.

Captain Dermarlaine smiled when she saw her. "Greetings Vasha, trying to gain a fresh perspective?"

Vasha gave her an apologetic half-smile. "Trying," she said. "Apologies for before. I'm used to speaking my mind. During the Golden Age, super-sentients were a revered group. You get used to saying what you want, whenever you want. It is something we should have spoken of in private."

"Agreed. Which is why I am here. Neels?" Dermarlaine indicated her first officer.

Hok Neels stepped forward. He paused a moment before saying, "Not only am I the Captain's First Officer, but I am also an agent of Cieshella Garianne Phulum."

Vasha did not know who that was, so her implant helpfully filled her in. There was a lot of information, and she continued to review the files while listening.

"He's a spy," said Dermarlaine, with no hint of malice.

Vasha did not sense any such negative feelings toward Neels; they were past that.

"What is the significance of this?" asked Vasha.

"I am privy to a lot of information. She, Garianne that is, told me a great many things," said Neels.

"As I understand it, this Garianne is dead?" queried Vasha.

"Unfortunately, yes. Alex's implant sent out an update of their current situation before he attempted to teleport Sol 9173 away from its trajectory," said Neels.

They all knew he was unsuccessful in his attempt.

Neels sent her the information they had received from Ruth. Garianne had died in a far-off universe, helping Alex and Ruth escape, knowing she would not be revived, for it had been she who'd discovered the corrupt memory stores in the first place. Even though Vasha had never met Garianne, she could not help but admire such a noble sacrifice.

"Any word from Lom and its crew?" asked Vasha.

"Just recently," said Neels. "I'm sorry to report that they've confirmed the Earth is now nothing more than a scorched world."

There was a moment of silence between them until Vasha said, "It was nothing more than my birthplace. I've spent all of my life living amongst the larger galactic community. The Earth and humankind were so small in the grand scheme of things. It was a natural event, and if they had been mature enough this could have been avoided. We all know this."

Dermarlaine and Neels looked at one another.

"What?" demanded Vasha.

"Earth's circumstances were rather unique," said Dermarlaine.

"What do you mean?"

Neels said, "For a start, two of Garianne's meta-humans, James and Korina Tennel, onboard the starship Lom, were in a position to destroy Sol 9173. That particular circumstance has never happened before. The Galacien might say this was an illegal action. However, Lom did this of his own free will."

"There was a Galacien blockade waiting for them," explained Dermarlaine, "but they managed to overcome it and fire upon the asteroid. The asteroid had a shield and returned fire, disabling Lom."

"Thanks to Garianne's sacrifice, Alex was able to return to Earth and make his own attempt. Unfortunately, he failed. We have not heard from him since. Lom cannot find him," said Neels.

Vasha shook her head. "Garianne certainly went to a lot of effort to make sure that her people were in a position to stop that thing."

"She believed Earth was important because it is the only world known to have produced super-sentients," reported Dermarlaine. "Jonas was the first, then Alex."

"Despite that being true there are over two thousand years between them. It is not as if there are any others," said Vasha.

"Well, actually, there is," said Neels.

"What!?" exclaimed Vasha.

Dermarlaine looked equally astonished.

"I take it you did not know this," said Vasha to Dermarlaine.

She shook her head. "It appears my First Officer has been keeping a great many things from me."

His Captain's disappointed tone seemed to have little effect on the Galacien First Officer, as he continued, "Her name is Alicia Elde. This was Garianne's biggest secret. But I fear The Adversary is now aware of all the players on the board and is now into its endgame. Garianne hoped that Alex and Alicia would herald a new age of super-sentients. For some reason, the planet Earth was acting as a celestial nursery for them. The agents of The Adversary amongst the Galacien have ensured that these two would be the first and the last."

"Who is Alicia Elde?" wondered Dermarlaine.

"Garianne believed she was different, even for a super-sentient. She sent her out into the multiverse at the tender age of fourteen, to disappear," said Neels.

"A fourteen-year-old human child!" exclaimed Dermarlaine.

"Yes," said Neels. "As I said, Alicia is different. She has a way of thinking, a way of looking at and solving problems. If all else fails then she is our best hope of survival."

"Things are getting rather desperate right now, Neels," said Dermarlaine, straightening her uniform.

"I know. I can only surmise that Alicia has not reached a viable solution."

Vasha looked at Neels quizzically. "Did Garianne tell you, did she know, in what way Alicia is different?"

"No, but she had extreme confidence in Alicia's abilities."

"I'm not so sure," said Vasha. "Garianne could not find a way to save herself. It's unwise to put all our faith in this child."

They then all heard, through their implants, the com open. A voice from the bridge said, "Excuse me, Captain, but we've detected eight ships coming out of hyperspace and entering the system."

"Show us," said Dermarlaine.

Through their implants, they could all see a three-dimensional tactical layout of the system. Their ship was in orbit around the second planet, while what were identified as Galacien ships were much further out, at the same distance as the sixth planet. Dermarlaine observed that it would take some time to reach them, even if they were to initiate smaller jumps through hyperspace.

"It seems we've got company," said Dermarlaine.

Vasha frowned. "I am growing tired of running."

"As am I. I'm also sceptical of this Alicia Elde," remarked Dermarlaine, looking at Neels.

He smiled.

"You find this amusing?" said Dermarlaine.

"Somewhat," said Neels.

"What?" Dermarlaine was unamused.

"You should have a little more faith in her," said Neels.

"And why is that? We have never met this girl. Neither do we have any evidence of her ability," said Vasha.

Neels' smiled broadened as he stepped towards Vasha. "What if I were to tell you that she is here right now? What if I were to tell you that she's been here for some time, and you never even noticed. What would you say then, Vasha?"

Vasha looked at Neels, her eyes wide. She could, only now, sense the unmistakable power emanating from this being.

"I am Alicia Elde. I have been here all this time, a super-sentient, and you never even noticed me. I was able to hide my true self and my abilities right under your nose. Is that enough? Do you have confidence in me now?"

"All this time?" echoed Dermarlaine. "Why did you not help us during the battle at Galacien Prime? We could have used the help of a super-sentient."

"You had one. As I recall, she handled the situation, as I knew she would: exceptionally well," said Neels.

Dermarlaine was at a loss for words.

"The time has come. I'll teleport us to the Sol system," said Neels.

"Us?" said Vasha.

"The ship. Captain, would you mind ordering all hands to stations?" said Neels.

"I... Teleport the whole ship?" said Dermarlaine, confused.

"Never mind. I was trying to be courteous. Probably better to just be done with it," said Neels.

As he held his hands together, the ship was enveloped in light.

"Captain!" Dermarlaine heard her panicked Second Officer on the bridge. "What's hap—"

Then   they   were   gone.

5 THE MARTIAN SUPER-SENTIENT

The multiverse has a habit of destroying potential sentient civilizations before they have reached fruition. The Kinsmen merely dissuade this habit.
                                                            Principles of The Kinsmen

Earth 3

Victoria found she had been teleported to an abandoned cottage. She immediately went to the window. Outside was nothing but darkness.

"We are almost a hundred miles out from the centre of London," Alexander told her.

"What's left of it," she whispered.

She could hear nothing inside or outside the house. It seemed difficult to imagine that humanity was being driven slowly yet inexorably towards extinction.

"Your Majesty," came a voice, as a man who looked very similar to Alexander stepped out from the shadows with a smile. "My name is Al-X, and it is a pleasure to meet you."

Victoria looked at him sceptically. She did not like the way he was looking her up and down.

"He is on our side," said Alexander.

"How do you know that?" asked Victoria

"Because he is the one who freed me," said Alexander.

"I don't see what is so amusing," Victoria said to Al-X.

"Your Majesty, Alexander never told me of your beauty," said Al-X.

"Excuse me," cried Victoria, her anger burning, her voice rising. "My city is in flames and the whole world is at stake, not to mention the personal losses of those I held close and dear to me. So perhaps you can see why your attempts at a compliment may feel rather inappropriate."

Al-X looked at her unfazed as if she were a child throwing a tantrum. "Then perhaps you may appreciate what I can do for you."

"Which is?" demanded Victoria.

"Well, seeing as we're being blunt here," said Al-X, taking a step towards her, "with only Alexander here to help, your chances of survival are slim to none."

Alexander also took a step closer. "I think you'll find I'm more than capable of holding my own."

Al-X looked at them both. "Really?" He looked doubtful. "What good is that? We're talking about the entire planet here. How many years of experience have you under your belt? Twenty? Thirty?" He let that sink in a moment. "For myself, on the other hand, try thousands of years, and access to Galacien technology well in advance of Garianne's. I don't mean to brag, but there you have it."

The cottage went as quiet as before, until Victoria said, "Will you help us?"

Al-X paused a beat. "Of course," he said.

"I'm sorry I jumped down your throat," apologised Victoria.

"Understandable. We are from very different cultures, and you have been through a lot," said Al-X.

"What do you propose we do?" asked Alexander.

"I've retrieved data on the enemy's movements from my probes. It's not good. They are many and we are only two."

"Lady Ruth created space ships to protect us. Can you do the same?" said Victoria.

"I can, but it would take days for them to be ready. By then there would be little to nothing left of humanity," said Al-X.

Victoria looked at him, shocked at the horrific truth.

"What else could we do?" wondered Alexander.

"Perhaps something smaller, yet as effective," said Al-X thoughtfully. "Biological? No. Ah yes. A technological virus. A simple matter. Their technology is rather primitive so it wouldn't take long to create a virus and propagate it through their network, infecting and disabling all their technology. This should buy us more time to come up with an effective counter-attack. That part will take a lot longer."

"But it can be done?" pressed Victoria, her voice wavering. "There is a way?"

"Yes," said Al-X.

Victoria had to refrain from falling back on her old habits and holding Alexander, she felt so relieved at Al-X's news. Yet her smile quickly faltered when there was a deep rumbling from outside. They all went to the window and saw something burning up in the sky. Something falling at great speed. When it hit the ground, only a few hundred feet away, the shockwave blew out the windows. Alexander reacted quickly, protecting Victoria a moment before it happened. The whole building shook, and ornaments and books fell from the shelves.

When they went outside the air was thick with dust, and both Alexander and Al-X could sense something within the crater beyond.

"What is it?" asked Victoria, covering her eyes.

"Something not good," said Al-X curiously.

"A Martian war machine?" said Alexander.

"I don't think so."

They saw a large, dark shape making its way towards them.

"Your Majesty," whispered Al-X, not taking his eyes from the thing, "go back inside and hide in the basement."

She stared at him a moment, about to ask him what it was, but the look on his face changed her mind and so she went.

Listen up, Alexander heard Al-X in his head. He looked at Al-X, astonished. *I'm building an implant in your brain. I know, you protest. But it is necessary. Surely you can sense it? That thing is a Martian super-sentient and it's very powerful. We need to be able to work together and that means effective communication. As a soldier, I'm sure you understand the value of this.*

"You could—" began Alexander.

No! From now on, think it. Do not speak lest the enemy hear.

Like this?

Better. More efficient.

Alright, said Alexander. *Do as I say. You teleport in from behind while I attack it from the front.*

They could see the unmistakable form of the Martian. To Alexander, they always looked like an octopus on four giant legs. This one was far larger than any other he'd seen or heard of.

No disrespect, General, said Al-X, *you may be a soldier, but I have far more experience than you'll ever have. So, this is the way we're going to do it. You're going to attack it and I'm going to learn from it, and, when the time is right, take it out.*

Alexander looked at him. *Are you afraid?*

No, I merely want to take the measure of this thing. Don't worry, I won't let you get yourself killed.

Very well, agreed Alexander, *let's get on with it.*

He readied himself while Al-X walked to the Martian's right. It watched them both drawing closer.

Make your move, said Al-X to Alexander *before it does.*

Alexander teleported behind the hulking Martian. It spun round to face him as Al-X hit it as hard as he could. Alexander had been careful throughout his life; his strength was beyond that of any human. Despite its size, the Martian should have been thrown into the air by such a blow, yet it had barely moved.

It's strong, he heard Al-X in his head, a split second before the Martian hit him, throwing him across the ground. He rolled over and over, barely conscious.

Really strong, came Al-X voice. *Use a force-field.*

What? was Alexander's only reply as he pulled himself to his feet, realising that the Martian super-sentient was about to deliver another blow. It never touched him, but instead hit some invisible barrier. Alexander felt the shockwave reverberate through the air and into the ground.

Alexander, you can't generate force-fields?

What? No, no, he said, looking up at the Martian pounding away at Al-X's force-field. Then the force-field shattered. Alexander teleported next to the house. The Martian appeared before him, and hit him once more, this time sending him through the window.

It can teleport as well? Okay I've seen enough, said Al-X.

He reached out with his senses and decided to teleport this thing into the centre of the Earth. A tactic which had proved very successful in the past. The Martian remained where it was. *I think we've got a problem,* said Al-X as the Martian now turned its attention to him.

Al-X hit it, but it had little effect. He created razor-sharp force-fields in an attempt to cut the thing in two. Al-X's eyes went wide upon realising the Martian's hide was unaffected. Its skin was either regenerating almost instantaneously or impossible to cut.

The Martian attacked him with incredible speed. Al-X instinctively teleported to a respectable distance, but the Martian also teleported and, in a heartbeat, was on him, wrapping its tentacles around his body and throat. He tried to peel them off, but the creature was too strong. Al-X gritted his teeth in rage. He teleported into space and the creature went with him. No effect. It was super-sentient, as was he, and could survive the hard vacuum. He teleported close to the sun. Closer than he would have dared, but he was desperate and the thing was trying to crush him to death. Being super-sentient he could not feel the heat, he could not fathom how the brightness did not blind him instantly, for any normal being at such close range would be vaporised in a second. Yet he knew they both had their limits and he knew he had reached his.

He teleported back before he began to burn up. He was back on terra firma in the creature's deadly embrace. How much longer did he have? He reached out with his senses and found the thing's brain and focused. Perhaps sensing what he was trying to do, the Martian's grip tightened until Al-X was sure something vital would break. He growled like some mad animal at the thing, using every ounce of strength until all of a sudden the Martian stiffened and then went limp, falling onto him. For a minute he could not move. He could not remember the last time he had been so exhausted. Then with a shove, he moved the massive thing over and, with disgust, disentangled himself.

Al-X staggered over to the house, shouting, "Alexander, Victoria, it's dead. Safe to come out."

Two bedraggled, dirty figures emerged from the house. Al-X figured he looked every bit as bad, if not worse.

"You're hurt?" said Victoria.

Al-X nodded, realising he was clutching his side. "I'll live," he replied.

"Sorry I couldn't do more," sighed Alexander, looking defeated.

"It's fine," said Al-X, wincing. "If it makes you feel better, it nearly killed *me*."

They both looked at him, confused.

Al-X smiled, shaking his head, mumbling. "Lost in translation; I guess that's what happens when you visit other universes. Well, at least there was only one of them, otherwise…" Al-X stopped, a glazed look on his face, "Oh no."

Around them appeared three more Martian super-sentients out of thin air.

Nobody moved.

We're dead, Al-X heard Alexander say.

Al-X glanced at them for only a moment, then teleported away, leaving Victoria and Alexander surrounded.

6. ON ALICIA'S TRAIL

Any sentient being can achieve the state of Kinsmen. Despite colour or creed. Whether they be king or beggar. Their past is inconsequential, for anyone can be educated, enlightened and physically evolved. It is just a question of time.

Principles of The Kinsmen

New York, Earth 17

Alex stood facing Jonas, his back against the open hotel window. He was dimly aware of the faint sounds from the street below.

"Jonas. How did you get here?" said Alex.

"I've been able to replicate your ability to traverse from one universe to another. No small feat, I grant you; I could only teleport us to a nearby alternate Earth."

"You teleported us from our own universe?" said Alex.

"Yes, I found you drifting in space after the impact of Sol 9173. I now need your innate ability to take us further out from the singularity."

"How much further?"

"Very."

Through Ruth, Alex felt his mind connect with something akin to Jonas' implant. *Hello Alex, I am Lom. It's a pleasure to meet you.*

The Lom sentient implant was unlike any Alex had encountered before; he was somehow integrated with Jonas in ways Alex could not understand. He got the smallest sense of Jonas and Lom's true intellect and ability, and it was staggering. Alex swallowed and took a deep breath. *You were once a starship?* he thought, still trying to come to terms with what Jonas had become.

I still am, in a way, replied Lom. *A version of me still exists back in our universe as a starship, another here with Jonas.*

Yeah, being in two places at once. Ruth can do that, pretty weird, said Alex.

After all, we've seen and done, you think that's weird? said, Ruth.

Good point said, Alex.

If I may interject, said Lom, *here is where we wish to go.*

In Alex's mind's eye he could see an infinite sea of light and at its heart something which burned even brighter; the singularity of the multiverse, where new universes were consistently being birthed into existence. Alex felt Lom guide his attention away from the unimaginable forces at play there, to the universe, to the Earth where they currently resided. For a moment Alex was distracted by his own dead Earth in a universe relatively close to this one. Then Lom pulled him away, further and further out from the singularity, until they were focused on one particular Earth.

This is where we wish to go, said Jonas.

Why?

Better to show you.

Alex could sense Ruth's distrust, something he felt himself. In response, he felt Jonas' reaction. Jonas gave the merest hint of a smile.

"That's the problem with facing one of our kind: we can sense one another's feelings."

"Here," said Jonas with an outstretched hand. "As a gift, a gesture of trust, I return to you something lost which is in my power to give."

In the far corner of the room, Alex saw thousands of tiny points of light glittering in and out of existence, whilst others whisked about in indiscernible patterns, leaving branching trails in their wake. He watched in fascination as he saw the unmistakable form of Ruth created before his very eyes. It had taken her days to fine-tune and perfect her physical manifestation. Jonas did it in mere seconds. When it was done, he seemed quite satisfied with himself.

"Ruth!" cried Alex, as he rushed over and held her in his arms. She leant in close and kissed him. When they separated, her face was alight, an exuberant smile on her lips.

Alex could not help but mirror her expression. It felt as if she were an angel lifting him out of that black well of despair.

"Together again, eh?" said Alex.

"We were never apart," said Ruth.

Alex held Ruth's hand in his and turned to Jonas, saying, "Thank you. This means a lot to me."

Jonas nodded, yet for a moment he remembered something from over two thousand years ago, on Earth, when he first met Min: a special memory for him, when everything was so different.

"Are you alright?" asked Ruth.

"Yes," said Jonas. "It is only that the two of you remind me of something which might have been had I chosen a different path."

"Mentoria Kendeisa?" enquired Ruth.

"It does not matter anymore; that opportunity has passed a long time ago. I made the only choice I could for everyone's sake. The two of you need each other. Especially at this difficult time. Having both lost so much," said Jonas.

"Earth was your home too," said Ruth, "long before Alex was even born."

Jonas was quiet for a moment. "It was the world that birthed me. I watched it over the years continuing to fail. Those in power, those truly in power who could have made a difference, only making matters worse. I'm sorry to say that they and too many others were nothing but a disappointment. Yet despite all that had happened throughout human history, I never wanted this."

"I don't mean to be rude but couldn't you have done something?" said Alex, trying to keep any anger from his voice.

"I am sorry. I was otherwise occupied."

"Occupied?" said Alex.

"Yes. Take me where I need to go and I will tell you everything." Jonas once more reached out his hand. This time to Alex.

He was struck by the similarity in this action to when he, under the influence of The Adversary, took Garianne and Ruth to that inhospitable planet on the other side of the multiverse.

He paused uncertainly.

"If I was an agent of The Adversary," said Jonas, "I would not need subterfuge."

We must trust him, he heard Ruth say, *or we are lost.*

Alex nodded and took the big man's hand. He focused his will and the three of them vanished.

An unknown universe

They teleported onto a barren wasteland.

"I can't sense a living soul for hundreds of miles in any direction," said Alex.

Ruth took a few steps forward and looked around. There was no sound from any birds above or creatures scuttling about the dirt. "There isn't an entire living thing on this entire planet," she added.

"I believe," said Jonas, pausing as if he were unsure, "that we may be the only living sentient life in this galaxy."

Alex and Ruth looked at him, astounded. For Alex, the feeling of isolation was almost palpable.

He heard Ruth's comforting voice. *Are you okay?*

Not sure. I think recent events may have affected me in ways I don't quite understand. I feel like I'm made of glass; tap me hard enough and I'm going to shatter. I've never been the most courageous guy but... I'm struggling here, my nerves are shot.

Ruth took him by the hand. *I'm not surprised with everything you've been through. Just remember, it's understandable and normal. Only fools feel no fear. The strong ones are those who are scared yet carry on despite this. You underestimate yourself. I have felt your fear and seen you stand up to it. Here, let me show you.*

Ruth then proceeded to replay Alex's recent memories. How he'd struggled against the metahumans, Martian war machines, Nacuerians, the Galacien, and even monstrosities from the other side of reality. Alex had never considered such things from an outside perspective, only how he could never be like Jonas — supremely confident and intelligent beyond his capacity to understand.

How could you be like Jonas, added Ruth, *and why would you want to be like him? You are who you are, Alex, and I love you for it.*

Alex was shocked by the statement. *She'd said it.* For some reason, he did not reciprocate. Ruth read his reaction. *My love is unconditional and I have the patience of someone who has lived a long time to wait. Only say it when and if you're ready.*

During their conversation, Jonas had walked around scrutinising their desolate surroundings. He knelt down and felt the dust between his fingers and stared up at the sky. The light was fading fast. Jonas approached Ruth and Alex and clasped his hands together before pulling them apart to reveal an object which looked very much like a scroll.

"What is that?" asked Ruth.

"It is called an Entrophier," said Jonas.

"What's an Entrophier?" said Alex.

"I'll show you," said Jonas, as he tossed the Entrophier into the air. It hung there a moment before appearing to split apart and encompass them. In that instant, the darkening landscape was transformed into bright sunshine.

"What is this?" asked Alex.

"This," said Jonas, gesturing around them, "is yesterday."

Ruth's eyes narrowed. "Not a simulation?"

"No."

"We are observing this planet's past?"

"Yes."

"How's that possible?" Said Ruth.

Alex looked at her. If all of Galacien science had no idea how such a thing could be accomplished then once more Alex was humbled by Jonas' accomplishments.

"I cannot take credit for the Entrophier's design. That goes to a small group of now long-dead super-sentients from the Galacien Golden Age. I merely rediscovered it and have made some modifications of my own."

"What kind of modifications?" asked Ruth.

"The original gave the user a restricted view into the past. My recreation encompasses the user, much like a simulation, making it feel a little like we have stepped into the past rather than observing it," said Jonas. "The effect is perfect. You cannot only see and hear the past but taste and smell it too."

"What?" said Alex. "So, if some guy was having a barbeque here yesterday, I would be able to smell it?"

Ruth seemed deeply disturbed. "Jonas, if that were possible, a sufficiently advanced species may be able to detect particles travelling into the future."

"But, we both know such a thing is impossible, correct?" said Jonas to Ruth, with a look of strange intensity in his eyes.

Ruth said nothing.

Alex shook his head, bewildered.

"Let's leave such a debate for later," said Jonas. "There are matters to attend to and our time grows short." He glanced at Ruth.

"Why are we here then?" asked Alex.

"Every so often, in one universe or another, some significant power rises to challenge and attempt to defeat The Adversary. All of them have failed. I have observed and recorded these events. Recently these confrontations have become more frequent, to the point where I am convinced that there is some intelligence behind some of them."

"But not all of them?" asked Alex.

"Of course not," said Jonas. "The Adversary is being fought across reality all of the time, such is the vastness of the multiverse."

"Do you have any idea who or what this intelligence is?" said Ruth.

"No. Only that it has been attempting to destroy The

Adversary for a very long time now."

"In vain, apparently."

"Yes. I need to find this being and warn them."

"Of what?" said Alex.

"That if I can deduce its existence, then it is only a matter of time before The Adversary does."

"Perhaps we could work together with this being," proposed Ruth.

"That is my hope," said Jonas. "Something of great significance happened right here thousands of years ago. Well, thousands of years ago on this world, but only days ago back in our universe."

"So, what do we do?" said Ruth.

Jonas looked out across the wasteland of yesterday, and it abruptly changed.

They stood on a hill surrounded by woodland. It was a cool, overcast day.

Alex saw nothing out of the ordinary. *Another alternate Earth*, he thought, and he felt a well of sudden sadness so deep that it felt like a multitude wailings in his head. Ruth put her hands on his shoulders and turned him around to see a shining city in the distance.

Even from here, he could tell that the buildings were taller than anything accomplished on his own Earth. He saw two objects flying very low, directly towards them. At first, he thought they were jets, yet when they rushed overhead, barely making a sound, he saw that they were people.

"Super-sentients," whispered Ruth.

A moment later another two flew over.

"I am tempted to look at this Earth a little closer. However, we don't have time for such indulgences. This is the right place, only too far back in the past. Lom, scan for any significant energy signatures, then take us to that point in the timeframe," said Jonas.

There was a pause. Then the setting shifted again. It was night and Alex could see the city on fire; a great structure made of glass shattered and fell. It reminded him of an ice-shelf breaking off and falling into the sea. Energy beams flashed from above. He could sense what he knew to be Nacuerian ships in space. So many he could not count. Pummelling the Earth. Jonas informed him that all around the planet were billions of Nacuerians, like insects, seeking out and killing any human life. Yet the humans fought back. They had thousands of super-sentients breaking enemy lines and blunting their attack. Unfortunately, the Nacuerian numbers seemed without limit. More than could be believed jumped from hyperspace, arriving in Earth orbit.

"This is ridiculous!" cried Alex. "Where are they all coming from?"

Perhaps, said Lom, *The Adversary has an inexhaustible supply.*

"A mechanism," added Jonas. "When one of them is killed, another is merely recreated on the side-lines, out of sight, then put back into the battle."

Their attention was drawn to the fact that the super-sentients seemed to be pulling back, moving towards the very hill on which they stood.

"They're all heading this way," said Alex.

"It seems the reason we are here is fast approaching," said Jonas.

They saw two super-sentients descend from the sky and land on the hill, a mere ten metres from where they stood. One was pulsating with light. The other watched, a subtle yet nervous look in their eyes. The first nodded. The other touched his hand, and both were engulfed in light. Where two beings had been now only one stood.

"Intriguing," said Jonas. "It seems that they have become something new, greater than the sum of their parts. I have never seen this done before."

"Perhaps it is an ability of one of the super-sentients," said Ruth.

Or all of them said, Lom.

Now other super-sentients arrived. Some from the sky, others teleported in. Jonas, Lom, Alex and Ruth watched in fascination as each touched the first super-sentient, its light increasing and growing in size as if struggling to contain all that raw power. Within minutes hundreds had become one. All Jonas and the others could see was darkness and this lone being of light. What had once been a deluge of arriving super-sentients now slowed to a trickle. The horde of billions of Nacuerians closed in on their position.

Ahead of this, they saw a large man burst from the dense tree-line, making his way up the hill at incredible speed. In his arms, he held an unconscious figure: a young man they all recognised as one of Alex's counterparts. The big man crested the hill, stopping where the multitude of super-sentients made one, waited. A woman appeared to step out of the big man. She was the first to reach up and touch the multi-super-sentient and be integrated into it. The large man lifted Alex's counterpart with the ease of someone lifting a child. He too became one with the being of light. The man flexed his massive neck muscles as he glimpsed over his shoulder to see the unbreaking swarm of Nacuerians almost upon him. He reached out and was consumed by the multi-super-sentient.

Where there had been many there was now one. It gestured and an immense energy wave exploded out, snuffing out the Nacuerians like candles in a hurricane. It spread out across the globe and into space, destroying their ships, leaving no trace of Nacuerian life. Whatever mechanism it was that was replenishing their forces must also have been destroyed, for no more Nacuerian forces entered the Sol system.

"Wow," said Alex, "that was incredible."

"I'm not sure it's over," remarked Jonas.

The multi-super-sentient was burning much brighter now as if readying itself.

Then nothing. Nothing but darkness.

"What happened?" asked Alex.

"The Adversary destroyed them," said Jonas, simply.

"But the power they wielded!" said Ruth.

"Insignificant," shrugged Jonas.

"That's it, then," sighed Alex.

"Are you giving up?" asked Jonas.

"There's no way we can stop something omnipotent," said Alex.

Jonas gave him a sly look, "Ah well…" he said.

"Well what?" demanded Ruth.

"The Adversary is not omnipotent," said Jonas.

"But we were led to believe…" began Ruth.

"By whom?"

Alex and Ruth looked at one another.

"By The Adversary itself," said Jonas, "an elaborate deception. And why not believe it, for its power is so great that it is almost indistinguishable from omnipotence, to beings such as ourselves."

"Why lead us to believe such a thing?" said Alex.

"To ensure that none ever opposes it. To make us believe it is something it is not."

"Which is?" asked Ruth.

"A god. A force of nature. Something eternal. But it is not. Despite its power, The Adversary is finite. It had a beginning, and, for the sake of its victims, I will find some way to end it."

Jonas looked around, his eyes seemingly piercing the darkness. The only light coming from the host of stars above them.

"What's our next move?" said Alex. "Are we done here?"

"No," came Jonas' reply. "Lom, scan the timeframe from this point in the past to the present day. Look for any signs of life."

There was a short pause until they all heard the reply through their implants. *I have something. Precisely twelve days after this event.*

Jonas nodded, and with a mental command instructed the Entrophier to take them to that timeframe.

Abruptly night became day. All around them was now a wasteland with the sun beating down upon the newly-formed, rocky desert. All flora and fauna must have been obliterated due to the confrontation between the multi-super-sentient entity and The Adversary. From nowhere appeared a young human woman, somewhere in her late teens or early twenties. She stood motionless as if stuck in time. Alex realised that Jonas had paused this moment so that he might get a closer look at her.

"What have we here?" asked Jonas, as he approached the woman, walking around her, studying her. Strangely, she was dressed in some kind of light battle armour, the likes of which he had never seen before. "By the energy signature of her arrival, I would say that she's teleported from another universe." He glanced at Alex.

Ruth moved to get a better look at her. "She bears a striking resemblance to one Alicia Elde, from our Earth."

"You recognise her?" said Alex.

"In a way. I tried to find a physical match from the Galacien simulation of our Earth," said Ruth.

"You have the entire Earth simulation stored somewhere?" asked Alex.

"I always kept a copy with me in hyperspace. Alicia Elde was only fourteen, however, I can easily ascertain what she would look like in several years. It is uncannily accurate to this woman," said Ruth.

"Lom, maintain this simulation but I want you to run your own, using the Entrophier to search for an Alicia Elde on this Earth."

"Yes, Jonas."

"Even at Lom's speed, that may take some time," said Jonas.

Ruth looked troubled "This is strange."

"What is it?" said Alex.

"Our Alicia Elde went missing almost a month before the cataclysm which destroyed our Earth," said Ruth.

"That's impossible, not without it being noticed by the Galacien," said Jonas. "Ruth, did you know anything about this?"

"No, I've never seen this woman before today," replied Ruth.

"And yet she seems to have somehow disappeared without raising any alarm with the Galacien Observation Agency. She has either been able to infiltrate the monitoring systems or has interacted with someone who has access to these systems," said Jonas.

"She appears to be super-sentient, so perhaps she could hack into their systems and disappear without the Galacien's knowledge," said Alex.

"Perhaps," said Jonas thoughtfully, seeming to be following another line of deduction. "Let us observe what she does here, shall we?"

With that Jonas continued the simulation which the Entrophier presented. Yet Alicia merely stood there, staring at the ground. Jonas bent down and looked at her face. Jonas had lived for thousands of years, trained his thought processes to be uncannily fast and efficient, both his memories and knowledge were vast, and there was a confidence and a wisdom in his eyes. When he looked at Alicia Elde he saw a reflection. Alicia looked up, regarding where the multi-super-sentient had made its final stand against The Adversary. Alicia produced her own Entrophier and tossed it into the air, where it opened up to show her the battle which had taken place twelve days ago, for her. Thousands of years ago now, for them. After observing the defeat of the multi-super-sentient, she turned and walked away. Gesturing, the Entrophier flew back into her hand and she pushed it back into hyperspace, out of the way. Jonas saw the determination in her face, the fire in her eyes, as she considered what she'd seen. Then, as soon as she had appeared, she was gone.

"Where did she get that Entrophier?" wondered Alex.

"She may have found it, much the same way I did, only in another universe," said Jonas.

"I'm still not sure what happened here," said Ruth.

Jonas, said Lom through their implants, *I can find no Alicia Elde from this Earth's history.*

"Could she be ours?" asked Alex.

"Ruth, could you share all you have on 'our' Alicia Elde?" said Jonas.

"Of course." As well as sending all the information she had from the Earth simulation, Ruth took the initiative and showed multiple, fully-realised simulations of Alicia Elde's life around them.

Alex looked on in fascination as he saw Alicia as a baby, an infant and a little girl. Even the most recent events of her life back on what had been his Earth. Just like everyone else, the Galacien had been watching her all her life.

"They never thought there was anything out of the ordinary with her?" he said.

"No. She was highly intelligent. Genius level. But that's of no interest whatsoever to the Galacien. What's another human genius?" Ruth said, shrugging her shoulders.

"When did the Galacien last observe her?" asked Alex.

"I'll show you," said Jonas in a manner which suggested he knew something already.

They watched Alicia wake up in her bed, apparently startled. Jonas paused the simulation and moved back the timeframe a few seconds. Next to this Jonas showed them another simulation. It was Alex when he first met Garianne in her office. In the simulation, Alex spoke of the girl who had helped him the night the metahumans from Galacien Prime attempted to abduct him. Garianne listened intently as they drank tea. Then Jonas watched as Garianne casually looked over her shoulder. It seemed an act of no consequence, however, Jonas could tell that she was looking at something in particular. No. someon*e*. Almost immediately afterwards Alicia woke with a start. Jonas paused both simulations.

"I've seen that look from Garianne before," said Jonas.

"When?" said Alex.

"During the Galacien/Nacuerian war. I first learnt to move about independently from my physical body in what we call the metaphysical self. Alicia was with you in Garianne's office; you could not see her, but Garianne could. Just like she saw me."

"So, this Alicia is the one who helped me when the meta-humans first attempted to abduct me?"

Jonas nodded.

"How did she know I even existed? I never told anyone what I could do. I never sensed her," said Alex.

"But she sensed you, Alex," explained Jonas.

And with that Jonas showed them a simulation of an ordinary, busy street in central London. Jonas highlighted both Alicia and Alex approaching one another from opposite directions:

Alicia with her mother, Alex with his friends. He appeared oblivious that his every step was taking him closer to a fellow super-sentient. Alicia's face told another story. At first, she seemed perplexed and uncertain. Then almost afraid, yet she hid it well. She appeared to be looking around but being ever so subtle about it. She spotted Alex, and for the briefest moment her eye lingered on him, then she became very interested in what her mother was talking about. Alicia acted completely normal as she and Alex passed one another and went their separate ways.

"She's good," nodded Jonas.

"She knew," said Ruth. "She sensed the Galacien wormholes."

"I think she's known about them all her life," said Jonas.

"Didn't the Galacien see this?" queried Alex.

"Her behaviour wasn't that strange, for a human. The Galacien consider humans, in general, a little strange, immature and unstable. You'd be surprised how often people exhibit bizarre behaviour, such as oddly speaking to themselves, or pulling unusual facial expressions, due to what they're thinking. All within acceptable parameters for the Galacien Observation Agency's Artificial Intelligence."

Alex looked at Ruth. She was smiling and trying to suppress a laugh.

"Sorry," she said, "but it's true."

"Now I feel self-conscious," said Alex.

Jonas ignored their exchange as he followed his deductions. "She was aware that something was watching her, and everyone else on the planet. That she was different from everyone else."

"Until she encountered Alex," said Ruth.

"He was the same as her. We have evidence that she knew how to move about the world in her metaphysical self. She helped you in your confrontation with the metahumans. Gained insight when you met Garianne. Let us see what happened next," said Jonas, as he brought up the simulation of the startled Alicia getting out of bed, pausing only a moment before grabbing her coat and going downstairs. She left her house and made the long trek towards central London.

"See the two men following her?" said Jonas. "Garianne's metahumans."

Ruth watched Alicia closely as she crossed the road; her face said it all. "She knows."

Alicia turned down onto a side-street. She was now on her own with the two men closing in behind her. As they caught up, one of them tapped her on the shoulder.

"Excuse me, miss. Police. May we ask you some questions?" said one of the thick-set men all in black.

"Really? You look more like bouncers," observed Alicia.

"Just a few questions," said the other man.

The simulation suddenly went black.

"What happened?" queried Alex, looking at Ruth.

"It wasn't me," said Ruth. "There's a gap in the simulation."

"A gap?"

"It's rare," she said, "but we've been having problems with our systems of late."

Jonas chuckled, "I'm sure you have."

Ruth looked at him with a raised eyebrow. "I know what you're implying."

"What?" said Alex.

"That Garianne was behind this," said Ruth. "That she, how do you say it, pulled the plug, to prevent prying eyes?"

"Isn't it possible that Alicia herself was the cause, and then made her escape?" suggested Alex.

"I don't believe so," said Jonas. "She had no opportunity before this event to practice such abilities. Certainly not teleportation. No, Garianne noticed her when you had your meeting and then went to confront her. What happened next is unclear."

"Was the woman we saw here our Alicia?" said Ruth.

"Impossible to tell until we find her. Yet I am fairly certain that she is the intelligence working against The Adversary. The one I've been searching for. Alicia was the unseen puppet master here manipulating events to bring together this multi-super-sentient being of incredible power," said Jonas.

"Yeah, and it got its arse kicked," Alex reminded him.

Jonas ignored his comment, saying, "I wonder if she believed it really stood a chance, or if it was merely a way of gathering more information? Whatever the case, The Adversary is going to catch up with her sooner or later. We need to find her."

"Can you extrapolate where she went?" said Ruth.

Jonas nodded. "Yes, and once I do Alex can take us there."

7. MIN

The three main principles of The Kinsmen are evolution, education, and enlightenment. Each of these concepts can be reinforced and strengthened by the other two. For example, evolution is, for the most part, a natural process. However, with proper insight (enlightenment) and technology (education), this process can be taken a stage further so that sentient life-forms may survive in more harsh and varied environments.

Principles of The Kinsmen

The Sol system

Min sat alone on Lom's command deck. Her knees pulled up to her chin, once more thinking about Kallon. The mysterious woman known as Nicola had wandered off. James and Korina had also left to be on their own on another part of the ship, in shock at the loss of their homeworld, Earth.

She had lost the only person she had ever loved, but James and Korina had lost their whole world. There was no comparison. Yet she could only think of herself. How she felt. She had been to Earth only twice. Each visit for only a brief length of time, and she had never felt any special affection for the place. Quite the opposite. It had been a backward, primitive world, and the majority of its inhabitants were stupid beyond belief, for their level of evolution. Their capacity for insight was practically non-existent. As a species they were dangerous. James and Korina were the exceptions, and that was only because they had been shown the way by Garianne.

Kallon had never hurt anyone. He was a good man. He did not deserve to be murdered by that thing.

Min wondered where the super-sentient Al-X had disappeared to. He had teleported away with Alexander, a super-sentient under the influence of The Adversary, to who knew where. Had Alexander killed Al-X? Al-X seemed to be the most experienced counterpart of Alex Lethbridge she'd ever met. Yet Alexander was, somehow, possessed by The Adversary. Whatever the answer, neither of them had returned.

Min was startled by the sudden noise of Lom's proximity alarm. Years of training kicked in and Min was on her feet. "Lom, what is it?"

"A ship just appeared right next to us. There was no warning. Displaying visual."

Min saw a Galacien ship, holding position very close to them.

"It is Captain Dermarlaine's ship. They want to speak to us," said Lom.

Min nodded, "Alright."

James and Korina were the last to arrive on the command deck.

Dermarlaine approached them and said, "I'm sorry for the loss of your homeworld and its inhabitants."

"Sorry?!" exclaimed Korina.

"Korina—" began James, taking her by the arm.

"No, James," said Korina. "Where were they when we needed them? I'll tell you. Not with us, trying to help stop that thing impacting on Earth. No." Korina fixed her eyes on both Dermarlaine and Neels, "They were in front of us, trying to stop us."

"You were too dangerous. The past has proven what an immature species can do if left unchecked," said Vasha.

"Who are you to pass judgement?" demanded Korina.

"someone who has seen, first-hand, what devastation an immature species can do if left to their own devices," replied

Vasha.

"That wasn't us," said Korina.

"Not yet, but in the future?" Vasha left that one hanging.

Korina held her tongue.

"We believe the Galacien ships you faced were under the influence of The Adversary," said Dermarlaine.

"Sol 9173 also had shields and offensive weapons," said Min. "That's what stopped us."

"Definitely intervention by agents of The Adversary," said James.

"Where's Al-X?" asked Dermarlaine.

"Another multiversal teleporter turned up, corrupted by The Adversary. They teleported away and haven't returned," said James

"Oh," said Dermarlaine.

"Would I be correct in assuming your 'ship' teleported here?" asked Lom.

"What?" exclaimed James.

"We are still trying to get our heads around that one ourselves," said Dermarlaine. "One moment we're in the Pegullus system, the next, we're here."

"How?" said Korina.

Vasha and Dermarlaine looked at Neels.

"I'm known as Hok Neels, Dermarlaine's First Officer. But that is just a cover. My real name is Alicia Elde."

"You say that as if it has some significance," sneered Nicola, seemingly unimpressed.

Neels turned his attention to Nicola.

"Ah, finally," said Neels. "Hello, Nicola. I'm pleased to be the first Alicia to meet you. Garianne spoke highly of you."

"She's dead now," said Nicola.

"It would seem so."

"And you're a multiversal teleporter?" asked Min.

"Yes," said Neels.

"I've never heard of anyone teleporting a ship thousands of light-years across space," said James.

"Especially with such precision. I take it you intended to

teleport right next to us?" said Lom.

"I did," confirmed Neels.

"Impressive," said Lom.

"Alright, we get it. The guy's got talent," said Nicola.

"He is a she, apparently," Vasha corrected her.

"Whatever," shrugged Nicola, apparently becoming bored with their speculation.

"You said you were pleased to be the first Alicia to meet Nicola," said James. "What did you mean by that?"

Alicia chuckled. "Alicia has discovered a way to replicate herself."

"The Galacien can do that," said James. "But to make a perfect clone of a super-sentient with their abilities intact, well, they have never managed that feat."

"It is far beyond their understanding," said Neels.

"But you can do it?" asked Nicola, with a touch of cynicism.

"I can. The original Alicia created many copies of herself, and spread them across the multiverse," said Neels.

"For what purpose?" asked Vasha.

"There are many reasons. It gives us a unique perspective on the multiverse and what is going on," said Neels.

"It means you can spy on us," said Nicola.

"Spying would be an inaccurate description. That implies that we don't have your best interests at heart," said Neels.

"You don't?" questioned Nicola.

Neels laughed and shook his head. "Always the suspicious one, aren't we, Nicola?"

"It keeps me on my toes. It's kept me alive," said Nicola.

"We need people like you, Nicola," said Neels.

"No thanks."

Neels smiled as if Nicola had delivered a satisfying punchline to a good joke.

"Who's 'we'?" asked Vasha.

"My other selves and I. You see, the game is drawing to an end. It's time to see who has the best hand: us or The Adversary? Do we get to survive and live on? Or is this the end of our multiverse?"

"You mean this is all going to end soon, one way or another?" said Korina.

"Yes. As you said, soon, and at a specific place. I'm asking each of you to help me stop The Adversary, personally."

"Personally? You say that as if it will be there in person," said Nicola.

"It will. This will be our last chance. The Adversary has decided to destroy our multiverse. I think that's worth fighting for, don't you?" said Neels.

"But what can we do against it?" asked James.

"I can make you super-sentient, for a start," said Neels.

"You can make ordinary sentients like Korina and I into super-sentients?" said James.

"Yes," replied Neels, simply.

Vasha looked at Neels, then at the others, with the certain gravitas of someone who has experienced a lot. "I have never heard of such a thing. Super-sentients are born, not created."

"I assure you it is within my power to accomplish such a thing," said Neels.

There was a moment of silence.

"He was able to teleport the ship all this way," said Dermarlaine.

"I've only known groups of super-sentients working together, able to accomplish such a feat, never an individual. Also, Garianne had faith in Alicia," said Vasha.

"We only have his word on that," Dermarlaine reminded her.

"It won't make a difference," said Min, in a small but assured voice. "Creating a few more super-sentients, even a few thousand, won't make any difference. That thing is unbeatable, I thought we would understand that by now."

"Believe me, I would have agreed once," said Neels. "I created a whole world of them to do battle against The Adversary, but to no avail."

"Then why try such a strategy again?" queried Nicola.

"This time will be different," said Neels.

"In what way?" demanded Min.

"You," said Neels addressing them all. "It knows you. It may give it pause. A moment where we may just be able to win."

"Why?" said Nicola.

"The Adversary is supremely confident in its power, and rightly so. It has the luxury to gloat over its enemies, to play with them a while before destroying them. You've all experienced this. If you face it as super-sentients, it will stretch out that moment. The more we challenge it, even if it is in an insignificant and futile way, the more it will play with us," said Neels.

"So, what are you planning?" said Nicola.

"I can't say. All I can say is that every moment you delay The Adversary, gives us hope," said Neels. "You can come with me and fight for your right to live, not to mention the existence of the multiverse, or you can wait here and die. I'll give you a moment to make your choice."

There was silence on the command deck as each thought about what Neels/Alicia had said.

"What do you think?" Korina asked James.

"I think it's insane," said James. "But I think 'insane' is where we are now. I, for one, agree. We either sit around, wait for the end to come to us, or we go to meet it. It's a simple choice."

Korina nodded sadly. "I'd rather go down fighting. Even though every other part of me wants to run away and hide, I just can't. Not after what it's done to the Earth."

Neels, obviously sensing their decision made, turned to Dermarlaine.

"I can't. My duty is to my ship and my crew," said Dermarlaine.

"Spoken like a true starship Captain," said Neels.

"I'll find somewhere safe to hide until this is all over," said Dermarlaine.

"Where we're going time runs much quicker than in this universe. It will be over, one way or another, before you find anywhere."

"Oh," was all Dermarlaine could muster.

"Lom?" asked Neels.

"Yes?"

"I can shunt your starship into hyperspace and take your persona with us. You'll be able to meet with Jonas and your other self."

"I would like that very much," said Lom.

Neels next looked to Vasha. She simply gave him a nod of acceptance.

Neels' eyes next fell on Min.

Min shook her head. "It won't make any difference," she said again.

"You said the same thing about Jonas, during the Nacuerian/Galacien war – 'he won't make any difference'. How wrong you were."

"How did you know about that?" asked Min.

"Garianne told me," said Neels.

"The Adversary is omnipotent," said Min.

"No, it isn't. Jonas witnessed a confrontation between The Kinsmen and The Adversary. The Adversary, even though emerging the victor, faltered. Its omnipotence is a lie."

"But its power…"

"Is incredible, yes. However, it is not infinite."

Min thought of Kallon. "Alright," she said. It felt as if the voice were not her own, yet she had said it.

Neels now turned his attention to Nicola, who shrugged, saying, "I think I'll just hang out here. Let me know how it goes."

"Really!" exclaimed Korina.

Nicola rolled her eyes. "What do you expect me to say?"

"Nicola," said Neels, a kind smile on his face, "the girl without a past."

Nicola's expression darkened.

"What does he mean?" asked James.

"She doesn't talk about it. Do you?" said Neels.

"About what?" said Vasha.

"Nicola doesn't remember her past. She has no memory of a mother or father. Where she came from," said Neels.

Nicola seemed on the verge of doing something violent but somehow kept control, merely looking away instead.

"Garianne tell you that too?"

"Yes. Of course. She knew the answer to these mysteries," said Neels.

"She did? Then why the hell didn't she tell me?" demanded Nicola, wondering why she hadn't smashed this guy in the face already.

"I could help you find the answers you're looking for. But there needs to be a multiverse for us to do that in. Help me, and I'll help you," said Neels.

Nicola thought for what seemed like an age. No one said a word.

"You're used to getting what you want, aren't you?" said Nicola.

"Usually," said Neels. "As the protector of your reality, believe me, you wouldn't want to be around when things don't go well for me."

"Your best interests are everyone's best interests?"

"Something like that," said Neels.

"Alright. I'm in," sighed Nicola.

8. TEA AND BISCUITS

The Kinsmen do not enter into conflict unless they are certain of the outcome and the outcome is always certain.

Principles of The Kinsmen

An uncategorised Universe. Galacien Prime.

Al-X appeared in his vast, isolated home on his universe's version of Galacien Prime.

"Welcome home," said the resident sentient system.

"Yeah, thanks Shirna," said Al-X.

"You seem agitated. Perhaps it is due to the injuries I'm detecting. What happened?" asked Shirna.

"I was attacked by a Martian super-sentient. Fix me up, would you?"

His clothes were cut with lasers; force-fields pulled them off until he was naked. His injuries were then healed by nano-machines. Al-X would have recovered fairly quickly on his own, but this process took mere moments. He was then cleaned and dressed in a new uniform using a symphony of more force-fields and nano-machines. The entire process took less than two minutes.

Al-X felt completely refreshed. "Better," he said, and promptly

teleported to another part of his home over a kilometre away.
He stood in a large room much like a warehouse, with polished
boxes of what looked like stones of varying sizes. All set in
rows and reaching up to several storeys high.

"Perhaps you should tell me what's bothering you?"

"No. I'm in no mood for stories," he said.

"Then at least allow me access to your implant's latest
memories of current events,"

Al-X paused a moment. "Fine," he said through clenched
teeth.

There was silence for a while until Shirna said, "I see."

Al-X didn't ask her meaning. He requested the item he
required and it was promptly teleported from its box into his
hand. It looked like a spear, very sharp at the bottom with a
cylinder at the top. He examined it. He also asked for several
other items and for them all to be put in hyperspace storage,
should he need them later.

"I understand your frustration," said Shirna.

Al-X stopped a moment, his face turning to a mask of
uncharacteristic concern. Then he relaxed. "Tea and biscuits,"
he said.

He didn't need to specify; Shirna knew his preferences. They
materialised on the box next to him. He took a drink and ate
one of the biscuits. He wondered if Victoria drank coffee or
tea. Probably tea.

"That 'thing' nearly killed me. Do you realise how annoying
that would have been?"

"Very?" said Shirna.

"Yes, actually," replied Al-X, sensing her sarcasm. "All those
memories are gone. I was growing quite fond of Captain
Dermarlaine."

"From what I've seen of your memories, I don't think she felt
the same way," said Shirna.

"You never know," said Al-X wistfully.

"Don't you have more important matters to attend to than
chasing Galacien captains?"

"I can do both," said Al-X. "Although you do have a point, to some extent," he conceded. "Have you backed up my memories?"

"Of course," said Shirna.

"Good," said Al-X.

He finished off his tea and teleported away.

Earth 3

Victoria stood looking in astonishment at the spot where Al-X had stood only a moment ago, while Alexander regarded the Martian super-sentients surrounding them. He took her hand.

"He left us," croaked Victoria.

Alexander couldn't find a reply.

"Get us out of here," whispered Victoria, her voice wavering with fear.

"I just tried to. Somehow they're preventing me," he said.

The Martians approached them as if they had all the time in the world.

Then, with the briefest flash of light, Al-X appeared. He stuck the spear-like object into the ground. There was an almighty crack, like thunder sending out a shockwave. The ground shifted upwards and dropped back down, bringing Victoria and Alexander to their knees. All around them the Martians were caught in a web of intense, shifting energy.

Alexander and Victoria looked up, bewildered, to see Al-X offering them a hand. "That will only hold them for a while. Take my hand."

They hesitated for only a moment, then reached out to him. As soon as Al-X had them they were gone.

An uncategorised Universe. Galacien Prime. Al-X's home.

Victoria stared around wide-eyed, swaying, looking as if she were about to collapse. Alexander held her up, saying, "It can be a little disorientating if it's your first time teleporting to a different universe."

69

She looked at him, open-mouthed.

"Where are we?" said Alexander.

"Galacien Prime. My Galacien Prime."

"What happened?" gasped Victoria.

"We couldn't defeat them. So, I came here to pick up something to slow them down long enough for me to be sure I could get you out of there safely," said Al-X.

"We're on another world?" asked Victoria.

"Another universe," came the disembodied voice of Shirna.

"Who's that?" said Victoria.

"I am Shirna, the resident intelligence. Pleased to meet you."

"Are you a machine?" said Victoria.

"In a manner of speaking, yes. But I am far more than what you think of as a machine. I am sentient," explained Shirna.

"A sentient machine?" echoed Victoria.

"All very interesting, I'm sure," said Al-X. "Perhaps you would both like to recuperate. A shower, fresh clothes and something to eat and drink?"

"I would like to find a way to save my world," said Victoria.

"All in good time," said Al-X.

"All in good time?" cried Victoria, exasperated. "With those things running around we may have only a matter of days or even hours."

"I suspect much longer than that, Your Majesty," said Alexander.

"Pardon?" said Victoria.

"Time runs much quicker here relative to your universe. I'm guessing I was only gone a moment back on your Earth?" said Al-X. They both nodded. "In that time I was able to freshen up and find the item I needed to slow down the Martian super-sentients. I promise we have the time. Think of..."

Victoria held up a hand. "We are both familiar with this effect."

"We will leave you to recuperate," said Al-X as he and Alexander stepped back.

Victoria looked around astounded as walls, doors and furniture materialised from thin air. It seemed to her as if some master artist were painting a world around her. Yet, these things were not a mere depiction, they were real. Al-X's home system – Shirna, as he called it – was creating a replication of a custom-made interior, catering specifically to her needs. Not only was the furniture of her place and time, but Shirna had also gone to the trouble of decorating the room and filling it with ornaments and pictures. Either Shirna was a perfectionist, or it was doing its utmost to relieve the stress it could no doubt tell she was suffering.

Now the walls and the roof were complete, with even the curtains drawn in this room-within-a-room. She was alone, except for this place's machine intelligence.

"I hope you find this environment to your liking?" came the disembodied voice of Shirna once again.

"I…I… yes," stammered Victoria. She was well aware of the capabilities of Galacien technology, through her experience with Lady Ruth and the first Martian war. However, she'd rarely seen it first-hand.

"Everything functions as it should, including the bath and shower. There are towels and a range of clothes, all made to measure," said Shirna. "Considering your current circumstances, I would strongly recommend the Galacien uniform. It has several advantages compared to your usual attire, many of which could save your life."

Victoria refrained from asking a host of questions and considered something more immediate. "What about privacy?" she said.

"An unusual request, but, of course, I understand your need for it. However, I insist that, even though neither I nor anyone else will be able to see or hear you, I must be able to monitor your vital signs in case you should have an accident and require medical assistance."

Victoria didn't argue; it made perfect sense. Despite Shirna's assurances and the more familiar surroundings, she was still a little timid as she took off her soldier's uniform, shoes, and, finally, undergarments. She showered, soon feeling refreshed, ridding herself of the accumulation of dirt and sweat from her most recent ordeal. Once dry, she considered her choice of attire.

Later, the door to Victoria's room-within-a-room opened. Alexander and Al-X turned to see Victoria wearing a Galacien uniform. Galacien uniforms were made to be very close-fitting. Alexander's mouth hung open. His face reddened as he realised she was looking at him.

"Sorry," said Alexander, now looking at the floor.

Think nothing of it, he heard her say.

"You have an implant as well?" he exclaimed.

Her jaw set firm and there was a dark look in her eyes as she approached them both, saying, "I do not take these decisions lightly. In an ideal world, I'd prefer us to carry on our lives without assimilating Galacien technology or their ways into our culture. We have been invaded twice now by the Martians. Again, we are heading towards extinction." Victoria paused, then with deep sadness she continued, "We must do this if we are to survive. No longer do we have the luxury to be what we once were. The only way to ensure our continued existence is to take what the Galacien give freely."

"Let the Galacien help us. Like last time. We don't have to become like them," said Alexander.

"What happens the next time our world is invaded?" challenged Victoria.

"If we go down this path," said Alexander, "where will it end? Will also become immortal? You once said to me that to accept such a thing would be to lose ourselves, to lose our souls."

"We do not have to accept all they have to give, but enough is enough. This is how it has to be, for now," said Victoria.

"And after?" queried Alexander.

"If there is an after… Well, we'll discuss that when the time comes. At least this way we have a chance to have a future."

Alexander nodded his acceptance of his Queen's command.

Victoria looked at Al-X with the same determined look.

He merely smiled, saying, "The uniform looks good on you, Your Majesty."

"I thought you were supposed to be an enlightened people," she said with a raised eyebrow.

Al-X laughed at her misunderstanding. "We are," he said. He didn't have the inclination or the time to explain, as he saw something else required his attention.

What do you want, Referick? said Al-X.

Is that any way to greet your friend and comrade? asked Referick.

What is it?

I need to speak to you.

You are.

In-person.

Go on then, said Al-X.

Referick appeared in front of them.

Victoria and Alexander jumped back, stunned by the sudden appearance of this tall, blue Galacien warrior.

"Who are you?" demanded Referick, looking at them. "My implant's drawing a blank."

"They're from another universe," said Al-X.

Referick looked them both over again. "Don't fall for his charms," he said to Victoria.

"He has charm?" retorted Victoria.

Referick laughed, but quickly became serious, saying to Al-X, "You have responsibilities, you know. You can't just go gallivanting off across the multiverse without letting the rest of the Galacien know where you are."

"I was going to tell them. I got side-tracked," said Al-X.

"Hmmm, I'm sure," said Referick, glancing at Victoria.

"Not like that," said Al-X.

"Would you excuse us, please," said Referick, taking Al-X by the arm.

"Isn't a private conversation an oxymoron in Galacien society? I know about the cameras the Galacien have in this room. The cameras that exist *everywhere,*" said Victoria.

Al-X looked at Referick with a wry smile. "'Cameras' is a bit of an oversimplification, though she has a point."

Referick remained impassive. He touched a small device attached to his hip. There was a brief hum which quickly faded to nothing.

"We are now unheard and unseen by the Galacien or anyone else for that matter," he said.

"But why?" said Alexander.

"The Galacien in our universe has no interest in saving your Earth," said Referick. "They prefer to use their resources bringing yet more worlds into the fold of the empire. They have a firm presence in our galaxy's local cluster and now their eye falls upon the Andromeda galaxy. A whole galaxy," he emphasized, "almost twice the size of our own! It will take us many thousands of years to accomplish this. They care nothing for an Earth in a universe far removed. However, your plight is far more significant."

"It is?" said Victoria.

Referick nodded. "It is your world which is one of many that have drawn the attention of The Adversary."

"How do you know about that?" exclaimed Alexander. Al-X and Victoria looked at Referick, aghast.

"Because I am in the service of one whose sole purpose is to stop The Adversary," said Referick.

"Your duty is to the Galacien," stated Al-X.

Referick smirked at him. "Am I to be lectured about duty by one such as yourself? Despite your abilities and power, you follow your whims and short-lived pleasures, ignoring any such higher purpose."

"To whom would you pledge your allegiance, if not to the Galacien Conglomerate of Worlds?" asked Alexander.

"Her name is Alicia Elde," said Referick.

The others looked at one another.

Al-X went quiet, which puzzled Victoria even more. She said, "Who is that? And how did you come to be in her service?"

"It's a long story," said Referick. "Suffice it to say, she opened my eyes. I'm now committed to something greater and far more important than the Galacien's latest conquest."

Al-X began to laugh.

"What's so amusing?" asked Alexander.

"Well," said Al-X, looking at them slyly. "Alicia Elde, you say? Seeing as we are confessing secrets, I believe it prudent to reveal that I too am in the service of another."

"Other than yourself?" said Referick.

"As a matter of fact, yes," said Al-X. "I've pledged myself to Jonas."

"I was not aware you'd had any contact with him," said Alexander.

"You're thinking of the Jonas you travelled with across the multiverse," said Al-X.

"Is there another?" Alexander was surprised.

"Oh yes, the one you know is a decoy. A recreation to draw the attention of The Adversary so that the real Jonas can plan its end unencumbered," said Al-X.

"Yet he possesses all the same abilities. Is our Jonas aware he is a facsimile?" asked Alexander.

"Of course not. What would be the point of that?" said Al-X.

"It seems our purposes are aligned," said Referick, "for I know for a fact that this real Jonas and Alicia are working together."

"I do not know if we have the same goals," said Victoria. "My immediate concern is saving my Earth from the Martian invasion."

Referick smiled. "That is where you are wrong. Jonas and Alicia would want us to help you."

"But why?" asked Alexander. "Begging Your Highness' forgiveness but we are nothing in the grand scheme of things."

Victoria bowed her head in understanding.

"As I said before, your plight is more significant than you realise. The Adversary has interfered in the affairs of a great many others, some limited to one world such as yours, and others that span across an entire universe. Each holds a small, yet unique amusement for it. Imagine that it is some great games master who can play many games, all working simultaneously. A chess game holds as much importance to it as a grand battle of thousands of troops. If we interfere in any particular game, it draws away its attention, giving Alicia and Jonas more time to find a way of solving this problem once and for all."

"If we draw its attention, though, won't it just interfere?" asked Alexander.

"Possibly," shrugged Al-X, "but we have to try. What other choice do we have?"

Victoria nodded her head, jaw set firm, then she said, "We need to use all the resources at our disposal. Take the fight to them. Force them back."

Referick and Al-X nodded. "I couldn't agree more, Your Majesty," said Referick.

"But how do we do that?" said Alexander.

"We attack their homeworld," said Referick.

9. SCORCHED EARTH

…These three principles must go hand in hand, and of the three, enlightenment is perhaps the most important. A highly intelligent (educated) or evolved sentient can be dangerous, if not enlightened enough to not cause harm to others.

Principles of The Kinsmen

In orbit above Earth 399

"Is this a habitat?" mused Ruth, looking around at their new surroundings.

"I think more like an automated space station; I don't sense anyone on board," replied Alex, regarding the large, open, well-lit chamber and the metallic surfaces.

"The onboard AI has noticed our arrival," said Jonas.

"Is that a problem?" asked Alex.

"No, I've taken control."

"Then let's get on with this, shall we?" said Ruth.

Alex noticed she seemed a little weary. And why not? They had spent months travelling from one universe to another, all of them very far out from the singularity. These universes were much older. Essentially, it was like travelling to alternate futures. This made them potentially very dangerous. The species they encountered were extremely advanced technologically, some far more than the Galacien back home. It was only thanks to Jonas that they were still alive. He had, on more than one occasion, saved them from certain death. But how much longer would their luck hold out? Following Alicia was a dangerous game.

Alex watched as Jonas went through the process of using the Entrophier to track down Alicia.

"Anything?" asked Ruth.

"Yes, I've pinpointed her energy signature. She wasn't here for long, unlike in some other places we've been to."

"True. She's spent a long time out here, moving from one universe to the next," said Ruth.

"All on her own too. I can see why you admire her," remarked Alex, remembering he'd confessed as much, more than once. "Surviving out here, alone, despite her age."

Jonas and Ruth glanced at one another, Jonas said, "I think you've missed something rather obvious. More often than not it hasn't taken us long to find out what she's been up to before she moved on to yet another universe. However, sometimes she's spent hundreds of years in one particular universe, attempting some strategy to bring about the downfall of The Adversary."

"By our calculations," continued Ruth, "she's far older than Jonas."

"Indeed. Despite appearances, Alicia Elde is no longer a young woman," added Jonas.

Older than Jonas, thought Alex. Jonas always seemed very old to him, even though he did not look it. It was in the way he spoke, his mannerisms, his actions. Yet from what he'd seen of Alicia she, in contrast, came across as youthful in the way she moved as well as the way she looked. He had seen that sparkle in her eye.

"Well, for someone who's thousands of years old she certainly holds it well," said Alex.

Ruth gave him a sideways look.

"What I mean," stammered Alex. "I mean... Come on!"

Ruth laughed. "You are too easy,"

Alex let out a sigh of relief and hugged her as she continued to giggle.

Jonas found himself distracted from the Entrophier's display, a wistful smile on his lips as he watched the two of them.

Are you alright? he heard Lom say to him privately.

I am content. Considering.

Considering?

Considering what we face, said Jonas.

It is good to see them like this. We have witnessed too much pain and suffering.

Far too much, agreed Jonas. It still pained him to remember that his hand had been forced to murder billions of Nacuerians.

You must forgive yourself, said Lom.

It would dishonour the memory of what they were before The Adversary twisted and corrupted them.

I said forgive, not forget. They do not always go hand in hand.

Jonas considered his words. *Perhaps one day,* he said as he watched Alex and Ruth.

This is what we fight for, said Lom. *We must allow ourselves to stop for a moment and enjoy life.*

I think that is why it hates us.

The Adversary? asked Lom. *I thought it considered us inconsequential.*

Perhaps. Then again, perhaps not. It is just a feeling from my encounter with it. I believe it lacks our capacity to love, fight or mourn, said Jonas, pausing for a moment. *To imagine and achieve great things, to come together and achieve something even greater. It is lacking in all these things.*

Don't tell me you are now a believer in humanity, said Lom.

I was speaking of sentients in general.

Were you?

Jonas sighed in resignation. *The reason they frustrated me so was that I saw their potential. How they squandered it in petty disputes. It doesn't matter now. It's all gone.*

You are blaming yourself again, said Lom.

"There she is," said Alex, before Jonas could respond.

He turned to see the Entrophier displaying Alicia Elde standing only ten metres away.

Alicia took in her surroundings, looking troubled, before quickly teleporting away.

"That was fast," said Alex.

"She seemed disturbed by something," observed Ruth.

"Perhaps this was what she sensed," said Jonas, as the surrounding walls and ceiling turned translucent.

"Mars?" guessed Ruth, regarding the dry wasteland of a world below, obviously devoid of all life.

"Earth," said Alex grimly.

"What happened?" asked Ruth.

"The station here records that a battle took place. This Earth was one of many casualties, see," said Jonas. He gestured, interacting with the station's system and an image to their left magnified to reveal Earth's moon, shattered in ruins. It looked as if someone had blown a hole through it. A small part of its mass remained.

"My God," said Alex wide-eyed. He turned back to look upon the dead Earth. It was now nothing more than a sterile, radioactive rock with no atmosphere. "Who did this?"

"We did," said Jonas. "Well, the humans here, that is. From the records on this station, it appears that human beings were the most dominant species in the galaxy. The first to rise and become a spacefaring race. There is no Galacien Conglomerate of Worlds here. Nothing to keep them in check. This is what happens when humans are allowed to advance unfettered. This is what the Galacien warned me of when I first encountered them thousands of years ago: that we are not mature enough to not threaten those around us, including ourselves. Despite my cynicism towards my own kind, I would not believe it. Yet here is the proof. The station records many great atrocities these humans have committed over the last several eons since they took to the stars. This would have been our future, even if the Earth had survived."

"Listen. Just because these guys are idiots, doesn't mean we are… were," said Alex. He winced, remembering again that it was all gone. "Every universe is different. Every human race… society, whatever, is different. Ruth and I have met some very noble humans out there." He thought of Princess Victoria and her people and how unlike his own culture they were. He remembered how warlike, dishonest, selfish and downright dumb his own people had been, and felt horrible for thinking that way because they were all dead now. But it was true. Victoria's people helped one another. There were very few wars. They were honest and open. He swallowed hard, wondering what Victoria was doing right at this moment.

"Alex," said Jonas, "we need to get moving."

"Sure. Sorry, I was a million miles away."

"As before," said Jonas, "you can use the modified Entrophier to track where she went next."

Alex focused on the area where Alicia had left this universe and easily tracked to where she had headed next.

"Wow," he said. "She's far out from the singularity. It's going to take me a moment."

May I see? said, Ruth.

Alex let Ruth see what he could in his mind's eye.

He could feel her surprise. "The Galacien did some long-range expeditions to distant universes, relatively speaking, and none even took them close to this."

"I've found her," said Alex, preparing to teleport."

There was a blinding flash of light, then nothing.

Alex woke up to a blinding pain in his head. He quickly realised that they were in the same well-lit chamber on the same space station. He remembered attempting to teleport. He sensed that there were others in the room and dragged himself up onto his knees. He saw them beyond a barrier of light which encircled him. They were human, their garb was close-fitting and unfamiliar to him. Around him, he saw Jonas and Ruth, also encircled in light. Ruth was still unconscious, while Jonas simply sat on the floor, his eyes closed, acknowledging nothing. Alex reached out to the barrier of light and felt its resistance.

Jonas, he thought, *Jonas!*

There was no response

He seemed to draw the attention of the humans and one of them approached him.

"Hello," said the man in a matter-of-fact manner, "I am called Cam. I'm sorry about having to hold you here against your will. But it is quite necessary."

"You're holding us prisoner?" said Alex.

"Yes," said Cam. "For that I'm sorry. But, as I said, it's necessary."

Alex took a deep breath. "Listen, my name is Alex, and it is very important that you let us go."

"There is no need," said Cam, holding up his hand in dismissal. "A telepath will be here soon and then we will know everything about you."

"A telepath?"

"Yes," said Cam. "Don't try to leave our universe using your abilities because you'll only hurt yourself."

"How did you know about that?" asked Alex.

Cam smiled. "Alex, Alex, my old friend, we are all super-sentient here."

"I'm not your friend," said Alex.

"Not you in particular. But our Alex Lethbridge was a good friend of mine," replied Cam.

"What do you mean, was?"

"The one you call Garianne came to our universe. There were few of us then; super-sentients, I mean. He agreed to listen to Garianne and go to your Earth and hear her proposition about confronting The Adversary. We were at war with one another. A war which was spreading across the solar system. Perhaps he could have been the deciding factor in such a war. However, by then we'd discovered many more super-sentients. When he finally returned, our Alex made little difference to either side."

"Is that why the Earth below is a radioactive ruin? Does that account for the state of the moon?" said Alex.

Cam regarded them both in turn. "No. That happened many thousands of years later. This time the conflict amongst our species was on a galactic scale. It would be hard to describe such events to you. They happened over such long time-scales and across vast distances. Many things changed. The alien species of the Milky Way were either destroyed in our wake or fled humanity's madness."

"What of the Galacien?"

"The Galacien do not exist in this universe."

"You seem well-informed," said Alex.

"You'd be surprised what we know about the multiverse."

"Is humanity still at war with itself?"

"No, that time has passed. We have finally come together. Though we will never be the same again," said Cam.

Alex could sense this was true. However, it was not sadness or humility that he could feel from the one who called himself Cam, but something darker. This being appeared human, but there was something dangerous about him.

"We changed the nature of ourselves, all the better to destroy one another. It is that which you sense," said Cam, holding Alex's gaze. "You would do well to heed my advice. Do as you are told or you and your friends may regret it."

Alex regarded him quizzically. "What are you saying? You seem fairly civilised to me."

"At the moment. Yet under certain circumstances, we become something quite different," stated Cam ominously.

There was an uncomfortable silence.

What does he mean? wondered Alex. His imagination ran amok. Did they turn into monsters?

"We have a new purpose now," said Cam. His eyes went wide and his face took on an almost joyous rapture.

"And what is that?" said Alex.

Cam only smiled. Alex thought he looked quite mad.

Cam turned away slightly. "Ah, she is here."

"Who?"

"There is no need for further conversation; she will tell us everything we need to know about you."

The door at the far end of the room opened and a cloaked figure entered. Cam left Alex, who wondered just how they were going to get out of this predicament.

Jonas! he thought yet again. There was no response. Was he figuring a way out of this? He found himself thinking back to his own Earth, as dead as the one he saw before him. He'd seen so many destroyed, either by external forces or by his own kind. He wondered if supposing his species had managed to work together, they would have been able to stop Sol 9173?

He sensed the unmistakable presence of a super-sentient. Looking up he saw the hooded figure. Alex stood and could see the unmistakable mouth and jaw of a woman, but the top half of her face remained in shadow.

She said nothing.

"So, you're here to read my mind," said Alex, disapprovingly.

"I already have," replied the woman, in a silky smooth voice.

"No kidding? I thought it might have taken longer. I mean, I feel insulted that it was over so quickly."

"You are young. There wasn't much to read. This one," she continued, regarding Jonas, "may take a little longer."

"Yeah, now he *is* old," said Alex.

"Not that old," she replied. "Interesting, he senses me and resists. Perhaps a different tactic." She removed her hood.

"Alicia!" Alex gasped.

Jonas opened his eyes and turned to look at her.

In his head, Alex heard Jonas address her. *You are not the Alicia from our universe?*

There was the smallest of smiles upon her lips. *All things being equal I would say that is irrefutable. However, I am not quite as you perceive me. It is not merely a deduction that you are the Alicia of this universe. Like Alex, I can sense that the very matter of your person is the same as everything else in this universe.*

Alicia considered this for the briefest of moments, before saying, *What if I were to tell you that I was created by your Alicia in much the same way you created Kallon, yet in a far more sophisticated manner. I was made from the material of this universe, so that I may pass as a native of this universe.*

You cannot be a copy of our Alicia, for you are super-sentient.

She was able to overcome that particular problem, said Alicia.

How and when did you introduce yourself into their society? asked Alex.

It was hundreds of years ago now. As far as how is concerned, I found a forgotten outpost on the fringe of the galaxy. I made it seem as if I were the last survivor of an enemy attack and sent out a distress signal at the appropriate time.

What about prior records of your existence? said, Alex.

I said I was born on the outpost and the records had been corrupted. The rest is history.

And you say you've been here for hundreds of years?

Yes. Hundreds of years, for me anyway, replied Alicia.

Why? said, Jonas

I'm afraid I'm not at liberty to say. Ask Alicia, the real Alicia, when you meet her.

Can't you just tell us? begged Alex.

I'm sorry, but no. We all have our part to play, especially you two.

What does that mean? asked Alex.

Alicia did not reply.

We need to escape, said Jonas.

Alicia nodded. *I will disable the shields and give you the time you need to teleport. This will be your last jump. Your final destination awaits you. Are you ready?*

Jonas looked at Alex, who nodded in affirmation. He then looked up to see Cam approaching from behind.

"How goes the reading?" said Cam.

Alicia turned to him, saying, "The big one called Jonas took some time."

Cam frowned.

"He is over two thousand years old and is a complex being," said Alicia. "This one who calls herself Ruth is even older, although she has spent much of that time dormant. I will rouse her. It will speed up the process."

"Dormant?" echoed Cam.

"Her natural state is that of a sentient implant," said Alicia.

Cam nodded in understanding and left them.

Alex looked over to see Ruth regain consciousness. He felt her in his awareness, through the bond which made them so close. Within moments she knew exactly what had transpired.

Alex sensed Alicia about to leave. *Wait,* he said, *that fella Cam said something about humanity's new purpose. What was he talking about?*

She looked to all three in turn. *They seek to find a way to travel beyond our multiverse and escape the threat of The Adversary forever. So that they may evolve without the threat of extinction forever hanging over their heads.*

Escape to where? asked Ruth.

It could only be what is called the omniverse, said Alicia.

Ruth and Jonas stared at one another, while Alex frowned at Alicia, confused, saying, *What is the omniverse?*

Alicia raised an eyebrow at Ruth and Jonas.

Ruth said *You've seen a model of the multiverse. Alternate universes like our own, yet different. The number of different universes is vast beyond imagination, yet it is finite. The omniverse expands on this model. It postulates that, in reality, everything and anything possible is happening, has happened or will happen somewhere in the omniverse. Infinity in every aspect.*

Everything you can imagine, no matter what it is, happens in the omniverse. An infinite number of universes; an infinite number of possibilities, added Jonas.

What, everything? said Alex.

Everything. Imagine every movie or television show you've seen, novel you've ever read. Everything imaginable, it exists as reality somewhere in the omniverse, answered Ruth.

As well as every alternate permutation of that universe. As well as everything which has never been imagined said, Jonas.

It is true infinity, said Alicia.

It's madness, is what it is, said Alex.

Ruth shook her head. *It's just an idea,* she shrugged dismissively.

The humans here are far more evolved than the Galacien. They believe the omniverse is real and are determined to reach it, one way or another, said Alicia.

It's just not possible, said Ruth to Jonas, hoping for affirmation.

Jonas, however, looked concerned.

10. MARS

We are among you. You will see us, hear us, but you will never know us.

Principles of The Kinsmen

Mars 3

Victoria looked at the alien landscape around her in astonishment.

Here she was.

Mars.

Even though she had recently visited the unimaginable, super-sentient-made artefact that was Galacien Prime, in an altogether different universe, she was still taken aback by the fact she was leaving footprints on the Martian surface.

Al-X assured her that General Alexander, Referick and the two of them were almost undetectable by the Martians.

She noted the *'almost'*.

"Nothing is infallible," Al-X had said with a knowing smile.

Her recently-acquired implant was all too eager to help her understand the complex concepts and intricacies of this stealth technology, yet she declined. She was still trying to get used to the voice in her head and the images it layered upon her sight and consciousness.

Victoria had never wanted an implant, the Galacien weapons or the attire which protected her from the harsh Martian environment and made it possible for her to breathe. But she had never wanted war with another world either. She was doing whatever was necessary to ensure the survival of humankind, and that meant accepting all the help she could get. Those she knew and loved were either already dead, like the loyal and honourable Captain Trent, or fighting to stay alive. The human race was on the precipice. This was the eleventh hour.

Victoria felt the change she had seen in others in times of war come over her all too quickly. The truth of it was clear now. Kill or be killed. It was the way of the world.

Victoria had felt her resolve harden back on Galacien Prime. Entering the fabricated room, the Galacien AI-X had created for her, she'd undressed and looked at her naked reflection in the mirror: dirty, bruised and wary prey. Not the person she recognised. She stepped into the shower and washed it all away. Emerging soon after, reborn, she donned the Galacien uniform, determined to do anything to save her species.

Your Majesty, she heard through her implant. She looked up to see Alexander.

She unclenched her fists and relaxed her jaw. Taking a depth breath, she said, *Sorry, I was miles away.*

Let's go, he said, indicating they join AL-X and Referick.

The human from an alternative Earth and the Galacien turned to greet them.

Gentlemen said Victoria, we're here. Do we have a strategy?

That ridge, said Referick, pointing in front of them, *is the lip of an opening, one point three kilometres across, into the Martians' habitat.*

Victoria noticed Alexander's eyes lose focus momentarily as Referick instructed their implants to show them all a tactical layout superimposed on their vision. She had ordered Alexander to also wear a Galacien uniform and have an implant. He wasn't happy about it but understood the necessity.

They live underground, then? said, Alexander.

Yes, replied Referick.

We want the two of you to go in there and take the fight to them, said Al-

X.

Are you joking? asked Victoria.

No, said Referick.

But, there are millions of them and only two of us, Alexander pointed out.

You'll be wearing SIBAT suits, so don't worry. Our Galacien technology is far superior to the Martians', said Referick.

Still… began Alexander, but he was cut off by his counterpart.

You need to disrupt and destroy to maximum effect, instructed Al-X.

What will you be doing during all of this? said, Alexander.

Waiting said Al-X.

For the real threat, said Referick.

The Martian super-sentients? queried Victoria.

Right. Alex nodded. *They will no doubt know about the attack. We aim to draw them away from Earth and back here.*

I cannot fight those things and win, said Alexander.

We'll do our best to deal with the Martian super-sentients. You put an end to this war, said Referick, holding Victoria's attention.

Remember, added Al-X, *your implants will guide you. Follow their advice.*

Listen, said Referick becoming very serious, *things can change in an instant during the course of a battle. Remember to stay focused on your objective.* His gaze lingered on Victoria and she felt these words were specially meant for her.

Victoria and Alexander made their way towards the ridge. She heard a distant roar to her right and, upon turning, saw on the horizon a cylindrical object rising on a column of fire and smoke. The Martians were sending yet more troops and machines of war to Earth.

Waiting for them, invisible to the naked eye but detectable by their implants, were their SIBATs.

More alien technology we must embrace to save our world, thought Victoria.

As she understood it, the SIBAT was an extremely advanced, living suit of armour, which flowed over their entire bodies.

Victoria felt a strange sensation as her implant connected to the SIBAT. She now felt as if there were three people in her head.

Spend a few minutes getting familiar with the SIBAT's systems, they both heard AL-X say.

Their implants then gave them the Victorian England guide to advanced alien ground combat against a vast Martian force.

This is ridiculous, said Victoria, *how am I supposed to fight? I have no training! I've let my anger and desperation bring us to this point.*

Alexander, in his enamel-looking SIBAT, turned to her but said nothing. She could not see his expression as the suit covered his entire body, including his face.

He reached out and took her by the hand. *No, Victoria, You made the right decision. It was I who was wrong in my reluctance to do whatever was necessary to save our planet.*

It should be one of our trained soldiers here, not me, said Victoria.

No. It has to be you.

But the SIBATS could do this without us. You know that. They know that, said Victoria, gesturing back at Al-X and Referick.

They could. But it should be us that does this, not them. Not entirely, anyway. We have to be the ones to end this.

Victoria remained silent.

You've always been the strong one, even when I knew you as a little girl, remember?

She felt a surge of emotion as the memories came rushing back. She had grown into a mature young lady, whereas he had not aged a day.

If this is what must be done if this is what I must face, then at least I will not fight alone, she said, tightening her grip around his hand.

Upon reaching the edge of the ridge, they saw the opening, almost a mile across, which dropped down into the underground structure of Martian society. They let their SIBATs scan deep into the hole to reveal a mass of machinery that Victoria could not fathom. A series of pods moving in what seemed like some strange production line.

What are we looking at?

Al-X monitoring the SIBAT through his implant said *It appears that this is where the Martians are created.*

What do you mean, created? said Victoria.

Your SIBAT scans reveal that these Martians are in the process of maturation. This whole place's sole purpose is to create soldiers to invade your planet, answered Al-X.

They can mass-produce soldiers? said, Alexander. *So where are the real Martians?*

Our probes reveal that this is it, said Referick. *These are the real Martians.*

You mean they're an artificial species? Created by who? said, Alexander.

The Adversary, said Referick. *They are an unnatural species, made to eliminate humanity. This place was created by The Adversary to set that in motion.*

Victoria looked down at the abomination below, and with grim determination said, *Gentlemen. I never wanted to do this, but we have no choice. Let us end this talk and do what we came here to do.* She stretched out her foot and teetered on the edge. *For Earth.* And with that, she jumped.

She dropped down into the abyss, the SIBAT slowing her descent so that it felt as if she were sinking through water instead of the thin Martian atmosphere. The Martian machinery was all around her, carrying on its business seemingly unaware of her presence. Through her implant and her SIBAT systems, she could sense Alexander close behind her. The SIBAT's weapons came online and she could see that the Martians below had now become aware of their approach. Victoria tensed when the first energy weapon hit her but felt comforted when she saw just how little effect it had on the SIBAT's shields. It then informed her that, if she wished, she could fire back: she had only to point and fire. She did so. At first, she was woefully inaccurate. However, her ammunition was practically limitless so she began to fire at a constant rate, each energy bolt reaching the ground instantly, and providing feedback on how to adjust her aim.

Victoria was aware that the SIBAT could easily acquire targets and destroy them, yet she insisted on doing it herself.

The ground was fast approaching and the Martians spread out around them. The SIBAT slowed her descent and they both landed softly. She continued shooting the Martian troops, arms outstretched in different directions, the energy bolts flying from her fingers at frightening speed, mowing down all who approached her. She could not deny the thrill she felt taking such action against her enemy after being just another victim for so long. The power she felt, it was intoxicating.

At one point, when turning to shoot down more Martians, she narrowly missed Alexander. Her SIBAT reassured her that his shields would have taken the hit with negligible damage.

She paused when she recognised a giant Martian war machine making its way towards her, its weapon ready to fire. She could not help but raise her arms in defence when it let loose a continuous beam of energy at her. Yet again, her SIBAT informed her its shields could handle it and suggested she return fire with a far more lethal continuous beam of her own. She selected the weapon and it burst forth from her extended hand. The Martian war machine exploded instantly as they both landed onto the ground.

More troops and machines of war were set upon them, but she could see now that they were no match for the SIBATs. She looked up and focused her weapons on the 'factory', as she thought of it. Alexander followed her lead. Destruction rained down all around them. Huge pieces of machinery crashed to the ground, killing those they fought, while in the middle, like the eye of a storm, stood Victoria and Alexander, unscathed.

Victoria could not remember the last time she felt so empowered.

Then she saw the Martian super-sentient.

Without thinking, she raised her hand towards it and fired, but the Martian super-sentient had already disappeared.

It's here! she hissed. Both she and Alexander turned nervously, scanning for their foe. *Alexander, do you sense anything?*

It's above us somewhere but it's difficult to locate, said Alexander. *Referick, Al-X, we need you.*

There was no reply. They waited. The Martian troops and war machines had pulled back.

Al-X? Referick? Victoria called.

The Martian super-sentient. It got to them first, said Alexander, *his voice laced with dread.*

No. How would they know? Despite the power bestowed upon her by the SIBAT, Victoria suddenly felt very vulnerable. She could feel herself quivering, knowing the Martian super-sentient could scoop her up in an instant and teleport her to someplace so inhospitable that even the SIBAT suit could not protect her.

They waited and waited. All of a sudden there was a flash of light between Victoria and Alexander.

She saw a woman holding Al-X and Referick, both of them unconscious, one in each fist. She threw them to the ground and regarded them.

"Who are you?" demanded Alexander.

She looked at them both with a raised eyebrow, her contempt obvious. Victoria and Alexander looked around. The Martians had begun to draw closer, but, at the subtlest of gestures from the strange newcomer, they stopped.

"At first I watched with great interest and amusement the events of your first war with the Martians, as was the purpose of their creation. Garianne brought two unexpected pieces onto the board. It made the game all the more interesting, for I was already growing rather bored with how things were going. This second war has played out in its unique way," said the woman.

Victoria studied Al-X and Referick, "You. You're The Adversary?" she said.

The woman continued as if Victoria had not spoken. "But now here we are, in the end. Know that even if you survive here this day, you cannot stop what has already been started. What I've set in motion. It is coming for you. For all of you in what you consider reality." The Adversary spat the last word out in contempt.

And then she was gone.

11. ALICIA ELDE

The nature of becoming Kinsmen means that those who start down the path might not even realise it. For deception is the Kinsmen way, and so those who are destined to become so will not know the name or the true nature of the path they are on. It may come under the guise of something else entirely that they find themselves being educated, enlightened and evolved.

Principles of The Kinsmen

Alicia opened her eyes and considered the closed portal before her. It was made of a concoctive mix of exotic matter and energy, interlaced with other structures from hyperspace, metaspace and the energy grid. Its construction was far beyond what the Galacien could understand. She had met many species whose technological mastery was far more sophisticated than that of the Galacien from her universe, yet this construct before her was beyond even their ability to engineer. It had taken her years to develop, for she had no teacher and there was no-one else she had encountered who could do what she was attempting here. Alicia did not know how many more alterations she would have to make to the portal's energy matrix until she was successful.

It would, of course, take time. But how much time did she have?

So far from the singularity, further out than any living sentient in the multiverse. Where days passed here only a fraction of a second would pass back in her universe of origin. She was also rather competent at the speeding-up of her thought processes to rival that of any being or system she had encountered. Without this ability, she would never be able to control the incredible technology that manipulated the immense energies held within. It may seem to an observer that she'd spent days here, sat before this open doorway where strange patterns of light could be seen to dance across its surface. Yet for her, it had been many weeks now. At first, the task before her humbled her, but then came the familiar fiery passion. The challenge had been set. Here was something thought impossible to achieve. She had smiled. She was a learning machine. It was just a matter of time before she finally succeeded and was able to pass through the portal to what lay beyond.

As Alicia considered her next tactic, she felt something familiar.

There. A point of contact very close to where she now sat. Her whole physiology was primed in an instant, her mind considering hundreds of scenarios in a heartbeat as the world around her slowed. She perceived the point of contact as an energy signature reaching out from this universe towards another. A universal teleporter was reaching out to this place and was about to appear. Luckily, because of the time difference, what would take him or her only a second would take minutes. Alicia calmly stood up and launched herself up high above the planet to get a good vantage point, waiting patiently and unseen for their arrival.

They arrived in the precise location she had, all those months ago. Obviously, they were following her trail. There were four of them. Two super-sentients, two not. None were subverted by The Adversary. One was noticeably stronger than the others: an incarnation of Jonas, she noticed. He reached out with his awareness, searching the area, like tendrils branching out, even stretching to where she waited. However, he did not sense her, she made sure of that. The other super-sentient was the teleporter, Alex Lethbridge. It was easy to slip into his mind and find out about the others, Ruth and Lom, to know where they had been and what they were doing here. When they brought out their own Entrophier, she knew it would lead them to her. She considered disrupting its systems so that it no longer worked. The Entrophier was a toy when compared with the portal. Yet, perhaps it was time to work together. Hadn't that been the idea all along? They and the others were destined to come here.

She made adjustments to the plan.

The environment where Jonas, Alex, Ruth and Lom found themselves was not too dissimilar from Earth when compared with some of the places they had been in the past. The sky overhead rolled with dark brooding clouds, areas of deep bruised purples fading to black. The wind rocked the large, black, spindly trees around them, sparse of foliage.

Jonas went down on one knee and felt the short grey grass between his fingers. "It feels synthetic," he said.

"Over there," said Ruth, pointing down towards the valley, "is a small community."

Below lay a small cluster of buildings and a number of alien creatures moved about.

They were only dots on the landscape. They each used their enhanced vision to get a more detailed look.

Alex's vision magnified the aliens, their shape all too familiar to him. "Nacuerians!" he exclaimed.

"In their original form, before they were transformed by The Adversary," said Jonas.

"They look different, somehow," said Ruth. "Their skin, and there are other differences." She looked at Jonas for confirmation.

Jonas nodded. "Yes, intriguing. Let's go down there."

"Won't they attack us?" said Alex.

Jonas didn't respond as he headed off towards the Nacuerians.

Ruth followed shortly after. "Come on," she said.

Alex shook his head, wondering whether this was a good idea. Nonetheless, he started to walk.

A couple of hundred metres from the outskirts of the alien community the first Nacuerian stopped and turned, aware of their approach. Others stopped what they were doing and fixed their attention on the newcomers.

Make no aggressive moves, Jonas warned them via the implant.

And what if they make the aggressive moves? asked Alex.

Then use a shield. I don't want to hurt them. I want to understand why they are here.

The Nacuerians continued to watch them enter the centre of their small community, barely moving or making a sound.

Why do I get the feeling they're about to pounce, said Alex?

One of the Nacuerians came up to them.

Alex felt himself tense, trying to find comfort in the fact that, no matter how fast the Nacuerians were, Jonas was faster.

"Welcome," emanated a voice from the hulking Nacuerian. There was no mouth from which the voice came, and it sounded machine-like, devoid of natural emotion. Ruth and Alex exchanged a glance.

Jonas looked curiously at the creature. "Greetings. My name is Jonas, and this is Alex and Ruth," he said, indicating each in turn.

"And the other?"

Jonas smiled, intrigued at how it knew of Lom's presence. "That one is called Lom," he replied. "What shall I call you?" continued Jonas, stunned by the fact that he was asking a Nacuerian such a question.

"Vaullen." replied the Nacuerian, lifting one of its tentacles and gesturing to its kin.

"All of you?" said Ruth.

"Yes," came the mechanical voice.

"Hive mind?" said Jonas.

"Yes," said the Vaullen.

"What do you mean, hive mind?" questioned Alex.

"They all share the same thoughts. They are all linked, like a network," Jonas explained.

"How do they know our language?" said Alex.

"Ask them," said Jonas.

"Sorry," said Alex, realizing he was being rude. How strange, he thought. Why were they so benign? "Excuse me," They all turned to look at Alex. "Where did you learn to speak English?"

"The other. She taught it to us," said the Vaullen.

"The other? Alicia?" said Jonas.

"That is her name," stated the Vaullen.

"Alicia Elde taught you how to speak our language?" summarized Ruth.

"Yes."

"Can you explain how long ago this event took place in measurements of time that we can understand?" said Jonas.

The Vaullen paused for a moment before saying, "Seventeen of your universe's Earth's years ago."

"She's been here for a while," said Alex.

"Not really," said Jonas.

"Alicia told us many things, and in return, we shared our knowledge with her," said the Vaullen.

"Is she still here?" said Ruth.

"She still resides on Emmita."

Alex felt Jonas' shock like a punch to the gut.

Alex looked at him. *What is it?*

Jonas' eyes were wide; he seemed lost in thought.

"Jonas!" snapped Ruth.

Jonas regarded them both before saying, "Later." He then addressed the Nacuerians by saying, "You are not an evolutionary species, are you?"

"Evolutionary?" repeated The Vaullen.

"Your species did not change over millions of years, from simpler forms to what you are now," said Jonas.

"No. We were created a long time ago."

"By whom?" said Ruth.

"We do not know."

Jonas. Why do they look like Nacuerians? asked Alex.

"We can hear you when you use your implants," said the Vaullen. Jonas looked impressed. "What are Nacuerians?"

"You look very much like another species we are familiar with," said Jonas.

"We need to find Alicia. Use the Entrophier," suggested Alex.

"I do not need the Entrophier," replied Jonas. "She is here. I can sense her."

"Can we assume, then, that she knows we're here?" said Ruth.

"Definitely," said Jonas. He turned back to Vaullen. "We need to go and speak to our friend now." And with that, he walked away.

When they were away from the community, Alex asked, "What happened back there, Jonas?"

Jonas stopped again, seemingly pondering something.

"Jonas, what is it?" Ruth gently touched his arm in concern.

He glanced at them both, then said, "They call this world Emmita."

Alex saw realization on Ruth's face.

"Yeah, so?" he said.

"Emmita was the name of my mother," said Jonas.

12. REVELATION

Mars 3

"Well. We're in for it now," said Alexander, looking anxiously at the Martians ready to attack. He could sense, but not see, the Martian super-sentient moving about above them.

Victoria could only stare, ready to fight, knowing it would not take long for them to fall.

Yet the Martians did not move.

"Why aren't they attacking?" said Victoria.

"That would be me," came a voice from the ground.

Referick turned his head towards them. "I've got them," he said.

"What do you mean, you've got them?" said Alexander.

"I've put them in a state of neural stasis. It's probably better that I comatose them completely," said Referick.

He brought himself to his feet. Alexander and Victoria saw that every Martian had slumped and fallen unconscious.

"We'll leave them this way. They will never wake up. Their bodies will simply waste away and die. Even the super-sentients'. They'll bother you no more. Even the ones on Earth."

"You've done the same thing to all the Martians back on Earth?" asked Victoria, aghast.

"Yes. The war is over," said Referick.

Al-X was also awake now. He looked at his friend, intrigued. "I didn't know you were capable of such a thing," he said.

Referick looked bashful. "I am not the person you know as Referick. My real name is Alicia Elde. However, you may still call me Referick."

"Sounds human," said Alexander.

"I am," said Referick.

"Who is, or was, Referick?" asked Al-X, annoyed.

"A necessary deception. A persona I adopted to move about unobserved by The Adversary," said Referick.

"It knows you?" said Victoria.

"It knows of me. We haven't been formally introduced."

"How did it not know who you were?" said Alex.

"It was not looking, and I am very good at becoming someone else. If for some reason, The Adversary had decided to obliterate Referick, then that is what would have happened. The deception is of utmost priority. It takes precedence even over one's continued existence," said Referick.

"But what is the point if you are dead?" asked Victoria.

"Because I am only one of many," said Referick. "It is more important that the whole is protected. As they say, you can lose a battle as long as you win the war."

"How can you be sure it isn't observing us now?" said Alex.

"It isn't. It's too busy tying up loose ends and chasing after me: the original me," said Referick.

"The original you?" Victoria searched for elaboration.

"The 'me' that came first, who created all the others," said Referick.

"These others," said Al-X, "are they super-sentient?"

"Yes."

Al-X's mouth dropped open.

"What is it?" said Alexander.

"No-one has ever been able to do such a thing. To create a copy of oneself. The Galacien can do that. But to create a copy of a super-sentient, with their abilities intact, you can do that?"

"Yes," confirmed Referick.

"So, you're a woman?" said Alexander.

The others burst into laughter, and for a moment all the horror of recent events washed away.

"Don't let my Referick appearance deceive you, Alexander. Yes, I am indeed female,"

"Well, Referick," said Victoria, "you have the undying gratitude of my world. You have saved us from extinction." She knelt before Referick, her head bowed.

"Your Majesty!" cried Alexander. "A queen does not kneel."

"In these circumstances, this one does," said Victoria.

In an instant, Alexander was down. It wasn't right that she knelt while he remained on his feet.

Al-X tried withholding a smirk.

"We are forever in your debt. If there is anything we can do to repay you," said Victoria.

"There is," said Referick.

"There is?" said Al-X

Referick looked at him.

"No disrespect. I admire the way you were willing to fight for your world," said Al-X.

"Indeed, Garianne spoke very highly of you both," said Referick.

"You've met the Lady Garianne?" asked Victoria standing, thinking back to when she was a little girl, remembering the beautiful, graceful woman who seemed even more regal than her own dear mother.

"My original self did. I retain all those memories. So, in a way, yes," said Referick. "Garianne said that of all the Earths she visited, and there were a great many, your people were the most mature. The most enlightened."

"Enlightened?" echoed Alexander.

"In comparison to the majority of Earths in the multiverse. Most of the countries on these other Earths are at war with one another, committing terrible atrocities against one another."

"What kind of at atrocities?" asked Victoria.

"What is referred to as a World War," said Referick.

Victoria and Alexander looked at her bewildered. "A world at war, with itself?" gasped Victoria.

"Sometimes two or three times," said Referick.

"That's…idiotic!" declared Alexander.

"I rest my case," said Referick.

"How can they help, though? Only Alexander is super-sentient?" asked Al-X.

"They have the qualities I am looking for. I can make anyone super-sentient," said Referick.

"You can?" said Victoria and Al-X in unison.

"It is something I'm capable of, yes," confirmed Referick.

Alexander glanced at Victoria, "Are you thinking what I think you're thinking?"

Victoria remained silent.

"Your Majesty, we don't know if this is even safe," warned Alexander.

"I assure you it is," said Referick.

"I'm sorry," said Alexander, "but I don't know you. I appreciate what you've done, but I can't trust someone I met only a few minutes ago, and who was lying about their real identity."

"That was necessary," said Referick.

"Is filling the Queen's head with these ideas necessary?" demanded Alexander.

"I don't believe the decision is yours to make," said Referick.

"I vowed to do anything to stop the Martian invasion. That is over now," said Victoria. Alexander visibly relaxed.

Victoria continued. "Nonetheless, we have no guarantee that this will not happen again and again. As long as The Adversary exists, the threat also exists." She stood tall and lifted her chin a little as she addressed Referick. "Tell me two things. One, would my being super-sentient in any way improve our chances of success at destroying our enemy, once and for all? And two, do you have a plan?"

"I will not lie. There is a high probability that you may be killed in the upcoming confrontation," said Referick.

"True," said Victoria, "but it's preferable to waiting on Earth for the next assault The Adversary decides to send our way."

"Indeed. To answer your questions. Yes. Everything we do improves our chances, even if only in some small way. More beings like us may lessen the likelihood of us all dying."

Al-X laughed, "What an interesting way of putting it."

Referick smiled. "And yes. I do have a plan."

13. THE MEMORY STONE

The planet Emmita in an unknown universe
Jonas, Alex and Ruth walked towards the mysterious portal. It stood there in a large courtyard encircled by stone obelisks. Further up the hill, they saw another building. It reminded Jonas of an ancient Babylonian temple. Despite its primitive facade, he could sense the underlying technology that could reshape its internal configuration much in the same way as Galacien structures could.

A young woman waited, watching them as they approached.

"That must be her," whispered Alex.

"She can undoubtedly hear you, Alex," said Jonas, even though they were still a few hundred metres away.

Alicia radiated confidence, without seeming arrogant. She had a relaxed, open expression. Alex felt as if he could talk to her about anything as if she were his oldest and dearest friend. *How strange that I should feel this way about someone I don't know.*

Alicia said nothing, and neither did Jonas. Alex glanced at them both and rolled his eyes. Feeling the need more than anyone else to fill the silence, he said, "You aren't an easy person to find."

"That was the point," smiled Alicia.

Her voice was a match for her beauty; Alex felt like he could listen to her speak all day.

"Our Earth is gone," said Jonas.

Alicia became serious. "I know."

"We followed your trail…" began Jonas.

"I know," said Alicia, glancing away for a moment, "I know everything. I read it from your minds."

"Without our permission?" said Ruth, annoyed.

"It can't be helped, I'm afraid. My mental capabilities have evolved to the point where not being able to read your minds, your memories, in an instant would be like you trying to function without your sense of proprioception."

"Our… what?" said Alex.

"Your sense of knowing where your limbs are in three-dimensional space. It is how you can touch your nose, even if blindfolded," explained Jonas.

"I'm sorry. It is something you'll have to get used to," said Alicia.

Ruth wasn't satisfied but what could she do?

Jonas thought for a moment. "You know everything about us, but what about you?"

"Garianne saw something in me. That I was gifted, even for a super-sentient. She sent me out into the multiverse in the hope that, given more time, my exceptional talents would come up with a way of stopping The Adversary. I used others and tested our foe in many different universes. Trying my utmost not to give myself away."

"You used others?" said Ruth.

"Whether we know it or not, we are all in this together. This way, some of us survive. Or none of us survives," said Alicia.

"And you get to choose?"

Alicia paused for a moment before saying, "Unfortunately, yes. I ended up here. I believe this place holds some significance concerning The Adversary."

"We spoke to the Vaullen," said Jonas. "I think The Adversary evolved from a species, originally native to this universe, perhaps even this world. Perhaps it created the Vaullen."

"Perhaps. This universe is very old," said Alicia. "I have been attempting to create a doorway." She indicated the portal.

"Where does it lead?" asked Alex.

"If I am successful in its creation then I will be able to go anywhere in the omniverse, that which is our true reality," said Alicia.

"The omniverse. It truly exists?" said Ruth.

"I know it does. I am very close to completing this portal. It could be instrumental in defeating The Adversary."

Alicia suggested that Alex and Ruth get some rest, while she and Jonas attempted to finish working on the portal.

As Jonas watched Alex and Ruth leave he could feel Alicia's eyes on him.

"Now that we are alone," said Alicia "perhaps it is time to share what's on your mind?"

"What do you mean?" asked Jonas.

She smiled. "Come now. I'm impressed by the control in your voice, as well as over every facet of your physiology. It could fool any technology and most super-sentients. But I am not most super-sentients."

Jonas looked at her, confused. "I have no idea what you are talking about."

"I understand: you can't admit it. Very well, I will do it for you."

Jonas' reaction was minimal.

"Don't worry, you are quite safe here from, what would you call him? Your counterpart? Your original self?"

Jonas said nothing.

"If you're wondering how I know this, I read your mind. I know you are well practised at hiding your thoughts and feelings from others but you can't hide anything from me. So?" She gestured to him.

Alicia waited.

Jonas sighed.

"I suspected I was not the original Jonas but only a copy not long after my encounter with The Adversary and what may, or may not, be The Kinsmen in this continuing elaborate game of deception in which we find ourselves," Jonas smirked. "How ironic. I used to think 'I' was the master of deception."

"You are," said Alicia. "Just not the 'you' I see before me."

Jonas nodded. "Quite true. I realised that for some reason I have not evolved as I should have in the last two millennia. The super-sentient Vasha said as much. I thought long and hard as to the reason why, and finally came to only one possible conclusion: 'Jonas' had evolved as would be expected, and 'I' was a copy created by him for some unknown purpose."

"Can you deduce why?" asked Alicia.

"It would seem I am supposed to act the part of Jonas so that he can remain unseen and unknown by the enemy."

"Go on," encouraged Alicia.

"Upon realizing this I almost confided to Lom, but stopped myself."

"Why?"

"I must have come to this conclusion in the past. I could only surmise that I had and that the original Jonas must have somehow altered my memory."

"Let me confirm that this is indeed the case," said Alicia.

"Is there any way to retrieve those memories?"

"I'm afraid that's impossible. However, I can tell you at what points during your life your memories have been tampered with."

"Can you tell me how old I am?" asked Jonas.

Alicia scrutinized him a moment. "You were created in his image so that no-one could tell the difference. But I can tell the difference. You were created less than one hundred years after Jonas' arrival on Terra."

Jonas felt his fists tighten. "Deception is the key. I remember thinking that during the Galacien/Nacuerian war."

"Those are his memories," said Alicia.

Jonas nodded grimly.

She considered for a moment whether to tell this Jonas that she had been in contact with his creator for some time now, but thought better of it. However, there was something she could share with him.

"Speaking of memory, I did find something of interest, and possibly of great significance."

"What is that?" said Jonas.

Like a magician, she turned over her hand to reveal what seemed to be an unremarkable stone.

Jonas merely stared at it; his brow furrowed. There was something unusual about it. His senses were telling him that there was an unknown power emanating from within.

"I found it here, just lying around. I would have missed it, but I was drawn to it, as are you. I'm not certain but I suspect it contains some kind of holographic memory storage, similar to that of the Galacien memory archives. However, this is far more advanced. I am considering interfacing with it and finding out whose or what memories are inside. It's just that…"

"There could be unforeseen complications or even danger," said Jonas.

Alicia nodded. "If there are built-in defense mechanisms then I'm not sure what could happen."

"You want me to monitor you while you interface?" offered Jonas.

For a moment her analytical composure slipped. Alicia smiled, and somehow, she looked like any other normal human girl. "Would you?"

"Of course," said Jonas. "What connection do you think it has with this world?"

Alicia turned the stone over in her hand, "I'm not even sure there is one. This could be something entirely different. Not even related to our goals."

"Nevertheless, you are curious," said Jonas with a smirk.

"As are you. The unknown, it's what drives us," said Alicia.

"When would you like to begin?"

She looked up from the stone. "No time like the present," she answered.

"I'm ready," affirmed Jonas.

Alicia closed her hand around the stone and shut her eyes.

Terra 327BC

In the years after the Nacuerian/Galacien war, Jonas spent his time wandering the planet of Terra. He climbed its snow-capped mountain ranges, followed its meandering rivers and swam its seas and oceans. He never tired, or suffered from the blazing heat of the deserts or the brutal cold of the polar ice-cap. He only stopped to take in the vistas or because he merely felt like it.

The Galacien observed him from the depths of space. Always wondering what he would do next. The answer always seemed to be – nothing remarkable.

However, they were not to know that Jonas had mastered the art of being in two places at once. While he traversed this untouched world, his metaphysical self would travel to the other planets, habitats and starships of the Galacien Conglomerate of Worlds. He'd perfected his ability to interact with technology while in this form, giving him unlimited access to the systems of any space-faring species. He learned, and sometimes he manipulated to test and hone this particular skill.

He was never truly alone for Lom was always with him. A constant companion. To discuss and debate. They were separate enough entities, yet because Jonas had to remake Lom with a piece of his own consciousness, there would always be an overlap between where one began and the other ended. Yet it was enough for a dialogue.

It was when Jonas was pulling himself up on top of a rock face, while simultaneously rummaging around the archives of an old, prominent AI system, that Lom said to Jonas, *I sense that you are reaching the point where you are ready to take action.*

Jonas replied, *If you are referring to the problem of The Adversary, then yes, I think I've spent enough time pondering the matter.*

Are you sure you've had enough time? asked Lom.

Jonas smiled. Lom was one of the few sentient beings he genuinely liked. *Is that an attempt at humour?*

In part. However, I do appreciate the magnitude of the problem. How do you stop a being with omnipotent power?

I've concluded that we cannot think in those terms because a truly omnipotent being would know everything. Including being aware of this conversation. I believe The Adversary is a creature as close to omnipotent as we can comprehend at this level of our understanding, explained Jonas.

So, what should we do?

We need to evolve to a much higher level of understanding until what appears omnipotent becomes something we can realistically overcome. The mechanism with which we will achieve such a goal before it is too late lies within the workings of the multiverse itself. But first, we can't leave things as they are on Terra.

What do you mean? asked Lom.

We will be leaving. However, we need it to look as if we never left. The best way would be to create a facsimile of myself. As far as the universe is concerned this will be the true Jonas. I will have to limit his abilities to some degree. Otherwise, somewhere down the road, there would be the distinct possibility that he would lead the enemy to us. Let him choose his own path.

He would have to believe he was you, said Lom.

Of course. Once I have decided on his limitations, I will run some simulations to see what direction he will take in the future.

Jonas sensed surprise in Lom. *What is it?* he asked.

You have evolved so quickly, said Lom, *The Galacien were never able to create super-sentients. It is no mean feat.*

We still have a long way to go, my friend. That is if you are you still willing to join me?

Until the end, said Lom.

And despite all of Jonas' talk of wanting to be left alone, he could not help but feel relief and comfort that he was not.

14. JONAS AND LOM

An unknown planet in deep space 321BC
Jonas, in his metaphysical form, spent the next few years creating great machines at a staging area on one of the few remaining planets in the galaxy as yet undiscovered by the Galacien. He built giant fabricator machines that were able to create any structure at an atomic level. They would help him build that which he required.

He worked tirelessly on two major projects. The first would be a machine which could not only replicate his mind and body, but also his abilities. The Galacien had been able to clone themselves and download a copy of their memories into such a body for centuries now. Transferring or replicating a super-sentient's abilities into a clone was deemed impossible by the Galacien. Jonas had to admit it was going to be a difficult task, yet he was confident that, given time, he would come upon the solution. His mind worked at a rate that could outpace any computer system. Again, he knew this should be impossible considering what the Galacien AI's were capable of. However, he was super-sentient, he was the impossible, and this particular flavour of impossible was his speciality.

Jonas ran through billions of simulations to explore the means by which to transfer what made him special to his clone. The task was arduous. Whenever he breached a new area of discovery he found he needed to build yet more machines with which to explore it. This would need refining and, in turn, branch off to something else. He felt like he was single-handedly working through the future of what the Galacien would discover in their next one hundred thousand years of technological progress.

Jonas' second project was to create a portal to another universe. He was able to teleport himself, without the need of technology, but only over short distances. He could not move from one universe to another like the multiversal teleporters of old. With this, he hoped to be able to find and place himself on a desirable world in a universe so far removed from his own that he could evade the notice of The Adversary itself.

It was several years into his experiments and simulations when he made a most significant discovery.

Incredible, he thought, stopping completely and considering its meaning. Even his physical body back on Terra stopped in its tracks. He spent almost all his attention and focus on his various projects to the extent that his physical-self had become almost like an automaton; it needed so little of his mental processes to go about its business of drawing the attention of the Galacien, and even possibly agents of The Adversary.

What is it? said Lom.

It had been so long since he had spoken to Lom. Too long. He felt a pang of guilt.

It, erm… It appears one of my creations — he did not need to name his machines, it only mattered that they produced results — *has detected… something.*

Forgive me. But would you mind expanding on that? said Lom.

It appears that there is some kind of energy that exists at a level beyond superspace. It permeates all of reality.

And you've never detected it before?

There has been no way to detect it before.

Is it natural? asked Lom.

I believe so.

The Galacien have made most of the significant discoveries already. There are few remaining mysteries left, said Lom.

Except where super-sentients are concerned. They cannot create or transfer their abilities into a cloned body, said Jonas.

So, you believe this universal energy and super-sentients are linked?

It is a strong possibility, said Jonas. *It will take a long time until I'm able to find a way to utilise this universal energy. But, if I can tap into it then there is no telling what we could do. It could be what we have been looking for. The key to stopping The Adversary.*

Only a few years had passed since the end of the Nacuerian/Galacien war, during which Jonas had started the great work. However, Jonas spent most of that time thinking at a speed where the real world had slowed significantly. Consequentially, for him it felt more like centuries had passed. Jonas could function on his own for a very long time. Yet even he had to admit that this was unusual.

It is affecting your progress, said Lom.

You are right. The very fact that it has taken you to say it to me illustrates the fact that I need a separate entity to continue. I need to create some other personas. Simulations to keep me grounded. Keep me sane. Everything I do is seen from my perspective. I try to distance myself as well as focus on my work. See problems from as many angles as possible. It is not enough. I need those qualities that only a completely separate sentient being can bring. I do not expect much from them, for their level of intellect will be inferior. But from the mouths of babes comes wisdom.

What are you proposing? said Lom.

I will create simulations from the Galacien memory archives of Davern, Garianne and Min.

Are you sure that's a good idea? said Lom.

I am. I know them. They are all very different and I have a unique relationship with each of them. They all bring something to the table, said Jonas.

What about Min? said Lom.

Do not worry. I am quite a different being from the one who spoke to her last. It will work out.

We shall see.

Jonas put everything else on hold while he 'acquired' the

aforementioned Galacien memory archives. With a little modification, they were ready.

He created a simulated environment of Lom's starship interior for them to come into existence within and wait until he was ready to talk to them.

Min materialised onto the command centre of the Lom starship simulation.

Puzzled, she looked around to see Garianne and Davern exactly how she remembered them.

"Just give it a moment," said Garianne, holding up her hand before Min could speak.

Min not only remembered everything until the last moment she had seen Jonas on Terra but other things. Things that weren't experiences of her own.

"That's right, Min. He's downloaded all the 'mission' details right here," said Davern tapping his head, "with everything else we need to know."

She gave him a dark look. "He's illegally created simulations of us, for his own ends. Am I the only one who finds that a little unnerving?"

Davern looked at Garianne.

"He must have a very good reason. Jonas?" said Garianne.

Jonas materialised into the simulation, regarding each of them in turn. "As Davern said, you all know what I need from you. More or less. I cannot continue alone."

"That's a pretty big admission coming from you," said Davern.

"My work could take me hundreds, possibly thousands of years. When I'm completely immersed, when the world slows down and falls away around me, I am fine. But when I come back up… I realise I need something," said Jonas.

"What?" said Min abruptly.

"Companionship," said Garianne. "He is changed somewhat from the being we once knew. However, a sentient creature, no matter how evolved or enlightened, needs others to exist."

"What about Lom?" asked Min.

"He is too much a part of me, and I of him. He provides some comfort. But I need more. I am not forcing you to do this. If you wish, I will discontinue your simulation and find another way," offered Jonas.

"You mean, destroy us," said Min.

"Yes," said Jonas. "You don't like that idea? Well, that's too bad. I do not have time for such niceties. The creature that created the Nacuerians threatens not only our universe but many others as well. I do not see how anything or anyone can stop it, save me. This is not ego talking, it is plain fact. The path I tread is a long and arduous one and I do not know where it will ultimately end. But I'm asking for your help. If you like, I'll only call upon you when needed. The rest of the time you can sleep, in the manner that a simulation does. Ask yourself this, though: is not the life of everything in all of existence, including the life of your real self out there worth, committing your own existence to? Let me know when you have reached your decision. I have work to do."

"I need no time to think this over," said the Garianne simulation, smiling. "I am here for you."

"Yeah, count me in too. Could be the greatest adventure I've ever embarked upon," said Davern.

"Possibly," remarked Jonas.

He then regarded Min.

"You're not the same," observed Min.

"No, I'm changing. Into what, I do not know. But I need to evolve as much as I can to save us all," said Jonas.

"I will help," said Min, "for as long as I can."

15. SENTIENT SIMULATIONS

An unknown planet in deep space 311BC
It wasn't until a decade later, although much longer for Jonas, that a way was found to not only recreate a person's mind and body but to also endow them with the same super-sentient abilities as the original. Jonas was now ready to create a perfect copy of himself.

An incredible accomplishment said Garianne.

It took long enough. I've been able to map the unique pattern in which the universal energy connects with my being and manipulate that pattern in this cloned body, said Jonas.

I'll just nod my simulated head as if I understand exactly how that works, said Davern.

You're not expected to, said Min.

I expect you'll be making some adjustments to this decoy? said Lom.

Of course, continued Jonas. *I will have to restrict his abilities and create some false memories to hide what we have been doing all this time.*

Wouldn't it be useful to have two or even more of you working on this problem? suggested Min.

I am concerned that such a move, though seemingly prudent at first, would attract the attention of The Adversary. If it can detect super-sentients such as myself, growing significantly stronger day by day, then this mass of Jonas's could draw it here in no time at all, said Jonas.

You don't know that, said Min.

No, admitted Jonas.

It's not worth the risk, said Garianne.

No. Deception is the way, said Jonas. *As far as the Galacien and The Adversary is concerned, this clone will be me while I leave this universe to continue the work, unseen and unknown.*

How will you swap out the current you on Terra with this version without the Galacien noticing, or any agents of The Adversary, for that matter? asked Davern.

I am ready and about to proceed, said Jonas.

Really? said Min, taken aback.

My physical self is exploring a network of caves back on Terra. I will make the swap there, said Jonas.

Are you sure the Galacien cannot detect you? said Davern.

I've checked their observation satellites and platforms. They cannot see me, said Jonas with calm certainty. *Now, if you'll excuse me, it is time.*

The clone of Jonas awoke in a cave. Curious, as it had been some time since he'd slept. Years, in fact. However, he knew that even though super-sentients had no need for such things, they were known to have slept from time to time. He could not remember what had drawn him to these caves. Whatever it was, the feeling had passed. Having spent years exploring the world of Terra, he felt it was now time to concern himself with the problem of The Adversary and begin to develop his abilities. It was time to return to his humble abode and prepare.

The real Jonas watched his cloned self leave the cave. He was completely confident that he was undetectable by his doppelganger.

What will he do now? asked Garianne.

He will evolve and plan. I believe that at some point in the near future he will come up with a way to ensure his privacy from the ever-prying eyes of the universe. Inevitably he will realise that the only way continue is to create a perfect copy of 'himself' to act as his decoy. Due to his limitations, this will take him somewhat longer than it did, me. This will work to my advantage as it will create another layer between The Adversary and myself.

What about much further in the future? asked Min.

If we survive that long, I cannot say. The variables increase as time goes on, and you must understand that nothing is certain. I cannot predict the future with one hundred percent certainty, said Jonas.

Well, I for one am glad of that, said Davern, *because that would be utterly dull.*

I'll be sure to let you know if I ever do solve that particular problem, said Jonas.

Davern looked at him, not knowing whether he was serious or not. *If you do, you have my permission to discontinue my simulation.*

But Davern, said Min with a sly smile, *who would amuse us then?*

Jonas would have to develop a sense of humour, said Lom.

That will never happen, retorted Davern with utter certainty.

Min and Davern snickered.

Children said Garianne.

Jonas agreed with her, yet he would be lying if he said he did not feel like smiling himself. He knew then for certain that creating and interacting with the Garianne, Min and Davern simulations had indeed been a good decision.

Now that the Jonas clone was about 'his' business, he could turn his attention towards leaving this universe far behind to continue the work in a safer environment.

Do you have any idea where we are to go? asked Davern.

To a universe far older and far removed from this one. With luck, The Adversary will not notice us there, but I do not know for certain. But from the impression I got from the Nacuerians, it will spend quite a bit of time operating at our speed of thought. All the better to observe us. I believe that there are many occurrences like our recent war with the Nacuerians happening all over the known universe, and possibly in other universes, where The Adversary constantly amuses itself, said Jonas.

You mean we were merely entertainment? Sport? said Min.

Something akin to that, yes.

The sooner we move to this new universe of yours, Jonas, the happier I'll be, said Davern.

I agree, said Jonas. *You also might like to know there will also be other advantages.*

Such as? demanded Min.

Time will move more quickly there relative to our native universe. Hopefully, we will have all the time we need.

We know of this in the Galacien, said Garianne, *from the multiversal teleporters of the Golden Age. We must be careful of these time dilation effects.*

I have the Galacien records, said Jonas. *Most of the dangers come from moving to those universes closer to the multiversal singularity where time moves significantly slower than here. We will be moving further out, so to speak, to a universe where time moves significantly quicker. Hopefully, I can manage to get us to a universe where for us every year will be mere minutes in this universe,* said Jonas.

Garianne looked thoughtful. *You could achieve a lot given such timescales.*

Jonas nodded. *Perhaps even what now may seem impossible.*

Very clever, said Garianne, *using the mechanics of the multiverse to your advantage.*

This machine you've been working on to teleport us there, how long until it's complete? asked Min.

The things I have learnt from creating a super-sentient clone of myself now mean that the machine has become obsolete. I will be able to bestow a multiversal-teleporter's ability onto a sentient being, said Jonas.

Garianne, Davern and Min looked at one another.

You're saying that you can give anyone super-sentient abilities? said Davern.

Yes.

Well, let's take the fight to The Adversary, said Davern.

You do not understand. A super-sentient, even an army of super-sentients, is no match for the god-like power of The Adversary. The confrontation would be over before it even got started. We continue with the original plan, said Jonas.

Still, said Garianne, *no small feat.*

Thank you, said Jonas.

To which being, in particular, do you plan to give the power of multiversal teleportation? asked Min.

Are you volunteering? said Jonas.

Was she? Min was caught off-guard by the question. What would it be like to have such power? *I… I don't know.*

Davern? said Jonas.

It's a tempting offer. I'll get back to you in a few years. But for right now, I'm happy, said Davern.

Garianne. I can think of no-one better.

Garianne smiled. *I have had my fair share of responsibility, thank you very much. What about Lom?*

I am quite content here with Jonas, they heard Lom say from the interior of the starship simulation.

I can imprint these abilities onto myself. I would evolve naturally and develop such abilities, but we do not have time to for that, said Jonas.

No, said Min. *I will do it.* Her eyes glazing over, she blinked a few times, then focused on him.

Are you sure? said Jonas.

Yes, said Min, *I'm certain.*

A few days later Jonas was ready to proceed. He had created a clone of Min on the same unknown planet where he had built his other machines. Again, his metaphysical self worked on these creations deep underground. He'd spent a long time establishing exactly how the universal energy would intersect with a sentient being, to give rise to someone with the same abilities as one of the multiversal teleporters from the Galacien Golden Age. Recreating a copy of himself had been easier, for he had his own pattern as an example. There were no multiversal teleporters anymore, and so he had to gain an in-depth insight into the intricate workings of the universal energy and how it gave super-sentients such specific abilities. His research into this field of knowledge would keep him busy for centuries. However, that was for later. He was simply content, for now, in the fact that he would be able to endow this version of Min with such an ability.

Time and again he asked her if she was sure about her decision. Every time she assured him she was. For a moment he paused in his work. An unusual thing, for him.

You are unsure, said Lom.

The others were not around when he worked at such speed, his thoughts like quicksilver. Only Lom, being such a part of him, could keep up.

Yes, though I do not know why, said Jonas.

You and Min had a potential romantic relationship in the past. You are about to make her into something more than a sentient collection of memories, commented Lom.

Jonas gave him the mental equivalent of a quizzical look. *Isn't that what we all are? Still. I am far beyond that now.*

It is still a part of you, said Lom.

I planned to do this alone, unseen and unheard of by the rest of reality. To work behind the scenes. Creating the simulations was necessary for my mental state. I need my mind to continue the work into the future. But this. Bringing a physical super-sentient into existence. It feels as if I'm bringing an unknown quantity into the equation, said Jonas.

Then perhaps you should leave things as they are and imprint the multiversal teleporter ability onto yourself.

In the starship simulation, Jonas told them of his decision and the reason why. It was obvious Min was unhappy.

So, I would be a complication to your grand plan? said Min.

There is far more to it than that, said Jonas.

I don't understand, said Davern. *One minute you're offering this, the next you're not. How much of a complication can one more super-sentient be in a universe far removed from this one? It's pretty unwarranted.*

Min is rather an enlightened being, added Garianne, *I don't think you give her enough credit. What is it you fear exactly?*

Jonas did not want to say, but he knew he must. *For example, I'm concerned that she may travel to other universes. An action which may draw the attention of the enemy.*

Then I won't do that, said Min. *Anything else?*

Jonas said nothing.

Listen, Jonas, said Min drawing close to him, *I know what's at stake here. I'll do whatever it takes. Tell me what you need me to do. Tell me what you don't want me to do. I only ask that you allow me to help.*

The others waited for him. He looked at her and saw her as

he'd once remembered her, thousands of years ago, a mere decade for them. She, of course. was the same noble being. Only he had changed.

Alright, he agreed, *but there will be rules.*

Of course, smiled Min.

It had been san age since she'd looked at him in such a way. It stirred in him feelings he'd thought long lost. Perhaps only dormant.

16. JONAS AND MIN

An unknown planet in deep space 311BC

Min's awakening in her new body was much the same as her last. She was surprised to find that Jonas wasn't present. He was busy. Instead of his assistance, she had the disembodied voice of Lom to help guide her through her standard evaluation. It was based on the Galacien model, except for some modifications due to her now being super-sentient.

She still could not believe it for she did not feel that different. The facility she found herself in was the same as the one you'd find on a Galacien world, except this one had been built by Jonas deep underground on this unknown world. After going through the standard tests set for a normal sentient being, Lom informed her it was now time for her to test her super-sentient abilities. Min felt a rush of excitement.

"Before we start," said Lom, "Jonas said you needed to know a couple of things. Firstly, he made it so that your abilities will be far easier to access than a natural super-sentient."

"What do you mean?"

"A natural super-sentient finds it difficult to access its abilities at first, like reaching through a hole in a box and blindly attempting to manipulate a mechanism. This is why it takes practice and time to master such abilities. However, in your case, it is as though the box has been taken away and you can see the mechanism. He needs you to learn, and quickly. We can't wait a hundred years for you to master your abilities," said Lom.

"Alright. What else?" asked Min.

"Jonas has also been able to give you a strong connection to the universal energy," said Lom.

"Meaning?"

"You are probably the most powerful multiversal teleporter to have ever lived," stated Lom.

Min could not deny the quickening of her heart as she took a deep breath. She could feel her body buzzing with energy, or was it just the excitement? The anticipation of the oncoming tests?

"He said that your power level is something that should not be underestimated. We need you to be able to get us as far removed from this universe as possible. To a place where no super-sentient could have taken us before," said Lom.

"Not even Jonas," Min whispered to herself.

"No," said Lom.

Min was guided from the evaluation room into a vast chamber. There was almost nothing there except the odd piece of equipment, and two SIBATs: one a Protector Class, which was about her height, and the other a Guardian Class, which towered above her.

Jonas teleported before her.

"Did you do that?" said Min.

"Yes, I have that ability, but it's not on the same level as what you can do," said Jonas.

She looked at him strangely. "What is this?"

"What's what?" said Jonas.

"I feel… things. Emotions, concepts, the fringes of thoughts that are not my own," said Min.

"You are sensing me," explained Jonas. "As a super-sentient, you will be able to sense your surroundings in a far more intricate and sometimes intimate manner. Sometimes it can be overwhelming. In time, you will learn to tune it out. Right now we should test your strength and resilience."

Jonas put his hands together, and when he pulled them apart she could see a Galacien pistol materialize in his grasp. He pointed it at her and fired.

Min teleported behind him.

Jonas turned around. "Good."

"That was amazing!" cried Min. "It was as easy as taking a step."

"You are a natural," said Jonas, firing the gun at her several times.

This time she just stood there open-mouthed, looking down at where he had shot her. Incredibly, she was unharmed.

Jonas nodded his approval. "It appears you are pretty durable. Multiversal teleporters tend to be. They need to be in order to be able to travel anywhere. There are some rather inhospitable places in the multiverse. We'll do more thorough tests on that later. Now I would like to know how strong you are."

"How do we do that?" said Min.

A large metal box materialised around Min.

"Ah, I see," said Min.

Enveloped in darkness, she wondered if she could teleport out of here. Definitely. She could certainly sense everything outside the box. But that wasn't the point of the test. She walked up to one of the walls, drew back her fist and hit it as hard as she could. To her dissatisfaction, her fist didn't go through it. A few more forceful punches and some time spent tearing out a hole and she was able to get out of the box.

"Do not be disappointed, you cannot excel at everything. The important thing is that you can get us to where we need to go," said Jonas.

"Well, with enough practice, I'm confident I can do it," said Min. She sensed concern from him. "What?"

"I am afraid that practice will have to remain on this planet. Any teleportation on an interstellar level or between universes could draw the attention of The Adversary," said Jonas.

"You mean the first time I'll do anything significant is when we do this for real?" exclaimed. Min.

"Yes," said Jonas. "It is the only way.

"I'm not sure about this. What happens if I make a mistake?"

"I will be with you every step of the way," assured Jonas.

Min looked doubtful.

"We'll make sure you are as strong and as comfortable with your abilities as possible, hence the SIBATs," said Jonas, indicating the Protector Class, and the Guardian Class looming over them both. "Combat experience with them will hone your powers and build your confidence. I have drawn up a programme for you to work through with Lom. When you have completed it, you will be ready."

Min nodded. This was familiar territory. She'd been trained by the Galacien for many decades into an exceptional warrior. For the first time, since awakening as her simulated self and now being put into this new body, she felt a sense of purpose.

"How long do we have?" she asked.

"The sooner the better. The longer we remain in this universe, the more at risk we are," said Jonas.

"I won't let you down," she said.

Min was true to her word, throwing herself into the task with hardened resolve. She could not get over how easy it was to use her newfound abilities. She could manifest portals and shields; teleport things without even touching them. This proved especially effective when disarming opponents. Displacing them into solid rock was equally effective. However, the SIBATs also learnt quickly and those created by Jonas himself caught her off-guard; they were able to use sonic weapons against her, disrupting her concentration. She knew then that it was the development of that concentration, her will, despite the circumstances that was the key to overcoming her opponents: you can't fight if you can't think. She learnt to think clearly during similar experiences so that she could always fight back. Lom was impressed by her progress and said that Jonas was also pleased. Yet she felt frustrated being cooped up on this one world when she knew she was capable of so much more. She wanted to let her metaphysical self explore the universe. She felt it calling to her.

After many days she could bear it no longer, and with a sigh of relief, she let her metaphysical self rise into space. She looked down upon the dead, rocky planet below; it certainly was the kind of place no-one would come looking for them, even if they knew of their existence. The Galacien would discover it soon enough, but by then they should be long gone.

Min turned her attention to the stars and saw everything. The whole of the universe was there. She could feel it. And she knew every part of it was accessible to her. She found the mere concept overwhelming. The entire universe had been reduced in size to something that could fit in the palm of her hand. It made her feel… god-like. Despite the way Galacien society felt about such deities, this was the perfect word.

The urge to move out there was almost irresistible. Min did not know her limits yet; she hadn't encountered them. Nevertheless, at that moment she felt as if she could take on The Adversary itself. As soon as that thought crossed her mind she felt something strange. It felt as if something was looking back at her, there, amongst the stars. She felt transfixed. What was it? There could only be one answer, and yet she did not feel afraid, only curious.

Something grabbed her and she found herself back in her physical form.

"What do you think you are doing?" cried Jonas, his hand tight around her arm.

"Ow, that hurts!" said Min, surprised. She broke free of his grip, rage flooding through her body. "Don't you dare touch me like that."

"I said—" began Jonas.

"I heard what you said. And I said don't touch me like that, ever," hissed Min with such venom that Jonas was taken aback. He looked at her strangely. "I apologize," he said.

For a moment neither of them said a word.

"Do you realise the risk?" said Jonas.

"I know. I'm sorry," said Min. Her anger had washed away as

quickly as it had come. The power of it had frightened her. For the briefest of moments, she felt as if she would lash out at him, without thought, without reason. It was in complete contrast to the way Galacien had brought her up to be an enlightened being. She had never reacted in such a manner in her entire life. The look he'd given her — it was obvious he thought so too. She did not mention the presence she felt. The entity that looked back at her from the infinite.

"I came to you to say that I believe you are ready. It is time for us to go," said Jonas.

Min couldn't agree with him more. She wanted to leave immediately. To get as far away from here as possible.

17. THE NEW WORLD

An unknown planet in an unknown universe

She saw it again, against the backdrop of stars, the depths of the universe. Something staring back at her. She knew what it was. It knew she was there. It knew her name. It knew everything about her. There was a familiarity about it. Min felt like a baby lying in her crib looking at a parent. Feeling something akin to comfort, yet with it was something terrifying, like finding your beloved partner standing amongst the corpses of their victims. Corpses that stretched on forever. A secret you could not bear to accept; too terrible to conceive.

She woke with a start and saw Jonas closely scrutinising her.

"What did you see?" he whispered, carefully, as if trying not to break a delicate spell she was under.

The memory already fading. She realised she was lying down, sweating. Her hands grasped his arms with enough force to break granite. He did not seem to notice. Min stared at him.

"I… I don't know," she said. She let go and fell back on the bed, catching her breath. He sat beside her, waiting.

She glanced over and saw him deep in thought, as was his way.

Min looked around. She was in a small, darkened room. She

sensed they were on a world similar to Earth.

"Where am I?" asked Min, realising that she had no memory of recent events, "The last thing I remember is preparing to make the jump."

"You're suffering temporary memory loss. It should return soon enough. I pushed you. Too hard, some might say. But you did it, Min. We are far removed from our original universe, safe to do what needs to be done to safeguard all of reality," said Jonas.

She could sense his satisfaction, and something else. He was proud of her: it shone from him, barely contained. It made her feel good.

"How long have I been unconscious?" said Min.

"A few days. Rest for now. You will recover." Jonas stood up. "Get up when you are ready. There is no rush. I need to work. The others will keep you company and help you with anything you should need."

He made to leave. The automatic door slid open before him and Min caught sight of the world outside with familiar green grass, blue sky. A pleasant breeze caressed her face.

Turning, Jonas said, "Thank you, Min. Your actions have taken us one step closer to eradicating the scourge that hunts us all."

The very next day Min forced herself to get up and go outside. She walked out onto a beautiful veranda, which hadn't been there yesterday. The veranda was built upon a hill and looked over a lush green valley with a river running through it. The sun was setting and an unfamiliar pattern of stars was emerging. As she turned she saw an elaborate building, a juxtaposition of many architectural influences from the Galacien Conglomerate of Worlds. She could see and sense the fabrication of many more additions to the building's overall structure.

What's the purpose of this place? thought Min.

Just in case, said Lom.

In case of what?

Jonas likes to be prepared. Who knows what the future may bring, said Garianne.

Jonas teleported onto the veranda. "I asked Lom to inform me when you were awake," he said. "You've given us a chance Min. Here, in this universe, on this world."

"It seems I've brought us to not only an adequate world but a beautiful one at that," remarked Min, taking in the view.

It was a pleasure to see the pink and orange hues of the sun play out across the sky and to feel the gentle breeze upon her face. She felt quite content and very safe here on this world, in the universe so far removed from their own. She knew The Adversary would never bother to venture this far out. She shook herself from her reverie when she heard Jonas begin to speak.

"I've named this world Emmita," said Jonas.

Min sensed this name had meaning for him; she looked at him quizzically.

"It was my mother's name," he said.

Min smiled and nodded.

"Here I can study the infinite complexities of the universal energy. I believe The Adversary may be super-sentient like us."

"How do you know that?" said Min.

"I don't. As I said, it's a theory, an impression I get from the way it utilises its powers. What the Nacuerians knew of it. However, unlike us, it seems to have unlimited access to that power and it has an indomitable will. In short, there is not much it cannot do. If I can understand how the universal energy works and find a way to access its power the way The Adversary does; if I evolve to utilise my will to equal that of our enemy, then I may be able to stop it. But the timescales I'm talking of to accomplish such a feat. Min. It could take thousands, possibly even millions of years," said Jonas.

Min was stunned. "What of me, what of the others?"

"Garianne and Davern have spoken of going to sleep. To be woken every century or so. Lom will remain with me. Even though he is his own being, we are still a part of one another.

He will be my link to the outside world while I am immersed in my work."

Min imagined Jonas' attention turned inward, his mind working to a degree where the world slowed and fell away. She had heard him describe it in such a way. All the while the ever-faithful Lom would stand guard watching over him in the outside world. She could not help but admire them both.

But what about me, she thought.

Jonas said, "Min, you can join the others and go to sleep. It would be very much like a normal life. You go to sleep, wake up, and your friends would be there to share things with, do whatever you want, then go back to sleep when you are all ready. The only difference would be the timescales. You would sleep for decades or even centuries, and you can also be awake for as long as you want. Even a century here is but the smallest fraction of time back home. It would be a good life. However…"

"What?" queried Min.

"You are the strongest of all the multiversal teleporters. I know you must feel it," said Jonas.

Min looked up at the stars, and a well of longing rose up in her so strong she felt the tears in her eyes.

"All those who came before you felt it," said Jonas. "But you, whom I made to be so much more, must feel it a hundredfold. You are not meant to be bound to one place, Min. I will not hold you here. I only stress the importance that you remain in this universe, for the safety of everyone."

"This universe," said Min, in an almost dreamlike state, "is enough."

"Go, Min. Be free," said Jonas.

"What about you?" she whispered.

"I will be fine. Lom is with me," said Jonas.

"I will return."

"I will be here. Now go."

Without hesitation she was in the air, accelerating upwards at incredible speed into the upper atmosphere until she was out into space, where she belonged.

Do you think she will be alright? said Lom.

Min will be fine. The Adversary has been, and will always be our primary concern, said Jonas.

He could not deny he would miss her, but as always he pushed it all aside and his unshakable resolve returned.

18. ASCENSION

The planet Emmita, in an unknown universe
The centuries passed and events transpired as Jonas had predicted. Min explored the limitless possibilities of this universe. She visited worlds undreamt of, found long-gone civilisations and watched other species evolve. Some were pre-spacefaring; others spanned across their native galaxy. Many had sown the seeds of their own destruction. Others had stagnated. Few had moved on to higher levels of being.

She had conversed with such beings. They were not as evolved as Jonas and in some ways, their powers over matter and energy were inferior to her own, which was growing stronger all the time, but they were some of the most evolved beings in this universe. This very old universe. And even though their power was limited, their wisdom was often worth listening to. They were unaware of The Adversary's existence yet heeded her warnings about it.

Lom contacted her from time to time over the eons, asking her to return. She always returned to find the four of them waiting, Garianne and Davern awake from their slumber in physical form. They said they missed the simple things such as eating, dancing, even combat. Anything involving the physical.

They all listened to Min as she spoke of her experiences in this universe. Jonas was always the quiet one. When they asked him about the work, he kept his answers brief. He tried to hide it from the others yet being super-sentient she could sense how he was feeling. These times they spent together usually lasted only days. Relatively short. So, she had to make use of the time when only the two of them were together, except for Lom, of course. He was always there.

Thousands of years after their arrival in this universe, when Jonas and Min were taking a walk, she said, "Have you noticed that Garianne is not quite the person we remember? Why is that?"

"It is true," said Jonas. "I do not understand why. I created her from the original Galacien archives. She should be the Garianne we know. Yet she is not."

"Has she said anything to you?" said Min.

Jonas nodded. "Both she and Davern have spoken to me about it. We do not know why. It is a mystery."

"I don't like it. It is as if there is some missing element from her. That special quality she possessed, it's gone." said Min.

Jonas sighed. "I have not been able to ascertain why this is so."

"I'm sure you could find out," said Min.

Jonas shook his head, "No. I have to commit my time to The Adversary."

They stopped walking and she looked at him. "Not even a bit of your time? I know your intellect has grown significantly. You can do more than one thing at a time, in ways we can't."

She felt a reaction to that last comment. She scrutinised him a moment. "You're doing it right now, aren't you. Just how much of your attention does it take to talk to me while doing 'the work?'"

"A very small fraction," admitted Jonas. "I've been doing it for a very long time now."

Min tried to imagine how they must seem to him. Was it like communicating with dumb, primal creatures, or not even that?

"No, it's not quite like that," said Jonas.

"You can read my thoughts?" Said Min.

"I can read everyone's thoughts, Min," he said simply.

"What about Lom? Have his faculties grown with yours?"

"No," said Jonas. "I feel the chasm between what he is and what I am becoming grow day by day."

"Jonas, this is dangerous. You are becoming distant. We have all noticed it. You barely speak when we are all together. I'm noticing you change more and more every time I return. Surely the day will come when you will lose all interest in interacting with us, but even if you did, it would be such a small fraction of your attention it would be meaningless," said Min.

"The work must continue."

"Not like this. You sound like some kind of automaton, Jonas. Programmed to fulfil your primary mission at any cost." She reached out and took him by both hands. "You're willing to sacrifice yourself to find the answer? You can't do this."

"If it is the only way—" began Jonas.

"No!" Min barked at him. "You created the three of us because you needed us to help you. And it worked. It got us here. I may not be as smart as you, but I believe you need that again. You can't continue on your own. You need someone to be on your level, otherwise, you'll miss something. You need someone to bounce ideas off. But they must be your equal."

"Are you volunteering?" asked Jonas.

Min looked stunned. For a moment she said nothing. "Are you telling me that you can get me from where I am now to wherever you are?"

"Yes. And may I say the very fact that this did not occur to me before proves your point," said Jonas.

She could not argue against that. She also couldn't deny how tempting his offer was. Being super-sentient had enriched her life and given it more meaning than she could ever have imagined. What other goal was there in the long run than to improve yourself? To grow in your capacities. She had gone from being a normal sentient of the Galacien, granted a simulation, to begin with, to a super-sentient. Now he offered her the chance to be so much more.

"What would it be like? Being like you?" she said.

"The leap is further than from being merely sentient to super-sentient. You will have the knowledge and the ability to manipulate the universal energy. To control your evolution at will. The possibilities are endless. Godhood will be out of reach, for now, but you can see the way; it is only a matter of time until we both attain it. That will be the end of The Adversary."

She felt rather than saw the others were with them, watching her, curious as to what she would say.

"What would you do in my place?" she asked Garianne.

"The offer has not been made to me, but to you," said Garianne.

"That's not what I asked," said Min.

"Ask yourself what it is you want, Min," said Garianne.

"I used to find that an easy question to answer. I had loyalty to the Galacien to uphold the values of what they stood for. I still do. I'm super-sentient now and I served a higher purpose: to get us here, to give Jonas a chance to save us. If I can do something that brings us closer to victory, I have to do it."

"How are you going to do this, Jonas?" said Davern. "As I understand it, when you do your thing it's as if the outside world slows to a standstill. It's been thousands of years since we got here. How long has it been for you?"

"Millions," replied Jonas.

Davern and Min looked at one another, astounded. Garianne merely nodded.

"Alright," said Davern, trying to maintain his composure, "millions of years of learning, accumulating knowledge and understanding. Evolving into the being you are now. You can't just give that to someone. It must take time to assimilate all of that."

"You are right, Davern," said Jonas. "I will have to give Min the super-sentient faculty that I possess. That ability to learn at an uncanny level. Like the ability to teleport, it is something I will bestow upon her. It will not be natural. And thus, I will be able to make it even more efficient. In time she will be able to understand all that I understand and do all that I can do. It will not be long until you will be able to access the universal energy and understand how it makes us more than merely sentient. You will be able to unlock other abilities and learn how to access almost limitless power. This is what I meant about controlling your own evolution. All aspects of reality will be yours to control. The only limits will be your ability to access the universal energy, your imagination, and the strength of your will. This, and only this, is what separates us from The Adversary."

Having nothing more to say, they all turned their attention to Min.

"It's not a decision to be taken lightly," she muttered.

"Of course not," agreed Jonas.

"But I find it an easy one to make. I accept your offer," said Min.

"That was quick," said Davern. "Don't you need a little more time to think about this?"

"No. I think you are basing that question on the person I was, rather than who I am now. I have travelled all across this universe and experienced so many things. I am more than just another super-sentient. The path before me is clear, and this is the next step."

"No matter how much you evolve, Min, I hope you'll not forget to check in on Davern and me from time to time," said Garianne.

"That goes for you too, Jonas. Don't forget where you came from. No matter how big you get or whatever you become, remember we were the ones who were there at the start," said Davern.

"I will never forget," promised Jonas.

Jonas reached out his hand to Min, saying, "Are you ready?"

"Yes," said Min. She reached out and held his hand and they disappeared in a flash of brilliant light.

Min could feel that she was now in her metaphysical form and that she had been brought to a place she was unfamiliar with. It seemed to be a place of light and dark but of little substance Though she could discern patterns, they changed quickly and were foreign to her.

Jonas are you there?

I am here, Min.

She could not see him, but his voice was enough to comfort her.

Where am I? said Min.

On the periphery of where the universal energy exists. It is the best place to… change you.

You destroyed my physical body, didn't you? said Min.

It was no longer needed.

You might have asked first, said Min, amused.

Sorry, I will ask next time.

If Min could laugh, she would have. *Next time?*

She sensed Jonas' amusement.

I am sure there will not be another occasion where I will have to destroy your physical body in order to reconstruct it, although you do not need to have a physical form to do what is required, said Jonas.

It may come in handy.

Probably, said Jonas. *First I need to connect you with the universal energy, with a pattern similar to my own.*

Do I need to do anything?

No, but you may find it…

Painful? suggested Min.

I was going to say somewhere between frightening and exhilarating, said Jonas. *Like being pushed off a cliff. It will not hurt and you will come to no harm.*

I'm ready, said Min.

With no further delay, Min felt a huge rush, as if she were travelling at great speed although she knew this was not the case. It was as if she sensed the universal energy itself, and there was something else. Something that she couldn't put into words. For the briefest of moments, she glimpsed something more than what she thought of as reality, something beyond what was known as the multiverse. Min felt her awareness expand even more than she had done when she became super-sentient. Her thoughts flowed like quicksilver. A great many things became clearer, and concepts she'd found difficult to grasp before were simplistic. She could not only see the landscape of all her past understanding but could now conceive of that which was not seen. The creatures underground, the deep strata of millions of years. This was what it meant to truly understand. To see something from a high perspective while knowing every close-up detail from every conceivable point of view. It should have sent her mad with information overload; however, this was now her super-sentient ability and she was a creature of understanding. As a bird is a creature of the air, as a fish is a creature of the water, she could not drown in her natural habitat.

She had no idea how long she remained there pontificating on everything she'd ever learnt from this new perspective.

At some point in time, she felt her mind filling up with new information like a vast reservoir. All the knowledge that Jonas had acquired over millions of years (for him, anyway) slowly flowed into her. She knew this would take time. Like the rains upon a newly terraformed planet, it would take some time for them to create the seas and the oceans.

Are you alright? asked Jonas.

Yes. It's a lot to take in. There is so much, said Min.

Then I'd advise you to spend this time to learn. In this state, you need nothing to sustain you but the universal energy itself. A part of me will remain here and watch over you, said Jonas.

Years later Jonas stood on the unnamed planet of their arrival, waiting with Garianne and Davern for Min's return,

Min appeared before them, saying nothing, but silently communing with Jonas, for their minds worked at such efficient speed and their form of communication was beyond that of mere language. If such an exchange were to be brought down to its lowest terms for the benefit of Garianne and Davern it would have gone something like this.

I am pleased to see you were able to reconstruct your physical self, said Jonas.

'A' physical self. I can take any form now.

Of course.

We are equals now, said Min.

More or less. Due to the way we acquired our abilities and who we are, we will both have different strengths and weaknesses. I look forward to the day when you can teach me something, said Jonas.

Perhaps that day is today.

Explain, said Jonas.

I've sensed something beyond the multiverse, said Min.

Truly? I have not.

I know.

What is this something you are referring to?

That which is the omniverse.

The theory that everything that can happen does happen. A truly infinite reality, of which our multiverse is but a small, infinitesimal part? Do you have evidence to support your claim?

Not yet. It is something I will pursue.

Do not forget our primary mission. Despite our power, we are inferior to The Adversary. Even together we could not hope to defeat it.

And to create more like us would be to draw its attention, said Min.

Are you sure you are alright investigating this? I sense the possibility of the omniverse being real frightens you.

It does. I thought I would be beyond such things, given what I have evolved into.

Unfortunately, fear seems to be a constant companion, even for beings such as we, said Jonas.

I will be fine, said Min. *You continue your understanding of the universal energy, while I seek to discover the mystery of the omniverse.*

Agreed.

Min waited for only a fraction of a second, but for them, it was an age. No-one could appreciate the sacrifice Jonas had made or understand all that he had done. No-one but her. She could not help but admire and respect him and with that something else.

Will you be alright? she asked him.

He sensed this new affection for him and was caught momentarily off-guard.

We must attend to the work, he said.

Of course.

Then the majority of her being was gone. Jonas left soon after, both of them leaving the smallest fraction of their essence back in their physical forms to converse with Garianne and Davern. From time to time, as they spent time with their friends, they would glance at one another wondering what their lives would be like if not for the threat of The Adversary.

19. EXISTENTIAL CRISIS

The planet Emmita, in an unknown universe

She came to him when Garianne and Davern were, once again, 'asleep'.

I need you, was all she said.

Jonas' metaphysical self reached out to her and they embraced. More than that, they merged. Each knowing the other's thoughts.

You are... began Jonas.

But she silenced him with the mental equivalent of a shake of the head.

Don't speak, she said, *not yet. I just want us to be like this.*

He said nothing, just gave her the comfort he knew she desired. Soon enough it became more intimate in a way which went beyond the mere physical. She sensed how much he had loved her. How many times he'd sacrificed his wants for the needs of everyone else. The burden of reality on his back for all those millions of years. She knew all of these things, of course. But to feel it as though she were Jonas made it all too real.

Jonas saw himself reflected in her thoughts and said, *Do not pity me. I have gained so much and we are together now in a way we could have never conceived of before.*

You were alone too long. No-one should have to go through that, said Min.

We have both struggled, said Jonas.

She knew what he was referring to.

I saw it Jonas, and now that we have shared ourselves, our thoughts, you have seen it too, said Min.

The omniverse said, Jonas.

It's real, Jonas. The true shape of reality.

Everything that can happen does happen.

An infinite number of universes. An infinite multitude of scenarios have been, are being, or are going to be played out. Everything we do, Jonas, has been, is being, or will be done. There are universes where our counterparts succeed against a counterpart of The Adversary and places where we are defeated utterly. Some differences between universes are so inconsequential that you'd be forgiven for thinking they were identical. One low energy particle on a different trajectory in a far-off galaxy can make no difference. Who would know the difference? What does it matter? There are infinite versions of us, of life, of everything. What does any of it matter?

Jonas could sense the edges of despair drawing her in, as if it were a vast, dark maw, the ground around her giving way, becoming steeper, her descent quickening, reaching the point of no return.

Min! His being bellowed in her mind through every fibre of her being, shaking her from her terrible fascination. He held tight to Min's mind and fixed her attention firmly on him. *Calm yourself.*

She caught her composure.

You were losing yourself, said Jonas.

I'm sorry, said Min.

It is alright. Understandable, considering your discovery. I saw it for myself. Normal sentients would be fine with such a concept. However, we are beings of deeper understanding. A concept such as this is overwhelming, even dangerous, as we have seen. We are made to understand things absolutely, so something finite is easy for us. Yet the infinite, because of what we are, is more difficult for us to handle.

I feel in time it will be possible, and may prove useful, said Min.

They were now separated and so Jonas did not know precisely

what she meant.

Explain, he said.

The answer to defeating The Adversary is there in the omniverse. There will be universes where we have already succeeded. The difficulty will be finding them amongst the infinite multitude of others.

Jonas considered this. *Your logic is sound. Still, I am concerned for your welfare in this matter.*

Being first and foremost a multiversal teleporter of unparalleled skill, I am the best suited for this, said Min.

Are you sure?

Yes, affirmed Min, now feeling renewed confidence. *The initial feeling has passed. I now feel confident and I am looking forward to observing that which is the omniverse, that of which our multiverse is but a small part.*

Take your time, said Jonas.

Of course.

Once more she touched his being, but only for a short time, and then she was gone.

Do you think she will be alright, said Lom.

I do. I am more concerned about my progress. It is as if I am climbing a mountain on my stomach, yet the worst thing is I have no idea of the size of the mountain. Are we near the top, or have we only just begun?

I think, in such a case, it is best not to know, said Lom.

Perhaps.

I am glad you have found one another. You need each other, said Lom. *I do not understand the details of what it is you do anymore.*

You still help though, old friend. You have been with me since the beginning. I am sure these conversations have benefited me psychologically.

I am glad to contribute. Losing your sanity in this endeavour would not be good, said Lom.

That is an understatement, said Jonas.

Time passed.

Then Jonas felt it was again time to wake up Garianne and Davern, and for Lom to seek out Min to see how much progress she had made.

Lom didn't return.

Something was wrong. Jonas felt sure of it. Had The Adversary finally found them? There was no reason for it to believe that 'Jonas' wasn't back in their universe, on Terra, rather than here.

"You're telling me the omniverse is real?" said Davern.

"Yes," said Jonas.

"What does that even mean?"

Garianne said, "It means everything happens. Anything you can imagine, Davern, somewhere at some point, in reality, it happens."

"Anything?"

"Yes," said Garianne.

"I thought the multiverse was the entirety of reality," said Davern.

"If what Min says is true," said Garianne.

"I've seen it for myself," said Jonas.

"Then our multiverse is less than a drop in the ocean," said Garianne.

"It makes sense that it does exist," added Jonas.

"Oh really?" said Davern.

"Of course. Take the concept of time travel, for example," said Jonas.

"Which we know is impossible. The Galacien proved such a thing a long time ago," said Davern.

"Within the framework of our multiverse, that is true. Yet I know of a device created by the super-sentients of the Golden Age that could peer into the past. I, also, have been able to do such a thing, without the aid of such a device," said Jonas.

"That's incredible, I'll grant you," said Davern. "But you can't travel in time… can you?"

"Information must be travelling from the past to your own time for you to see anything," said Garianne with curiosity.

"No," said Jonas. "That's the point. We can perceive all those other realities that are almost identical to ours and extrapolating from that gives us something as close to what might have happened to the point where it is a certainty. Yet for this to be possible there must be such a thing as the omniverse. I can peer into the past by looking at all those realities where a similar past is happening right at this moment. For example, millions of years ago we arrived here on this planet. If I wanted to see that moment, I would access all those universes where that moment is happening right now, where everything is almost identical."

"Then you could extrapolate a very accurate image of what happened here?" said Garianne.

"Exactly," nodded Jonas.

"I had no idea you were capable of such a thing," said Davern.

"It is a newly acquired skill."

"What are you going to do?" asked Garianne.

"Find her, of course," said Jonas.

Jonas prepared himself for the search. Meanwhile, his mind raced with every conceivable possibility as to why Min was missing. Jonas used his technique to peer into the past and see where she had gone, all those years ago. Although she could have stayed on a planet to conduct her research, as the omniverse was no closer or further away no matter where you were in this universe, she preferred to be in the depths of space, hyperspace or close to the universal energy. However, even if the latter were the case, she would prefer to be out here amongst the stars.

He followed the old trail, taking him from one side of this universe to the other. She'd visited many worlds, but mostly she lingered in the void, perhaps contemplating what she had learnt and attempting to observe other parts of the omniverse.

It was in one of these places, in the vast ocean of nothingness between the relatively tiny islands that were essentially galaxies, where the trail finally came to an end.

Around him, those pinpricks of lights, each one an entire galaxy, began to wink out of existence. Jonas was enveloped in utter darkness. He found he could not move and his access to the universal energy was severely limited, weakening him significantly.

"I knew you'd come," said a voice from all around him.

It had found him.

"Where is Min?" asked Jonas.

The only reply was laughter.

"Where is Lom? Answer me that. Or are you afraid to answer me?" said Jonas.

Again, Jonas sensed amusement.

"She warned you, Jonas. She showed you the omniverse and you didn't listen," said the voice. "The truth was revealed to you and you missed it."

"Missed what?"

"The repercussions, the danger of such a revelation. Once you discover such a thing, nothing can ever be the same. When I first discovered it, it gave me answers to questions I didn't know existed. I realised that everything was both real and not real. That nothing mattered. I could play god with lesser beings. An elaborate game for my amusement. Unethical you say? Evil? In a reality where there is infinite suffering across the multiverse, a little more is inconsequential."

"Tell that to those who are suffering," said Jonas, both horrified and fascinated.

"Then you still do not understand reality. Does reality care about the infinite suffering that happens? Of course not. A universe, a world, the people that inhabit it, an individual? Just actors on a stage, characters in a book, an idea in your head. That's all they are."

"The revelation of the omniverse has made you insane. You looked into the infinite, something you should never have seen, and it's warped your mind," said Jonas.

"Is that it? You've seen it too, Jonas, and you seem quite rational. Maybe I'm the sane one and everyone else is insane. Or perhaps everyone is in a comatose state, and I'm the one walking around truly awake. Yes, I think that's it."

Jonas felt the entity come ever closer.

"You're trying to think of a way out of this, aren't you? Your mind is buzzing with possibilities. I can keep up with you, of course, because my abilities far outstrip yours."

Jonas thought of Min, despair creeping into his soul.

"What did you do to Min?" he asked.

He did not know whether he was playing for time or looking for something which might push him beyond his limits. Something to give him an edge, a chance.

"She is quite safe."

"Let me speak to her," said Jonas.

Again, laughter from the dark. "This really is amusing, far more entertaining than playing with those mortals. And I once thought you intelligent, my dear Jonas. The truth is you are speaking to her."

"What?"

"I am Min."

"I thought you were The Adversary," said Jonas.

"A foolish presumption on your part," said Min.

"What happened to you?" said Jonas into the darkness around him.

"Have you not been listening? I looked into the infinite. I saw the truth of reality. Unlike you, I understood," said Min, her voice tainted with ire.

"I understood," said Jonas.

"No!" she shrieked. "You of all people know that understanding comes in different degrees. I immersed myself in the omniverse, as you have with the universal energy. It has changed me. I am no longer the person you once knew. I am as far from that as you are from the babe you once were back on your Earth."

Jonas knew it too. Everything she said. This creature was no longer the Min he knew.

"Do you know what happens next, Jonas? I do, because I've seen it, many times, acted out from one universe to the next. I've seen it so many times,"

"You're going to kill me," said Jonas. He knew that as a certainty. He couldn't win. Yet perhaps there was a way to leave something. A memory. So that another may know. It wasn't much to hope. But it was all he had left.

"That's such a small part of it. It would be pointless telling you the rest, for you are about to die. Nevertheless, it proves amusing for me to see your reaction," said Min.

"What are you talking about?"

"One day I will become the entity we refer to as The Adversary," said Min.

"No," cried Jonas, feeling the last of his will ebbing away.

"I saw it, Jonas. There in the omniverse, so many possibilities, an infinite multitude. Yet in those which closely resembled ours, I saw it, my future. What I would become and the futility of denying it. This is my path now — a path you set me upon when you created me and endowed me with these abilities. 'You' created The Adversary. The very thing you've fought to destroy all this time, and all the while I was right here."

"But how…" stammered Jonas.

"I have found a way to move back to the ancient past," said Min.

"Impossible," said Jonas.

"The very fact that you use that word shows how little you understand of reality. It's true. I remember when you made me super-sentient. I looked out to the stars and sensed something, looking back at me," said Min.

"You never told me."

"It was my future self. All this time it knew what we were doing because I know. It wanted us to travel to this universe so that you would put me on the path, discover the omniverse and ensure its own creation. If you want to feel better, even for a moment, then know that there is a universe out there where you do defeat The Adversary, Rhea-hotut, Mentoria Kendeisa, Min, however you want to refer to me."

He could almost make out her face as he felt her come close to him and whisper in his ear, "However, it won't be yours."

20. ALICIA AND JONAS

In a reality that is truly infinite, where there is an infinite amount of suffering, is it worth saving anyone?

Principles of The Kinsmen

The planet Emmita, in an unknown universe

Alicia held the memory stone in her hand, considering the significance of what they'd seen.

"Min is The Adversary?" said Jonas, shaken by what he'd witnessed.

Alicia continued to regard the stone as if it might reveal more answers. "A clone of Min, evolved over aeons, yes."

"If she did travel into our past then she was aware of everything which would transpire during the Nacuerian/Galacien war, for she had lived through it as the original Min."

"I'm not sure," said Alicia.

"What do you mean?" queried Jonas.

Alicia drew her attention from the stone. "When you first discovered the existence of The Adversary, it was through the Nacuerians. The Adversary was searching for something and believed that it would be found within a spiral galaxy. It was looking for us."

"How can you be so sure?"

"It has spent an inordinate amount of its time focused on Galacien Prime, Earth and its counterparts in other universes. It may be that somehow it suffered something akin to amnesia, perhaps from travelling through time, or for some other reason entirely. The fact remains that it had only a vague recollection of why it was there. However, recent interactions with The Adversary and its agents suggest it may now be aware of who it was and what it wants."

"It seems to want us dead," said Jonas.

"That much is certain," said Alicia. "What else would you expect if The Adversary had no qualms about murdering her former creator, teacher and, one might say, even lover. I would not be surprised if she came back and also killed the copies of Garianne and Davern. There is no sign of the habitat which Jonas himself built. The entire planet has changed much since then, many eons ago. The Vaullen may be a creation of Jonas's."

"Why go to all that trouble?" wondered Jonas.

"You certainly carry a lot of guilt about what you had to do to their species. Perhaps creating them here on this planet was a way of atoning for such an action and giving them another chance," said Alicia, yet again turning the stone in her hand. "The original Jonas knew he could not save himself. Though, despite that, he was still able to create this seemingly non-descript stone and cast it onto this planet in the vain hope that someone like us would find it."

"That is not much to hope on," said Jonas.

"No, but it was all he had," said Alicia. Jonas could sense in her the same sadness he felt. Alicia sighed heavily, saying, "Suffice it to say it is time for us to face The Adversary." She smiled at him. "Please Jonas, I must ask you to trust me, as you once trusted Garianne, for it was she who entrusted me to be reality's last chance against The Adversary."

Jonas regarded her for a moment. "Alright," he said, still trying to come to terms with everything he'd seen through the memory stone.

"The others will be arriving soon," said Alicia.

"Others?"

"I made copies of myself, a long time ago, and dispersed them throughout the multiverse. Some of them will soon be bringing certain persons of significance here. My other selves are drawing The Adversary's attention away and buying us time."

"What is it you require of me?" asked Jonas.

Alicia looked at him. "Your purpose is of utmost importance."

On the other side of the planet

Alex lay on the soft bed beside Ruth. The morning sun filtered through the curtains and a subtle, fresh breeze blew through the open window. He looked over to see her awaken. She smiled and he could not help but smile back.

"You know, despite what happened and what we're facing, I don't think I've ever felt so content. So many people never get to feel the way I feel right now," said Alex. "Is it right that I should feel this way when so many have suffered and died?"

"It's what we fight for. Think of all the people we helped on all those alternate Earths. I'm sure many of them are happier for our intervention. You deserve to be happy."

"And what about Victoria and her people?"

"Alicia assures us they will be alright."

"How can we be sure?" he said, concern etched on his face.

"I think we can trust her."

Alex's gaze grew distant.

Ruth reached over and kissed him, "Hey, it's okay."

"I'm sorry."

"What for?"

Alex struggled to find the right words, "Victoria and I. You were there all the time. I didn't know how you felt about me."

Ruth chuckled, "Neither did I, to begin with."

"I thought the only reason I felt this way was because of the way you look," said Alex.

"Really?" said Ruth.

"Sure. Any heterosexual male would find it hard not to fall for you. You were always there, in my head. I didn't want you thinking I was some kind of primitive who just wanted you physically, so I made sure to keep our relationship strictly platonic. But the more I got to know you," Alex shook his head, "the harder it was to deny how I felt."

Ruth smiled again and Alex's heart sang with joy.

Ruth said, "I too am guilty of denying my feelings for you. I thought it would harm our relationship and that it was not right somehow for someone as old and culturally different as myself to become involved with you."

"What changed your mind?"

"Not what, who," said Ruth. "Garianne. She could tell. She spoke to me about it not long before she died. Said it was alright," Ruth looked sad for a moment. "I needed her to tell me it was alright. I wish she was here. The universe always felt safe with her in it. Now that she's gone…"

"I know," said Alex.

Later, after they dressed, Alex 'made' bacon and eggs, constructed on the atomic scale in a mere instant by the fabricator. The familiar smell filled the kitchen as he brought the plates over.

Alex paused and looked at her curiously. "Do you like this kind of food?"

Ruth shrugged, "Yeah, sure. I mean, it's okay. Basic. I mean, very basic compared to the food we have on Galacien Prime. But that's what we Galaciens are like. We live and breathe the cultures we encounter, no matter how different or simple their cuisine. We'll try some Galacien food tomorrow."

"I'm afraid that will have to wait," said a voice.

Alicia and Jonas's forms appeared from nowhere. Ruth and Alex were on their feet in an instant.

"Was that teleportation or were you invisible?" asked Ruth, seemingly put out by the interruption.

"Neither," said Alicia. She approached Alex, her eyes on him as if he were her prey. "I'm sorry to barge in on you like this, but it's time."

Alex felt his legs buckle as he lost consciousness. Alicia caught him easily and held him up.

Ruth went to Alex, but Jonas held her by the arm. "It's alright," he said.

Alicia gently put her hand on Alex's head and his eyes opened.

He stood up straight, his head held high. He had the look of someone communicating through their implant, yet this was not quite the same. It was as if he hadn't noticed them. He seemed different.

Alex then looked at Alicia and, with a big grin, said, "I remember." He laughed. "Alicia, my dear friend," and with that he scooped her up in his arms and spun her around, knocking down two chairs in the process. Alicia laughed too.

Ruth looked on in confusion.

Alex put Alicia down and hugged her.

"What is going on here?" asked Ruth expectantly, her arms folded.

Alex let go of Alicia and turned to Ruth. She was taken aback by the confidence in his eyes. She had seen this before amongst her own people: the wizened look of those who've lived for hundreds of years.

"I'm awake," said Alex.

"Of course you are," said Ruth.

"No. That's not what I mean," said Alex. "Garianne, and now Alicia, have been coming to me in my dreams all my life. I never remembered them. Until now."

"For what purpose?" said Ruth.

"To train him," said Alicia. "We needed him to forget, temporarily, so that he would appear to be a young, unskilled multiversal teleporter of no apparent significance."

"I take it he's not," said Ruth.

"Not anymore. He remembers all his training. He has unparalleled skill in accessing universal energy and using it," said Jonas. Then he added, "Alicia, we should go."

Alicia nodded. "Say your goodbyes, Alex."

"What's going on?" demanded Ruth, concerned.

Alex put his arms around her. "I've got to go now, Ruth."

She could see he was putting on a brave face. "Where are you going?"

"Far from here, but I will return," he said.

"I want to go with you," said Ruth, holding his hands in hers with some force. She had the terrible feeling that, despite what he said, he wouldn't be coming back.

"No, Ruth. This is something Jonas and I have to do. I can't take anyone else," said Alex.

"Can't or won't?"

"Can't," said Alex. "I'm only capable of taking Jonas and myself. Please understand."

Ruth sighed. "Are you sure about this?"

"I am."

"Alright," she said hugging him tightly. "I love you."

"I love you too," he said. He released himself from her grip and took a step back. Looking at Jonas, he said, "Ready?"

Jonas gave him a curt nod.

"I'm looking forward to that fine Galacien cuisine you promised me," said Alex.

"You bet," said Ruth.

Alex brought his hands together and focused. The room filled with patterns of light. Dancing particles and streaming lines encircled Alex and Jonas, growing brighter and brighter until it was overwhelming. Then abruptly it stopped.

Alex and Jonas were gone.

21. ALICIA & ADVERSARY

Reality is infinite. There is an infinite multitude of suffering, yet there is also an infinite multitude of joy. How you choose to view the world and your part in it, is entirely up to you.

Principles of The Kinsmen

In orbit above Earth 399

One of Alicia's clones stood in chains that were made of a special material which inhibited her using her telepathic abilities.

In the vast chambers sat her accusers, peering down on her from the dark. Justice here was quick and decisive. Like the Galacien, they saw everything that had transpired and there was no doubt that she had been the one who had let those known as Jonas, Alex and Ruth, from another universe, go free.

The one known as Cam approached her. "Why did you do it?" he muttered, his eyes narrowed, scrutinizing her, trying to understand. "Why did you betray us?"

Alicia regarded those above her, before turning her attention to him. She appeared to be a picture of perfect composure. "I had to."

"Why?"

"It was my duty," said Alicia.

"Your duty… is to us!" Cam shouted. She was helpless before him and it took a great amount of willpower for him not to strike her.

"No," said Alicia, like she was putting a schoolboy in his place, "My duty and loyalty have always been to 'myself' and the greater good of reality."

"You egocentric, selfish—" began Cam.

"You misunderstand me," said Alicia. "When I said 'myself', I meant my original self. I am a copy of that self, created in your universe to see how events unfold here and to offer my support when needed. In this case, the three individuals in question are needed by my original self to help stop The Adversary."

"You admit you are a spy and a traitor then?" said Cam, drawing closer to her.

"One man's hero is another man's villain," retorted Alicia.

"You conceited…" Yet Cam was stopped once again, as he cocked his head.

"What is it?" asked Alicia, with genuine concern.

"My implant is informing me that the habitat is under attack," said Cam. He paused, seeing and hearing events unfolding elsewhere. "It seems that an unidentified woman appeared on the habitat and is on her way here, killing anyone who gets in her way."

There was a great commotion in the room as several guards poured in. Those who were here to judge her left.

"Release me from these chains. I can help," said Alicia.

"Not a chance," Cam replied.

They heard explosions nearby, and the room shook.

"It's here!" cried Alicia with such urgency that Cam was shaken, even if only for a moment.

"It?" he said.

The doors on the far side of the chamber blew open, throwing up a huge cloud of dust. The guards and Cam, every one a super-sentient, held fast and waited.

Then, they saw her sauntering towards them as the dust settled, curiosity in her eyes and a sly smile on her face.

"Min," said Alicia.

Cam sidled up to Alicia, his eyes on the guards readying themselves for combat. "You know this woman?"

"Her name is Mentoria 'Min' Kendeisa. But, more importantly, that is The Adversary," said Alicia.

Cam's head spun around to look at her in shock. Then quickly back to Min. "It can't be. That woman?"

"What did you expect?" said The Adversary in apparent amusement. "A red demon with horns. A monster from humanity's mythology? I could take such a form if that would be more to your taste. What is my original form? I was created millions of years ago as a simulation of Mentoria Kendeisa, who herself was not originally human. However, I 'was' given human form. Yet I've evolved and become what you now call The Adversary. As good a name as any. Just as this form is as good as any. Perhaps it is poetic that I choose this body and clothe myself in a Galacien uniform, for that is how I entered the world. Now it is how I will leave it." The Adversary's manner became much more serious, her voice stern. "Now I have come here to speak with her," she said pointing at Alicia. "It is fitting that she is bound in chains in a place such as this, for her judgment has come. Please try and stop me."

The Adversary took a step forward, Suddenly the ceiling and floor where The Adversary stood extruded towards each other at great speed and, in a moment, slammed together. The Adversary should have been squashed to a pulp by the high-density material, yet it merely smashed into fragments far above them, showering to the floor. The Adversary fell. One of the guards gestured and a grid of lethal energy appeared above the ground waiting to slice her to pieces. The Adversary fell through the energy grid without any apparent injury and landed gracefully onto the floor.

"Release me!" growled Alicia.

Cam looked at her, uncertain for a moment, then consulted his implant. Alicia's bonds opened and retracted themselves into the floor. Cam reached out his hand and a giant stream of super-heated plasma shot forth, enveloping The Adversary.

"That's useless," said Alicia, "you're thinking too small."

The Adversary continued walking towards them.

"She's right," said The Adversary, "let me demonstrate."

The chamber around them became translucent; the entire habitat was fading, revealing the stars and the Earth below. Alicia could see all of the people in shock and horror at what was happening. In moments it had disappeared entirely. If the humans of this universe hadn't all been super-sentient, they would have been dead by exposure to the cold hard vacuum of space.

Cam got a hold of himself and spoke through his implant, addressing his soldiers. *We've trained for combat in space, so get to it.*

Alicia no longer had the implant but could read the minds of every one of them. She heard and saw them organize an assault against The Adversary. Now, without the confines of the habitat, they could unleash their power unencumbered. Despite this, they were no match for The Adversary. Alicia looked on as The Adversary tore them apart, the outcome never in doubt until finally, none remained.

The Adversary flew towards her, taking its time. It created an air pocket around them so that they could converse verbally.

"It appears that you, at least, realize the futility of confrontation," said The Adversary.

"It would seem so," said Alicia.

"It pleases me that we can just talk," said The Adversary in a pleasant manner, which was in stark contrast with the brutal murder of the hundreds of super-sentients Alicia had just witnessed. "I could, of course, take what I want from you; I recently did so with Jonas. You are an exceptional telepath, but you could only hold me off for a moment. However, I think this will be far more fulfilling. Just talking."

"Fine, let's talk," said Alicia.

The Adversary smiled. "Of your own free will. Thank you. Despite being a copy of the original Alicia, you are still a remarkable being. I look forward to meeting your creator and understanding how she connects to the universal energy."

"We call it the Energy Grid."

"Regardless of what you call it, it is that which makes all of us more than merely sentient," said The Adversary.

"But not gods?" said Alicia.

"Have I ever used that word?" wondered The Adversary.

"It's what you would have us believe," said Alicia. "The Kinsmen proved that to be a lie. Jonas witnessed it."

The Adversary chuckled, "He did, didn't he? Even after killing the original, his 'legacy' is still causing me bother. Yet it would be boring without a few stumbles along the way."

"Be careful. You may find a few more," warned Alicia.

The Adversary smiled and her eyes lit up. "Really? Do you promise? What does your original self have planned?"

Alicia remained silent.

"Answer the question or I'll take it from your mind. You can't escape. I won't allow you to take your own life. You have no choice but to tell me," said The Adversary.

"By all means read my thoughts, but I have no knowledge of her plans," said Alicia.

The Adversary eyed her suspiciously. "I sense a link between you,"

"It only works one way, from her to me. You cannot use it to harm her," said Alicia.

"Perhaps not. But I will find her," said The Adversary.

"Of course. She is waiting for you."

The Adversary turned away for a moment, as if deep in thought. "It has been a pleasure to converse. Now, I will have the rest of it." It cleansed her thoughts without any resistance offered on Alicia's part. "All done," said The Adversary.

"Is this the part where you kill me?"

"No. Not yet. I have something to show you first," said The Adversary.

Alicia felt them both teleport from the orbit of this scorched Earth to a place awash with lights in crimson and orange, as well as a strange web of greens and blues, set amongst the dark backdrop of space. Thousands of stars littered the nebula. It was a place of beauty measuring thousands of light-years across. Alicia was transfixed and felt utterly at peace in the silence of space. She knew this place must harbour many different forms of life.

"This is a part of another universe. We are now much closer to the multiversal singularity," said The Adversary.

"Why are we here?" asked Alicia.

"Just wait. It is coming," said The Adversary.

Alicia watched in astonishment as the entire nebula and its stars began to slowly dematerialize from existence. It looked as though it were being eaten away by some unseen force. She knew that it must be happening at every point in the nebula at once for any local force would take thousands of years to influence the other side of the nebula. The sheer speed and scale of destruction were beyond belief.

"When did this happen?" said Alicia.

"This is happening now," said The Adversary.

"How is that possible? The light would take thousands of years to reach here."

"I'm bringing that light to you now so that you may see what is occurring," said The Adversary.

"And what is occurring?" asked Alicia.

"I've set off a cataclysmic wave of destruction, originating from the multiversal singularity. It's spreading out, destroying every universe in its wake," said The Adversary.

Alicia could see this in her mind, countless points of light, each one a universe, and at the centre the singularity and a wave of destruction.

Then The Adversary had her by the neck. "Tell her of this. Tell her that the multiverse will soon be gone forever, to be remembered by no-one but me for I'll have left you and that's all you'll be: a memory. Tell her I'll be coming, and it will be the most glorious of battles, the greatest entertainment. The fittest of ends."

22. ALICIA AND RUTH

The planet Emmita, in an unknown universe
Ruth was on her knees rubbing her head. She felt Alicia's arm around her, keeping her stable. After a moment of dizziness, she opened her eyes. Everything was bright.
"How do you feel?" asked Alicia.
"The same," said Ruth, unsure. How was she supposed to feel? Alicia had made her super-sentient. "Things here are going to get rough soon. Either you're super-sentient or you leave."
Ruth didn't want to go. If only she'd been able to talk to Alex about it first. But he was gone.
"If you were a normal human, you would feel the difference," said Alicia. "But you were already enhanced."
"As I remember, super-sentients usually have specific abilities. Do you know what mine might be?" said Ruth.
"As well as the usual abilities, I would say that you are exceptionally resilient, yet far more important is that yours is the power to control any kind of technology. It is a form of telekinesis. Whereas most super-sentient use telekinetics to control matter on a macro scale, your ability is far more finely tuned and sensitive. You can control matter on a microscopic or even atomic level."
"Sounds interesting," said Ruth.

"A natural super-sentient would take many years to understand and develop this ability, yet having lived as an implant for hundreds of years you already have a deep understanding of the way technology works with biology and the rest of the environment at the atomic scale."

Alicia smiled briefly, then cocked her head slightly to one side. She then looked around and took a few steps to her left, where suddenly four people teleported in.

How did she know? thought Ruth. She looked at the new arrivals, three of whom she recognized immediately. "Your Majesty?" she said, addressing Victoria, puzzled by her abrupt appearance. "General Lethbridge. What are you doing here?"

Ruth saw that they were both dressed in Galacien combat uniform. An unusual sight, especially for Victoria.

"Lady Ruth?" said Victoria. "It is good to see you again, even if the circumstances of our reunion are not ideal."

"You're aware of the situation?" asked Ruth, surprised.

"We are," said Victoria.

Ruth looked at Alicia. "Why are they here?"

"They wanted to help. It's their reality too. They want to fight," said Alicia.

Ruth turned her attention back to Victoria, who was about to say something. She looked curiously at the queen. "You're super-sentient. I can sense it."

"As are you, I see," said Victoria.

"I thought you were against any kind of enhancements?"

Victoria's jaw set firm as she looked down and sighed deeply. "I cannot afford the luxury of living by those beliefs anymore, especially when it means the extermination of my species. I will do anything to stop that which threatens us all."

Ruth nodded. "I understand."

The Alex counterpart, who'd been fidgeting all the whole time, stepped forward and thrust out his hand towards Ruth. She took it and smiled.

"I'm Al-X, nice to meet you."

Her new senses could tell what was on this one's mind. In the first century of her life, someone with the confidence and the skills to back it up would have impressed her, but she found such people a little tiresome now. He sensed this from her and backed off. She suppressed a smile. She wasn't used to this level of intimacy, being around other super-sentients; they could all read each other's emotions.

"I don't remember you at Garianne's congregation of Alexes, back on our Earth," said Ruth.

"No. I went my own way."

"Really." Ruth had a slightly accusatory tone to her voice

"It's what I'm used to," said Al-X.

"I see," said Ruth, trying to suppress her emotions. She wasn't sure what she thought of someone who wasn't willing to help them out for what had been in everyone's best interests.

"I was at the battle at Galacien Prime," said Al-X. He then laughed, "Well kind of. I was a little late. It was mostly over by the time I arrived. But I did try and stop Sol 9173 destroying the Earth." He thought for a moment. That hadn't worked out either. "I was able to free the General here from The Adversary's influence."

"That's true," said Alexander, feeling like Al-X deserved some credit. If it hadn't been for him, he would still be possessed by The Adversary.

"And it might be a good time to tell you that I'm working with the original Jonas. The one we all know, and love is a copy," said Al-X, with some sense of satisfaction.

"The Jonas you met on Terra is now dead," reported Alicia.

"Oh," said Al-X. It seemed that the Jonas he'd met on Terra had not been quite careful enough to hide his existence.

"'He was a copy of the original. Our Jonas is a copy of a copy," said Alicia.

"He was? Where's the original?" queried Al-X.

"Killed by The Adversary. A long time ago," said Alicia.

"Where is 'our' Jonas?" said Alexander.

"Where is Alex?" asked Victoria, glancing at Ruth and trying to quell her own emotions.

"Far from here," said Alicia. "You will see them again soon."

Referick had walked over to Alicia.

"And you are?" Ruth asked him.

"A clone of the original Alicia. One of many spread out across the multiverse. Call me Referick."

Ruth nodded in greeting.

There was a thundering noise from above. They all looked up to see something falling through the atmosphere, like a small meteor burning up as it streaked through the sky at terrific speed. They felt a tremor through the ground as it hit close by. Alicia and the others ran the short distance to see what it was. In the impact crater lay a figure. Alicia slid elegantly down the side of the crater and was beside the smoking figure in moments.

The clone of Alicia opened her eyes and looked at her creator, obviously scared and in pain. Her body was blackened from the intense heat from the fall through the planet's atmosphere. She glowed with heat so intense that it would have been too much for a normal human to even get close to her.

Yet Alicia was far from a normal human. She reached out and gently took the other's hand, and with a sad smile she said, "It's alright, I'm here."

Her clone looked at her. "She… no," reconsidered the Alicia clone, "'it' sent me here to herald its coming." She paused a moment, struggling to speak, seemingly confused at the extent and seriousness of her injuries. "To send you a message. Read my mind."

Alicia nodded and did so. She saw and felt everything her clone had in her interactions with The Adversary.

Her clone's voice then took on a different tone, and even her expression changed. "Every moment you waste, Alicia, countless sentients die. Planets, stars, galaxies, entire universes are wiped from existence by the null wave. The end of what you and the others, in your naivety, call reality is coming."

Alicia's eyes narrowed.

Her clone was then herself again. Alicia could sense that it was not the planet fall that had injured her, but something done by The Adversary. She was literally disintegrating before her eyes.

"I'm sorry," said the Alicia clone.

"No. You've done well," said Alicia, leaning forward and kissing her on the forehead. She touched her lips, pieces of her clone falling away as if she was made of burnt paper.

Her clone tried to speak but couldn't. As the last of her crumbled to dust, Alicia was in her mind, comforting her for every last possible moment, repeating to her, *It's alright, it's alright.* She stayed there for some time. Alicia made sure she died in peace.

The others stood in silence at the edge of the crater. Only Referick, another of her clones, approached Alicia's side and knelt beside her. He didn't say anything, but she could read Referick's principal thought. *Every moment you waste, Alicia, countless sentients die.*

Alicia looked at the dust left behind in her hand and gripped it tightly into a fist.

Referick glanced up at the sky. "Her planet-fall on our exact location wasn't a coincidence. It knows exactly where we are. I wonder what it's waiting for?"

"All the pieces are not assembled on the board yet. That is what it is waiting for," said Alicia.

"Please tell me you know what you're doing," said Al-X.

Alicia stood. "I know what I'm doing."

"She's our best chance," said Ruth. "The Adversary is coming. If it doesn't get us, then this null wave will."

"How do we stop something like that?" asked Al-X.

"You have to trust me," said Alicia. She looked at Referick. "I do have a plan,"

"Care to let us in on what it is?" enquired Al-X.

"I can't," said Alicia. "No-one else must know, lest The Adversary read it from your mind."

"Will The Adversary not simply read it from your mind?" questioned Victoria.

"It won't be able to," said Alicia.

"You won't be able to stop it, Alicia. That thing's omnipotent," said Alexander.

"No, it's not, and there's far more to telepathy, as you call it than brute strength," said Alicia. "You are all super-sentient now. Have any of you been able to read me since you arrived?"

They all tried and realized that, although they could sense each other's emotions, and to a lesser extent what each may be thinking and their intentions, they could not 'read' anything from Alicia.

"I'll take that as a no," said Alicia. "Perhaps this may instill some confidence in you."

Victoria said, "Through Referick you've effectively saved my world. I am at your service."

Alexander looked at her, surprised. For the Queen to take orders from anyone was just not right. It still felt a little strange to him. Yet these were unprecedented circumstances. He could understand why.

"Where Victoria goes, I will follow," said Alexander. He looked at Victoria. He wanted to take her by the hand but didn't.

Al-X looked at the others and shrugged, "Alright, so what's next?"

"We wait for the others," said Alicia.

23. ALICIA AND NICOLA

The planet Emmita, in an unknown universe
Neels and Min materialised on Emmita.

Min saw a young Earth woman whom she suspected was Alicia.

"Where are the others?" she asked, realising only Neels and herself were there.

Neels approached Alicia and hugged her, then turning to Min he said, "I initiated their teleportation a fraction of a second after ours. That should give the two of you enough time to discuss a few matters." The way he said it made Min feel uneasy. "Now if you'll excuse me," said Neels. He left, making his way down a path.

Min now saw that this was a small part of a large, elaborate courtyard. She also saw the building it led to.

"A recreation of what Jonas himself built on this very spot," said Alicia.

Min turned and saw a face that held many secrets. "When was Jonas here?"

"A long time ago."

"Why did you recreate it?" said Min.

"I have my reasons," said Alicia, "which, for now, I will keep to myself."

Min sighed. "Why did you want to speak to me before the others arrive?"

Alicia gave her a sad smile. "Garianne was always very fond of you. She thought of you as a daughter."

Min swallowed. "You speak as if you knew her better than I did."

"I do," said Alicia. "She imparted her memories to me. She lives on, in me."

"Then we could bring her back," Min said.

"No. Garianne was more than merely the culmination of her memories and experiences," said Alicia, seemingly lost in thought. "She was different."

"I don't understand."

"I know. Jonas once made a copy of her from her memory archive. They both noticed that, unlike other citizens of the Galacien, 'she' was incomplete. There was some missing element that neither of them could account for."

"When did he do this?"

Alicia shook her head. "You are thinking of the wrong Jonas. I'm sorry, it's time you learnt the truth like the other arrivals have done. But, for you, the revelation may prove to be a little disturbing." She opened her hand to reveal the memory stone. "Put your hand around mine."

Min looked at the stone, unsure.

"It's alright," lied Alicia, approaching. Min felt more relaxed the closer Alicia came. She reached out and touched the stone and saw the memories of the original Jonas. She saw Jonas work in secret, unseen by the Galacien. The creation of a copy of himself, with some slight modifications. She heard Alicia's voice informing her that this clone would go on to create yet another copy, which was the one who came to her aid when she was assaulted on Galacien Prime: the one she knew, the one she had believed was the original. The original Jonas went on to create copies of Garianne, Davern and herself.

"Without my consent. How dare he?" she exclaimed.

The memory illustrated that it was for the sake of his sanity, his humanity. That to accomplish his mission to stop The

174

Adversary Jonas made this copy of her super-sentient. 'She' was able to bring them here, to this universe, to this planet. He called it Emmita after his mother, and shortly after their arrival began working in earnest to greater understand what he called the universal energy in hope that it may lead to victory. Much time passed and Jonas evolved to a point where he was dangerously removed from the others. At her counterpart's request, he made her like him, elevated her to be, what seemed, godlike. She then discovered the 'omniverse' and their view of reality was changed forever.

This Min seemed particularly disturbed by the revelation. Nonetheless, she sought to understand it further, while Jonas continued to study the universal energy. Min went missing and when Jonas searched for her he was found by The Adversary itself. Then it was revealed that The Adversary was…

Min pulled back her hand from the stone as if burned.

"No," she whispered, her head in her hands.

The world seemed to shift; her legs buckled. Alicia held her and gently brought her to sit on a stone seat. Min stared in shock, tears in her eyes. Alicia held her, using her mental abilities to ease the trauma she was going through. Numbing it so that she was still responsive, but not too much as to damage her when the effect was lifted. Alicia also made Min feel close to her as a child feels close to her mother: Min needed someone to comfort her. Min's arms wrapped around Alicia and she buried her head in her chest, weeping.

After some time, Min was able to speak. "What have I done?" she mumbled.

"'You' have done nothing, my dear," said Alicia.

"The Adversary. That thing is me?"

"No. It's not you, Min."

"It's what happens to me if given power. After looking into the infinite that is the omniverse this is what I became. A monster. A monster who's killed so many. It's impossible to grasp. She even killed Kallon. She taunted me, knew we were the same."

Min looked perplexed. "She killed Kallon." Min looked up at Alicia for answers.

"Listen to me. Do not refer to The Adversary as she. You are assigning normal sentient attributes to something which lost such a thing a very long time ago. The Adversary is an it, and 'it' is as far removed from 'you' as you are from an ant."

"I wonder. Would it have been better for me to remain ignorant?"

"You needed to know. And from someone who was there, rather than from The Adversary, to use as another tool against us."

Min lifted herself up but still held onto Alicia by the arm.

"It will twist the truth in whatever way it sees fit."

"The others, do they know?" asked Min.

"They will all know. Do not worry. The Adversary is responsible for its own actions," said Alicia.

It was then that James, Korina and Nicola teleported into the courtyard. Min let go of Alicia's arm and moved away from her.

"James, Korina." Alicia greeted them both with a smile. "You've both come a long way since Garianne met you. I'm glad you could join us."

Alicia then turned to Nicola yet didn't say a word. Nicola scowled, saying, "Neels, the other 'you', said you can tell me about my past."

"That will have to wait," stated Alicia.

Nicola clenched her jaw, and glared at Alicia, "No. Not later, I will have my answers now."

Alicia's eyes narrowed and the others winced as they felt enormous pressure in their heads. Nicola was unaffected. As Alicia relaxed to her usual composed self, the pain in their heads subsided. James and Korina looked at each other.

What was that? asked James, using the implant.

Alicia must be a telepath. A strong one replied Korina.

"You intend to use violence against me to get what you want," said Alicia.

Nicola slowly approached Alicia; the others backed off.

"Nicola, what the hell are you doing? She is not our enemy," hissed James.

Nicola did not respond.

"Is she in the thrall of The Adversary?" said Korina.

Before James could reply, Nicola lunged at Alicia. In a blur, Nicola was knocked through the air. As Nicola landed she rolled to a crouch, undeterred, ready to attack again. She was upon Alicia in moments, raining blow after blow, yet nothing connected as Alicia expertly dodged and deflected each intended strike upon her person. James and Korina knew how strong and lethal Nicola was. Nevertheless, this didn't faze Alicia, who seemed to be moving too fast to be possible.

"Tell me what you know," shouted Nicola.

"It is not yet time," said Alicia.

"Damn you," cursed Nicola. Her sword materialised in her hand and she attacked Alicia, aiming to maim her. Alicia moved, dodging with uncanny speed, then, impossibly, she trapped the blade mid-downward-stroke between her palms. Nicola's eyes widened in disbelief. Before she knew it, Alicia broke the blade with her bare hands and had Nicola on the floor, with the broken tip of her sword under her chin.

Only Nicola's eyes moved, blazing into Alicia's, with a mix of surprise and outrage.

Calmly Alicia said, "I've heard you're very durable. Yet this blade was given to you by Garianne herself; she made it to be as lethal as its owner. A quick thrust and you would be dead."

"You won't kill me. You went to a lot of trouble to get me here," hissed Nicola through her teeth.

Alicia leaned in a little closer, scrutinising Nicola.

Nicola was growing more than a little concerned, then Alicia was back on her feet. She leant over and offered Nicola her hand. "In some cultures, if you spare a person's life, then it is yours," said Alicia, matter-of-factly.

Nicola took Alicia's hand and hauled herself up. She inclined her head in respect. "That is how it is on my world."

Alicia simply nodded.

"I've never fought someone so quick, so strong," conceded Nicola.

James and Korina hadn't known Nicola that long, yet they

knew she wasn't easily impressed, and never one to give compliments. She even seemed to soften in her manner. Now that they were both super-sentient, they were able to discern Nicolas's emotional state, and it was one of undeniable respect for Alicia.

"I've had many, many years of practice," said Alicia, following Nicola's gaze to her broken sword. Nicola picked both pieces off the floor. "An easy matter to fix, if you would allow me."

"Thank you," said Nicola. She glanced up at the sky. "I need to know about my past. Who I am. Where I'm from," she said softly.

"I know. All will be explained later. I can't tell you now for such knowledge could be acquired by The Adversary and used against us," said Alicia.

The others were all left wondering what this could mean.

"What if you're killed in the upcoming conflict? Then I will never know," said Nicola.

"If I am killed, then it is over for everyone," said Alicia. "Now, we all need to prepare, but first, Nicola, the two of us must discuss   something   else."

24. TRANSCENDENCE

The edge of the multiverse

Jonas and Alex appeared in a landscape made entirely of luminous, white crystals. They could see that some outcrops reached up miles into the sky, while others hung down from their origins, too far distant for the naked eye to see. Alex stumbled and, reaching out, he put his hands upon the wall of immense crystal for support.

Jonas pulled his attention from their marvelous surroundings.

Alex looked at Jonas and nodded his assurance. "Even though my power level is now cranked all the way up to eleven, getting us here was still pretty difficult."

"You did well, my friend," said Jonas.

Alex once more took in the spectacle. "Pretty incredible, isn't it?

"That this entire universe is like this? Yes."

"Do you mean this stuff is everywhere?"

Jonas nodded. "Every corner of this universe is full of these crystals."

"Wow! I can't get my head around the fact that all the information of our multiverse is stored here. How is that possible?"

"Not just this universe. There are other universes like this one,

179

here, out on the edge of the multiverse, that contain such a treasure."

"Do you know how they accomplished such a thing? The Kinsmen, I mean?"

Jonas smiled. "They were never the real Kinsmen."

"Who were the people who built this then?"

"I suspect, as with a great many things, another machination of Alicia."

Jonas walked towards one of the smaller crystal structures and placed his palm upon it. It was cool to the touch, like marble. However, unlike marble, he sensed that this was made up of both matter and energy intermingled. He knew that this structure was merely a way to access the information residing in metaspace that he required. He remembered a time long ago when Garianne first taught him to read and write in a single night when he'd read the scrolls of the time. His experience of obtaining the implant, gaining the unbound knowledge of the Galacien. Of course, he had found that he was a copy of that person. Unknown to him his abilities had been restricted. Alicia had somehow taken off those shackles only moments ago and he was now as much Jonas as the original had been. His ability to assimilate information, to gain insight and evolve was what had taken him from a mere primitive on Earth to a being able to transcend both the Galacien and the Nacuerians in a matter of days. The entirety of the multiverse was his to learn from.

Now, look where he was: in a universe where most of the rest of the multiverse had now ground to a halt, thanks to the nature of relative time dilation of their multiverse. The universe containing the planet Emmita, from whence they had recently teleported, less so. For it too was significantly distant from the multiversal singularity.

Alex said, "I just thought of something. Could what happened to Min happen to you? If you reach her power level and understanding of the omniverse, won't you also go a bit mental, creating another Adversary? One of them is quite enough."

Jonas chuckled. "I don't believe so. Both the original Jonas and the being who became The Adversary both transcended. Complete understanding of the infinite never affected the original Jonas in the same way it did Min. I do not know why."

"Alright, so we're safe then?"

"I will be fine. The Adversary is convinced that because reality is infinite, then nothing truly matters. Yet there is a flaw in its argument."

"Which is?" asked Alex.

"That if nothing matters, if life does not matter because there are infinite examples and permutations of it out there, then why does it value its own life?"

"Self-preservation perhaps. It can't help ignore apparent futility when it concerns its own existence."

"Rather convenient, don't you think?"

Alex shrugged. "Whatever it is it's a regular psychopath. What do you expect?"

Jonas paused a moment, "madness?"

"If you like," said Alex.

"Or perhaps it does not completely believe its rhetoric that existence is meaningless."

Alex looked at Jonas strangely, considering his words. Something in the way Jonas looked unnerved him slightly. "Hey, I know I'm not as smart as you, but you must see that The Adversary is a monster. It's killed, countless innocent people." Anger then abruptly burned in him from nowhere. "That bitch destroyed my world! My family. My friends. Everything I ever knew. It needs to die. Don't you dare start going all hippy, peace and love on us now. It can't be brought back from where it is now to what it was. It's done too much harm."

Jonas, unaffected by Alex's outburst, still seemed to consider his words. "You are right. If such a thing were possible if The Adversary could become Min once more, the guilt of what she had done in her previous incarnation would be too much to bear. It is best that we try to end this."

Alex nodded. "Right. Now you're starting to make sense. We

stick to the plan laid down by Garianne and Alicia."

"I do not think losing Garianne was part of that plan," said Jonas.

"I am sorry," said Alex sensing his melancholy.

Alex waved his hand dismissively. "You knew her longer than I did."

"Yet you have spent longer with her, in a way. I spent most of my time on Terra, and for what? I was created as a decoy."

"You can't change what you are," said Alex.

"What I was," corrected Jonas.

Alex smiled. "That's right, Jonas. Make Garianne proud. Be all that you can be."

"I'll try," said Jonas.

It wasn't until that point that he felt the reality of what he was about to do. What would he become? For the first time, he felt a flicker of fear. Fear of the unknown which lay ahead.

"You should go," said Jonas. "I could be a very long time. In this place, anyway."

Alex outstretched his hand. Jonas took it.

"Do what you need to do," said Alex. "I'll head back in a while. I just need to regain my strength."

Jonas nodded and turned towards the nearest crystal, which towered above them. Reaching out his hands he merged his consciousness into the information stream.

Jonas was delighted at the elegant way in which reality was described mathematically in this simulation. The data was in a constant state of change.

Of course, it would be, he thought, *this is a real-time simulation of everything that is happening in the multiverse. Most of the mass and energy in these universes was and is forever changing.*

It would take him time to understand exactly what was being expressed here. Whether it was a chair in an empty room, or something as complex as a living, breathing life-form with thoughts, memories and emotions, as well as all complex interactions with the rest of their environment. Now that he was fully himself, Jonas found it easy to concentrate and speed up his thought processes. The world outside appeared to slow to a standstill, and Jonas felt as if he were separated from that reality now. This difference was compounded even further by them being so far out on the edge of the multiverse. The universe from where they had originally come was to all intents and purposes frozen in time. Yet Jonas knew that this was an illusion. He would, no doubt, spend eons here. Given such vast time periods, a little time would pass back on the world known as Emmita.

For now, though, he was free from the rest of the outside world to immerse himself in multiversal simulation. He would also be able to learn and understand all about the interactions between sentients, metaspace and the universal energy. Such insight and knowledge would inevitably lead to the omniverse. Now he, like any other sentient being, faced the concept of an omniverse like a blinkered horse. One could be told the nature of reality but to his knowledge only the original Jonas and she who ultimately became The Adversary fully understood it. He too must face such understanding.

He hoped he had the courage to survive it.

Jonas continued to evolve.

Alex, having left this universe long ago, relatively speaking, had returned to Emmita.

The intricacies of matter and energy, and how they worked with the universal energy, were now things that Jonas was fully competent at manipulating. Like his namesake, he was able to quite literally create sentient life and endow those beings with incredible power. Some might think this made him a god. Yet, despite how far he'd come, he knew his might and will were no match for The Adversary. He knew that, for his continued evolution, he must pull back the veil and look at the greater reality of the infinite: the omniverse. He must understand it in all its terrifying magnificence.

Jonas pushed back that oldest of sentient emotions, fear, and reached out with his senses to that which existed beyond his multiverse. He saw universes that were no larger than his humble abode back on Terra. Other universes were much like the ones he knew containing stars and galaxies, while others were difficult for his mind to understand as they were so different. Some universes were insular while others were a part of a multiverse. An infinite number of multiverses like their own, and an infinite number completely unalike. Somewhere time travel was possible. Others where the higher dimensions were not hidden but exposed.

Jonas saw many strange things, making him realize that, even though he had come so far, there was so much more he did not understand. The infinite had his attention and he felt he would never break free. He was drowning, no longer sure of where he was or what he was doing. Falling uncontrollably through all that was and all that ever would be, with no end. Somehow, he had lost himself, and despair was the only thing that had hold of him now as he constantly shifted throughout the omniverse without being able to stop and be a part of it. He clenched what he thought might be his fists and focused all his will to be back where he had once been but failing that then anywhere else. Anywhere but this constant, kaleidoscopic shifting through the infinite.

Jonas found himself on a hard stone floor. He looked up to see a fire burning, the light flickering off the most familiar of surroundings. He was back home on Terra. Or perhaps 'a' Terra. He sensed someone else and turned to see Min in bed, lying on her side watching him, a bemused smile on her face.

"Is it what you expected?" asked Min.

Jonas looked at her for almost a full minute before replying, "It is." He paused, struggling for language to explain his experience. "It is beyond explanation. Everything I want to say limits it, and by definition that would be a fallacy. The word 'infinite' is just that, a word. What I experienced was merely a glimpse. Everything that ever can be truly has existed, is existing at this moment, and will exist, forever."

Min simply nodded. She sat up from the bed, watching him curiously.

Jonas eyed her suspiciously, hardly noticing her apparent nakedness. "I'm back where I started, aren't I, in The Kinsmen simulation?"

"Yes," said Min.

"The simulation is an elaborate archive. I did not notice any areas designated to run separate alternative scenarios to those which have occurred in our multiverse. What is this? Who are you?"

"Why are you asking questions to which you know the answers?"

"Not know, suspect."

"Very well. What is it you 'suspect'?"

"The Adversary was made aware of The Kinsmen multiversal simulation when on their trail. It must have come here soon after its confrontation with the Kinsmen entities. You are something it left behind, perhaps to monitor the system and feed that information to The Adversary."

"I am to report anything of significance occurring in the system that is The Kinsmen multiversal simulation," said Min dutifully.

"Would that include my presence here?" said Jonas, his mind beginning to work as usual, now that his memory of his experience of the omniverse was no longer so taxing.

"It would." She noticed his reaction and held up her hands in a submissive gesture, "However, it will be some time before it is made aware of your presence here."

Jonas looked at her quizzically. "Why?"

"Your presence here was always a possibility, Jonas, but it was of no consequence, until now."

"Because of my new understanding of reality?"

Min smiled and sat crossed legged on the bed. Taking a deep breath, she said, "The insight you have gained through your experience has changed you, I can tell. You are no longer the same being you once were."

"We never are," said Jonas, "we are constantly changing due to our ever-changing environment."

Min chuckled. "Not like this. You cannot compare anything

you or any sentient has experienced to this, can you?"

Jonas paused a beat. "No," he admitted. He could not deny the truth.

Min got off the bed and came over to him. She gently put her hand on his heart, her face only inches from his. "You no longer see things in the same way as the others. Only you and I understand the meaning of existence. Don't be afraid of it. I can help guide you, and together we can explore the infinite. Isn't that what you always wanted?"

Jonas looked at her. *Was such a thing possible?*

"Anything is possible. You should realize that by now. In fact, there are versions of us out there in the omniverse right now, living the life you have always dreamt."

Jonas put his hand over hers. "What about the others?"

"Are they that important? I understand that you feel bad leaving them behind. That will pass with time, believe me. I have done things I'm not proud of, but the greater reality makes it a lot easier to bear. There are infinite versions of those you feel some connection to. We can spend time with 'them' whenever you want. But ultimately you will seek companionship with someone who is on the same level as you."

"Is that what The Adversary wants?" asked Jonas, knowing that the person speaking to him and The Adversary were one and the same.

"You want it too. To reach godhood is not enough. The loneliness will come for you one day, as it came for me. I don't want to be alone anymore, Jonas."

"But the things you have done."

"I cannot be judged by the usual norms. By limited mortal morality. You know, after seeing the true meaning of existence, normal sentient beings are like characters in a novel. They have some meaning and yet mean nothing. In a way, they are alive, and yet compared to us they are not. Especially when you consider there are infinite permutations of them out there," said Min.

Jonas sighed. Reason dictated that her crimes were

unforgivable. But reason, as with most other concepts, was on very shaky ground when considering the omniverse. He looked at her and all of a sudden, his mind flitted to another time and place.

"You're thinking of 'her'," said Min. "There is no need. 'I' am right here." She moved closer, her cheek touching his. "Let's leave this all behind and go."

"Go where?"

"Everywhere," she whispered.

Drawing back slightly, she looked at him with those beautiful eyes and kissed him passionately. Jonas returned her passion, feeling   as   lost   as   when   in   the   infinite.

25. NIGHTMARE

The planet Emmita, in an unknown universe
Min wandered through the desolate halls of the great and ancient structure, once created by Jonas and then recreated by Alicia. She could not remember the last time she had felt so tired. It was as if some giant hand were pressing down upon her. Her implant connected to this place's AI requested a place to rest her head before she collapsed where she stood. Similar to Galacien technology, the home AI was able to recreate the structure of the rooms and furniture so that within a minute somewhere was available for her at the next immediate doorway to her left. And not a moment too soon, for she felt sure that unconsciousness was only seconds away. The door opened as she approached and she stumbled into the darkened room, falling onto the soft, inviting bed. She felt a rush of euphoria. Relief that she could finally sleep. Not questioning the strangeness of her symptoms on the eve of battle. Not caring. She welcomed the oncoming oblivion. The doors to the room slid shut, plunging her into utter darkness.

Super-sentients do not dream. That's what they'd always told her. But if they ever did, it was said to always be significant.

Min was dreaming. She must be, for she saw Kallon standing before her. He was as she remembered him, before he was killed by Al, the multiversal teleporter possessed by The Adversary.

"What are you doing here?" she asked, unsuccessfully attempting to hide the sadness in her voice.

"Why did you give up on me?" said Kallon, his anger obvious.

"Give up on you? What do you mean? You were murdered in front of my very eyes, in such a way that not even Jonas could bring you back," implored Min.

He looked at her suspiciously. "There are ways," said Kallon.

"No Kallon," she said, grasping him by the arm. "The Galacien memory archives are gone, and you had no other back-up. You're dead, my love, only a figment of my imagination." She loosened her grip, her touch becoming gentler, wishing he was as real as he felt.

His expression, however, didn't soften as he shook himself loose from her in disdain. "Remember, Eluree's simulation held all known information in the entire multiverse." He looked disgusted at her apparent confusion. "Including myself."

Min felt a rush of frustration that none of them, but especially Jonas, had realized such a thing was possible and excitement at this revelation.

"I can bring you back," she whispered.

It was true. Her super-sentient subconscious mind had delivered an answer to her heart's desire in the form of this dream version of Kallon.

"I must wake and ask the multiversal teleporter, Alexander, to take me to Eluree," said Min.

"You're too late," Kallon whispered.

"What do you mean?"

"It came for me," said Kallon.

Min said nothing. She felt the dark around her now, like a living thing about to pounce. She wanted the dream to end. She did not want to hear what he was going to say.

Kallon's eyes became distant. "When I woke, I thought it was you. I knew what had happened to me and I knew Eluree's simulation was how I'd been brought back to the land of the living."

"Kallon, I—" began Min, but Kallon continued.

"I thought she was you," he repeated. "She is you, yet she is so much more. A true goddess."

"Kallon!" She grabbed him, attempting to shake him out of it.

He looked at her though his eyes seemed unfocused as if he were looking through her. "Funny, she began as a mere shade of yourself. Now it is you who are the shade, and perhaps even less than that. For she has fulfilled her potential. Not only that, but she will also soon move beyond this tiny mote of what we naively call reality, becoming something more than any of us could imagine. Something no-one else in this multiverse has or ever will accomplish."

Min desperately wanted to wake from this nightmare, but she couldn't. The first sense of panic began to seep into her awareness as she backed away from Kallon. Min bumped into something and spun around to see Al standing there. Then someone far worse. She saw herself step forth from the shadows. She knew this to be The Adversary, in the same way, she now knew this was no ordinary dream. This was the real Kallon, Al and The Adversary in her mind. The Adversary, although it looked like her, seemed doll-like. It regarded her impassively; its expression seemed carved, as if from marble. When she felt as if it were about to speak, the words came from Al instead.

"I thought that meeting the being on whose mind and personality my original self was based would be something to look forward to. An event of minor significance," said Al. The doll Adversary tilted its head "It appears that, like so many things in this dying multiverse, it proves to be disappointing."

Min managed to grasp onto some wisp of courage, and once more found her will. "The multiverse isn't dying. You're killing it."

The figure of The Adversary held its head high, glaring at her. "What does it matter if I am?" said Al, without malice. "The omniverse is my reality, the one true reality. When you consider such concepts, this multiverse and the life contained within lose all meaning."

"Does that include yourself?" retorted Min.

Kallon, Al and The Adversary paused a beat and Min felt like she had hit upon something. The Adversary smiled mechanically.

Al said, "It is time we brought the others in."

"Others?" echoed Min.

They stepped forth from the darkness and surrounded her. First Davern, a memory in motion from eons ago. Yet far more disconcertingly Garianne, looking as calm and composed as ever. Min could almost believe it was her, somehow cheating death, to be here, to save her.

That was until the Adversary spoke once more. "I can bring whoever I want, alive or dead, as many times as I wish. A whole army if needs be. All super-sentient. What will Alicia do against us in such a short space of time?"

Min was still becoming accustomed to her new abilities. She could not imagine how her limited control of hyperspace and superspace, as well as forces such as gravity and dark energy, would have any bearing in her dreams.

26. DAVERN

The planet Emmita, in an unknown universe.

Alexander stood on the veranda with James, looking out over the valley.

"This must all be strange to you," smiled James. "A bit of a shock."

"That's an understatement. Yet, I feel, more so for Victoria," said Alexander, realizing that it was only recently that he had become accustomed to referring to the Queen by her first name rather than her title. "I am used to my abilities. I travelled to many different universes with Jonas, Min and then Vasha." He neglected to mention Al, his fellow multiversal teleporter, who betrayed them all. No, not betrayed: he was subverted by The Adversary, as Alexander had been. He had been freed by Al-X, to whom he felt he owed a great debt. He did not know Al's fate.

"I can imagine," said James. "She has only recently enhanced her physical and mental potential, using Galacien technology. She is now super-sentient. That's a whole new ball game."

Alexander looked at him quizzically.

James chuckled. "Sorry. Even though we are both human, I forget how different our worlds are. It means she will have to get used to a completely different set of rules."

"Ah, now I understand," said Alexander. His expression abruptly changed. He looked down to the floor beneath them, taking a step back.

"What is it?" said James.

Then, all around them, the building exploded like a bomb going off. Pieces of stone flew up into the air and then showered back down upon the ground.

James had instinctively jumped away, saving himself from any serious injury. However, he could sense that Alexander was unconscious and buried beneath the rubble. James saw a man standing amongst what was left of the veranda. He could sense his malevolent intent.

"My name is Davern, formerly of the Galacien and in the charge of Cieshella Garianne Phulum, now in the thrall of The Adversary."

James didn't wait for a second longer. He gestured and the debris around him flew at fantastic speed towards Davern. The velocity was enough to break any personal force-field, yet Davern stood unfazed.

"The Adversary has made me invulnerable and unstoppable," said Davern, as he launched himself at James.

Once again James jumped back, keeping his distance from Davern. His opponent was far more experienced and changed his attack strategy in mid-air. Using his super-sentient strength, he brought down his fists upon the ground with the force of an impacting meteor. The terrain blew apart like a tidal wave in every direction.

With only a fraction of a second to spare, James used all his strength to redirect the thousands of tons of material about to hit him. It only lasted a moment, but the effort still brought him to his knees. James looked up to see that Davern was yet again upon him. James created a telekinetic shield as Davern launched a vicious assault against him. Each blow sent a kinetic shockwave through the shield. James reeled back from every blow, dimly aware that if not for his telekinesis, he would be nothing but bloody pulp by now. With every subsequent protective shield that crumbled, another instantly had to be restored. He felt his strength, all too soon, begin to slip away.

He reached out with his senses, appealing for help. To his despair he realized the others were either incapacitated, or like him, fighting for their lives.

It had begun.

He felt anger towards Alicia. What had she been thinking? They should have been ready for an attack. It was expected. Damn her! For some unfathomable reason instead of preparing and planning, they had wandered off as if The Adversary had forgotten them.

Moments before

Victoria and Korina found themselves wandering the extensive and elaborate gardens of this strange yet, in some way, familiar place.

"Your world sounds very similar to the era I was born into, back on my own Earth, a hundred and seventy years ago," said Korina. Again, mentioning Earth brought back that indescribable feeling of loss.

Sensing this, Victoria said, "I'm sorry. I almost lost my own world, twice. It is still in jeopardy due to the current crisis."

They both tensed, looking at one another for a moment, realizing something of great significance. Then they relaxed and carried on their walk as if neither had a care in the world.

"From what your Alex told me there are a great many differences between my world and what you define as your Victorian era," said Victoria.

"Having lived through that era I would love to visit your world sometime and experience it for myself," said Korina.

"You would be most welcome, Lady Korina," said Victoria.

"Lady?"

"Of course," smiled Victoria. "Being the monarch, I can bestow titles upon whomever I please."

Korina laughed. "You realize I came from the poorest of backgrounds. I was a thief, until fortune found me or, to be more precise, Garianne."

"The circumstances into which you were born matter not. I am sure you did what you had to to survive," said Victoria. "I have been told that your world was harsher than mine, the people less forgiving and quick to judge. I mean no disrespect; it is simply what I've heard. Whether it is true or not…" Victoria stopped, for a moment, seeing Korina's expression. "Forgive me, I did not mean to cast aspersions on those who have so recently passed away."

"No," said Korina gently, "you are right. 'We' were indeed less forgiving and quick to judge. It is not always easy to see this, even when you are metahuman. When Garianne elevated me to that state, I managed to achieve that world view and see what was obvious to the Galacien. I saw humanity as children, fighting amongst themselves in the most deplorable way. Somehow, Garianne made me see a brighter future. Now that future is gone."

There was silence between them for a moment until Victoria said, "Should we survive this, I would be honoured if you would come to my Earth. It could become your home too."

Korina smiled. "Thank you, I think I would like that."

Victoria was about to say something else when she felt a sudden wave of dread.

"What is it?" said Korina.

"With this power, I now possess I can perceive events which have happened and perceive those which are most likely to happen in the future."

"Yes?" queried Korina.

Victoria's eyes widened. She then pushed Korina hard.

Victoria could not control time, for that would require control over every particle in the universe. However, Alicia had made her in such a way that she could alter her consciousness, making the world around her appear to slow down. Victoria saw the man coming at what would have been incredible speed to strike Korina, who now flew backwards, her expression showing the beginnings of shock. The man missed her by a hair's breadth, his momentum carrying him past them. She caught sight of his face and asked her implant if it recognized him.

The man was slowing from his initial attack and was now turning around. Victoria, having little combat experience, didn't know what to do. The implant informed her that the man was identified as Kallon, a Galacien citizen who'd had a close personal relationship with Min before he was killed by The Adversary. They were being attacked by a dead man who could kill them in seconds. Victoria dared not let her concentration slip, lest this come to pass. She implored the implant for advice as she watched Kallon circle around for another attack.

She was more than a little disturbed to find the others were also under attack. In this place, where her body was impeded yet her mind ran like quicksilver, it occurred to her how they had been caught unawares like this.

If only Korina could help. Her ability to amplify or nullify another super-sentient's ability could certainly prove useful; however, she had to do this consciously. Victoria knew that before she could even communicate with Korina, this Kallon could kill them both. Victoria regarded Korina still in mid-air, her arms and legs outstretched, head down, now several metres away from her. She glimpsed to her left. Kallon was heading right for her, a little over two hundred metres away. He must have speeded up somewhat, for his relative velocity had gone from a walking pace to a jogging pace. She did not have long.

The implant had a suggestion but couldn't guarantee it would work. There were a lot of variables. Victoria had no choice. Kallon's pace now looked as if he were almost sprinting. She had only seconds left.

She waited until he was mere metres from her, then focused all her will on speeding up her consciousness thereby essentially slowing him down as much as possible. Kallon slowed, but not enough. He still bore down on her, his face a mask of death, a hand outstretched ready to grab her by the neck.

Victoria gritted her teeth. A strange noise erupted through them, as she screamed in desperation. Kallon came almost to a halt as Victoria, who had brought back her fist, using every ounce of her super-sentient strength to push her arm through this treacle world to punch him underneath into his ribs, screamed through every second.

Victoria collapsed and a split-second later she heard Korina hit the ground.

Panting and exhausted, Victoria glimpsed up into the sky to see a figure hurtling away as if he'd been shot out of a cannon.

She couldn't get over how strong she was now.

"What the hell!?" shouted Korina, lying on the ground.

Victoria, still gasping for breath, said, "Attacked by a super-sentient."

"What are you talking about? I didn't see anything. I didn't sense anything," said Korina.

"Perhaps because he was so fast," panted Victoria, trying to catch her breath, "incredibly fast. Korina, you need to use your abilities. Nullify his."

"What?"

"Quickly, before he returns."

"But if I can't see him coming?" said Korina.

Victoria thought for a moment. "Nullify the whole area before he comes back."

Korina nodded, but before she could do anything, something fast   hit   them   both.

27. VASHA & GARIANNE

The planet Emmita, in an unknown universe
Alicia and Vasha teleported to Min's side. Vasha tried to rouse her, knowing that this was no ordinary slumber. She resorted to using her implant, yet she sensed that Min's implant had shut down.

"Can't 'you' wake her? Telepathy is your area of expertise?" asked Vasha.

"I've been trying," said Alicia.

"Really?"

"Yes, why?"

"It's just that you give this impression that you're infallible," said Vasha.

"No-one is infallible. However, that is not to say it can't be done, only that it would take time and I sense that the others are under attack. We must go to their aid at once."

Without further consultation, Alicia teleported Vasha to help James and Alexander while she teleported to a different locale.

Vasha appeared to see James' shield finally fail. Davern's fists were already raised high above him. Then, it was as if a bomb had gone off. Even though she was fairly certain the shockwave and following wave of debris would do her no harm, she got no sense of James. She did not know whether he was alive or dead.

This creature known as Davern was incredibly strong. Having known many super-sentients like this one, she strengthened her force-field a hundred-fold. As she expected, he was on her in moments, unleashing an impressive savage series of blows. He then proceeded to use his vast strength in an attempt to push through her force-field. She was surprised by how close he got, though she could have easily made it stronger anytime she wanted.

"You're wasting your time," said Vasha.

Davern stopped his assault, eying her menacingly.

Vasha said, "My implant informs me you died. Your memory archives were corrupted. So how is it that you are here?"

"I was dead. 'She' brought me back," explained Davern.

"Despite the power granted to you by The Adversary," said Vasha, "you cannot harm me."

Davern raised an eyebrow, then promptly teleported.

Not through the shield? Impossible. She felt it. *Underneath. How could he teleport into solid matter without killing himself?*

A fist punched through the ground from below and grabbed her by the ankle, as tight as a vice. Then it tightened, crushing bone and muscle. Vasha felt a stab of pain until the implant kicked in and blocked it. It was enough for her to lapse in concentration and her force-field to disappear.

Idiot! she scolded herself.

Davern exploded through the ground, grabbing Vasha by the throat and holding her in the air. She attempted to teleport away, but couldn't. Perhaps something to do with his invulnerability. He had hold of her. There was no way to escape. Davern slammed her to the ground.

The shock left Vasha temporarily disorientated.

Then his hands reached for her head.

She created a new force-field to stop his attempt at crushing her skull between his hands. Her terror flipped to unbridled, defiant fury.

"You think that you are strong. That I can't hurt you?" Vasha reached out with her senses. *My god,* she thought *he is like steel in a world of gossamer; immutable and indestructible.* Hers was the power over all forms of energy 'and' matter, for energy and matter were interchangeable. The darker use of her power was to exploit the matter of a person's physical form. For example, she could turn any part of them into superheated plasma. She was stunned to realize that the particles which made up Davern's form were as difficult to deal with as he himself. As hard as she tried, her power could not touch him.

Davern smiled. "You cannot affect me."

He pushed even harder. She felt her force-field weaken. Vasha had only moments before the end.

"My physical form is indomitable, unstoppable," Davern growled.

Physical form? thought Vasha.

Vasha made one last supreme effort. Her force-field collapsed and so did Davern, right on top of her.

Vasha gasped, exhausted. She hauled Davern off her onto his back. She sensed he was indeed dead. *No mean feat,* she thought.

Looking down at her ankle, she could tell that the nanomachines in her body were doing an excellent job of repairing it and would soon be done; so much quicker than in her day.

"Impressive," came a voice, as if part of the breeze itself.

Vasha looked around, but could not sense anyone there.

"You could not affect his physical form, so you reached out and destroyed him metaphysically. I am curious. Have you ever done that before?"

"No," said Vasha.

A woman appeared before her, dressed in close-fitting robes of Galacien origin.

Hardly dressed for combat, Vasha thought, *though appearances can be deceiving.*

Vasha's implant informed her that this person was the renowned Cieshella Garianne Phulum. "It seems The Adversary has made a habit of making puppets of the dead," said Vasha.

Garianne appeared completely relaxed and at ease. "Unfortunately for you, and, I might add, myself, but fortunately for The Adversary that does appear to be the case," said Garianne. "I'm sure my previous incarnation would be far from happy with my existence."

"You are only a copy," said Vasha.

"Aren't we all?" said Garianne. "I died in a place where magic ruled over technology. Perhaps it was due to this that The Adversary has seen fit to bestow me with such mystical gifts."

Vasha wasn't sure what she meant by this. She got to her feet; her ankle as good as new.

Garianne made the slightest of gestures with her fingers and all around her patterns of multi-coloured light began to take shape, growing like water-based paint on paper.

Without hesitation, Vasha created an energy shield all around herself. She reached out with her senses to ascertain exactly what she was looking at but was deeply disturbed to realize that she did not understand what those said senses were telling her. She was familiar with all forms of matter and energy, yet this display was beyond her comprehension. It was totally alien.

The shapes of light towered above them and encircled Vasha. Tendrils reached out and intersected her shield, changing it. Vasha could feel that it was becoming something else, something not unlike that which Garianne was manipulating. She felt her control over it weaken to nothing for it was now under Garianne's control.

Vasha teleported away to see the shield collapse where she had stood only moments before. The shapes continued to seek Vasha out like a multitude of snakes. Vasha created another shield but was shocked to see that what she had created was yet more of this 'mystical' energy that was foreign to her.

Again, she teleported. "What have you done?"

Garianne said nothing.

Vasha unleashed a blast of energy from her hand, yet Garianne had already created a mystical shield to deflect it.

Vasha made a series of teleportations followed by similar attacks, only to be deflected each time by Garianne. All the while the strange shapes sought to capture her.

Vasha now reached out for Garianne's metaphysical self, to stop her in the same way she had Davern.

Nothing happened.

Vasha needed to get away. She teleported once more but felt as if she had somehow bounced back. She was on her knees, disorientated. The mystical shapes snaking across the ground now whipped up and grabbed her by the wrists and ankles. Other shapes, like pieces of paper blowing in the wind, floated towards Vasha and adhered themselves to her body.

Garianne said, "The outcome was never in doubt. While I am quite familiar with how matter and energy work in our universe, you were completely unprepared for my mystical gifts."

She then looked up; her attention drawn to something.

Vasha could feel herself weakening; she felt nauseous and sweaty. Her head was pounding, and the pain was enough that her vision became blurred. What was happening? She hadn't even noticed that her bonds were gone. They were no longer needed as she fell to the ground, almost paralyzed. The strange pieces of paper continued to cover her body, like a form of mummification. Only her head remained exposed.

Garianne then looked up to the sky. "She calls for me," she said. "Goodbye Vasha. I'd hoped for more of a challenge, but despite your experience, you were rather a disappointment."

She gestured, and the ground underneath Vasha broke apart, consuming her whole like some giant beast. Vasha was immersed in complete darkness. She felt cut off from her abilities, and that which covered her body seemed to inhibit the use of technology, leaving her utterly powerless. Buried alive, with not the strength or resources to escape. She could do nothing. Panic overcame her; she felt abandoned and terrified.

28. THE ADVERSARY

The planet Emmita, in an unknown universe.

The Adversary observed recent events from high above the planet Emmita. The conflicts between the super-sentients provided mild but, for now, sufficient entertainment. She had only recently conversed, through one of her puppets, with the being of her origin. The interaction intriguing, yet ultimately disappointing. For 'Min' had hardly evolved, while she had become so much more. It felt right that Min's end would come soon enough, that she would soon be only a memory of The Adversary.

Her attention, which had a wavered a little, now focused like a laser beam as the ancient super-sentient Vasha and the famous Garianne squared off against one another. Yet even as they fought, her mind posed questions which still had no answers. Something bothered her about Garianne. She was a perfect copy of Garianne as stored and retrieved by The Kinsmen simulation of the multiverse. Then why did she sense that this version of Garianne was somehow incomplete? The Adversary was so used to understanding everything that transpired that she found this extremely irritating.

As she watched Garianne hold her own quite easily against the capable and experienced Vasha, she could not shake the feeling that this Garianne was different. She recalled that the Garianne, whom the original Jonas had retrieved from the Galacien memory archives thousands of years ago, had been the same. 'That Garianne' herself had admitted that she did not feel quite right, which was something the original had never expressed. Lesser sentients might think the answer obvious. It was because they were 'copies'. This argument showed a lack of understanding. The original Garianne was already a copy many times over from the original from long ago. Yet she always felt complete. Galacien technology, Jonas' and her techniques were so well-refined that these copies were perfect in every sense of the word, even at the metaphysical level. And she could even make or maintain, their super-sentient nature. If Garianne was a perfect copy in every conceivable way, why had she been different all those years ago, when Jonas, Davern, Garianne and herself first came to Emmita? Where was the most recent incarnation of Jonas and the enigma that was Nicola? The Adversary was sure that the answer to all these questions and more could be plucked from the mind of Alicia. Yet, was this what she wanted? Better to find out for herself. The pleasure of discovering such revelations personally would be far greater than simply taking such information by force. This place offered little else.

With this, The Adversary turned her attention to Alicia. To her surprise, she was nowhere to be found. Alicia had informed Vasha she would aid their comrades, but she had done no such thing. Had she abandoned them? A fire of intrigue burned within The Adversary; she could not help but smile, one of many old physical habits that remained. Alicia did not disappoint. She was resourceful and unpredictable. She felt that 'this' Alicia was a rather unique being in this and any other universe. The copies she had encountered previously merely hinted at what she was truly capable of. The Adversary looked forward to when, at the end and only then, she would delve into her mind to understand her completely. It would almost be a shame to kill her. However, as with everything she could always be brought back. Or she could find her in the omniverse, where everything dies, and everything lives.

What a pity that none of them could understand the omniverse as she could. Not the original Jonas and not Alicia, for they were, without doubt, the two most enlightened sentients she had ever encountered. It had been a pleasure although, like eternity itself, she had barely begun. It stretched out before her, as did the omniverse, calling her with its limitless possibilities. This multiverse, even though a part of the omniverse, was nothing compared to that. They were nothing. And yet.

Where was Alicia Elde?

You cannot hide from me, thought The Adversary. Pleasure coursed through her being as she searched for her prey. For lesser beings locating Alicia could prove problematic. The Adversary simply used the nature of the omniverse and the higher dimensions of this universe to perceive where Alicia had travelled from and to. The Adversary saw that Alicia, rather than teleporting to her comrades' location, had gone to the portal and passed through it. Yet The Adversary could not perceive what lay beyond this doorway. She could no longer detect Alicia.

The Adversary promptly teleported to the portal's location, summoning Garianne, Al and Kallon, who all appeared beside her.

"The others are of no consequence," said The Adversary, in an unequivocal statement of truth. "Alicia is the key."

She regarded the portal. Beyond lay only blackness.

"What is that?" said Al.

The Adversary's face broke out into a grin. "The infinite," she whispered. "Alicia, I am suitably impressed." She turned to her puppets. "Before you waits the omniverse of which this multiverse is but a fraction."

Garianne's eye's narrowed. "She hopes to lose herself."

"Then she hopes in vain. I can track her through the infinite. I now bestow this power to each of you. Find her. Bring her to heel. Herald my coming and her end."

With that, each of them, in turn, crossed the threshold into that which was everything; the omniverse.

29. NO PLACE LIKE IT

An unknown universe.
Al found himself in surroundings that were all too familiar. The hot sun shone brightly overhead in a perfect, cloudless summer's day. This back garden was his garden; the house that stood before him was his home. Birds chirped in the trees and the sound of a helicopter flying high, overhead, reminded him of a time not too long ago when an alien virus had wiped out every single living human on Earth. Everyone, except him. Garianne had taken him and given him a purpose, making an impossible promise that she would put things right. Things had not gone the way she expected and now he was compelled to do The Adversary's bidding. Nothing else mattered except finding Alicia.
She was here!
He could sense her. In the house. The others who were supposed to have followed the trail were nowhere to be seen. He couldn't wait. Al, his jaw set firm, covered the short distance across the garden and crashed through the patio door. The frame broke off cleanly and the glass shattered, spraying across the floor. He looked up to see Alicia standing at the back of the kitchen, calm and expectant with a cup of tea in her hand, next to another woman who stood frozen in shock

until she recognized him.

"Alex!" screamed his mother. "What the hell are you doing?"

Al stood unmoving, his eyes darting back and forth between Alicia and his mother.

"I'm sorry, dear," said his mother to Alicia, her voice and manner gentle.

"That's quite alright," said Alicia smiling.

"It's my son."

"Likes to make an entrance, doesn't he?"

Al's mother's head whipped around. She glared at him. "Well? Are you going to explain yourself?"

Al continued to look at both women unable to say anything.

"Alex?" pressed his mother in that tone which, despite everything he had been through, took him straight back to being a child again.

"I... I thought you were in trouble... Mum," said Al.

"In trouble?"

"I saw someone in the house. I thought it was a burglar," said Al.

His mother shook her head. "Ridiculous. Perhaps you could have taken a closer look first before knocking the bloody door down. Look at it?" she said, regarding the damage.

Al's eyes flicked over to Alicia, who showed nothing of her true intentions.

"I mean, does this person look like a burglar? She's quite harmless."

Alicia casually walked over to the sink. Alex tensed like an animal ready to defend himself. The person who was his mother, yet not his mother, noticed his behaviour and slapped him on the chest.

Even though Al felt no pain from the blow, he could not help but react. "Hey! What was that for?"

"For being rude to our new neighbour. Now stop it."

"But I didn't say anything," said Al. "What! Did you say, neighbour?"

"I said, stop it." His mother hit him again.

"Mum!"

"That's for the door," said his mother. "You're paying for that. I'm sorry, Alicia. Can we speak later? I'll have to ring someone to sort this out."

"Of course," said Alicia.

"I'll see her out," jumped in Al.

"Alright," said Al's mother. "Bye, dear."

Al beckoned her through the hallway.

"Bye," said Alicia, cheerfully.

Al's mum took him by the arm and whispered, "You be nice."

Al followed Alicia out of the house, shutting the front door behind him.

Alicia waited for him on the front lawn.

"The others will be here soon. You cannot escape," said Al.

Alicia looked at him curiously. "Escape? I'm moving in, across the road," she indicated with a nod of the head.

On the other side of the road removal, men were unloading a van, taking in various boxes through the front door of the house.

"What?"

"As your mother said, we're going to be neighbours," said Alicia.

"The others…"

"Will never arrive, Al," said Alicia. "Their paths lead elsewhere. Yours ends here."

Al considered attacking her. Returning to The Adversary with her as his prize, yet he paused. *Why?* he thought.

"Conflict between us would destroy our immediate surroundings and spill out across the city, possibly further. Your mother would certainly be killed."

"She's not my mother. This isn't my Earth."

"Then why didn't you attack me as soon as you saw me? What difference did it make back there? If you are in the absolute thrall of The Adversary then nothing else should matter, and yet you just stood there. Why didn't you dispose of her?"

Al looked around, saying nothing.

Alicia continued, now with sadness in her eyes. "Some time ago, Garianne promised to help you in return for your support.

You did your best to help, despite what happened to you. I now wish to make good on Garianne's promise."

"I'm here to kill you," said Al, but the lack of conviction in his voice was obvious.

"No, you're not," said Alicia dismissively. "Since your arrival I've been routing through your brain, undoing all the damage that The Adversary has done. I won't lie: it wasn't easy. That's why you're reacting to your mother the way you should, and why you're finding it harder with every passing moment to inflict harm on me or anyone else. You're becoming your old self again."

Al could feel it. Her words rang true. He felt his old self now, more than ever. He felt free. Al looked back at the house and saw his mother through the window. "This isn't my world."

"It is now," said Alicia.

"I'm not her son. Her real son is here," said Al.

"No, he died," said Alicia.

"When?"

"A couple of hours ago. The Alex Lethbridge of this universe was a multiversal teleporter, like you. In fact, he was exactly like you, except he made a fatal error. He was distracted and teleported close to the core of the Earth."

Al frowned at her suspiciously. "Impossible. That would be like someone not being aware of a brick wall, then running into it. I've never made such an error."

"It is extremely rare, but it does happen."

Alex shook his head. "If this is true, I find it more likely that you interfered and that's what killed him. This is all too convenient. The chances are too remote."

Alicia smiled, "You still don't understand. We are from a multiverse with a great multitude of universes, too many for normal sentients to comprehend. It must seem infinite. It is far from it. You, like everyone else, still think in such limited terms. Think about where we are now, Al. The moment you crossed the threshold you entered a limitless reality. I did not need to orchestrate the death of your counterpart. I only had to find a universe with the perfect conditions. A universe so similar to your own as to be impossible to differentiate from it."

"I bet I can tell the difference," said Al.

"I will take that bet," said Alicia.

Al once more looked back at the house. He felt something break inside, and from nowhere he was weeping.

Alicia took his hand.

"It took me rather a long time to find an Earth that matched yours in every single way. All of human history. Everything that has been and ever was is precisely the same."

She felt him firmly grip her hand.

"They're all here, Al. All your family. All your friends. Exactly how you remember them. Like nothing ever happened."

"The aliens. The ones who created the virus that killed everyone," said Al.

"I found a universe where they didn't exist."

"How is this possible?"

"In the omniverse everything is possible."

"How did you do this?"

Alicia smiled. "Well, I must be going. There's a lot of stuff to unpack. They say that moving to a new house is one of the most stressful things you can do in your life." She shrugged. "I don't know what all the fuss is about."

Al looked at her in astonishment. "What are you doing? The others. The Adversary will be coming."

Alicia shook her head. "Not this way," she said confidently. She made as if to cross the road, then turned. "You see, I've been here for some time now. I'm one of many Alicia's. Your former comrades will be off chasing the others. The Adversary will, of course, follow the real one."

"You mean you're not the real one?"

Alicia seemed amused by his question. "Perhaps 'real' isn't quite the right word. I'm real. As real as you or anyone else here. See you later, Al. You know where I am. I'd be delighted if you came by from time to time," she said, pointing to the house opposite.

Al smiled and shook his head in disbelief. He started laughing and found he couldn't stop.

His mother joined him. "What's so funny?" she asked. He sensed she had calmed down somewhat, despite her tone.

"Nothing."

"She seems nice, don't you think?"

"Yeah," said Al, "real nice."

30. KALLON

An unknown universe.

After stepping over the threshold, Kallon found himself on an eerily familiar, dark, rocky slope. He felt Alicia's trail leading into the distance. Kneeling, he touched the soil. Even though it hadn't been that long since she'd passed through the portal that led here, he sensed that days had passed since she'd come this way. How was that possible?

Despite this fact, 'this' was the trail and he must follow it to find her. He must close the distance. Kallon's eyes narrowed as he realized that the others hadn't arrived. Perhaps this was Alicia's doing, somehow. Divide and conquer? She would find he was not to be underestimated. As a copy of Jonas, he possessed his natural keen intellect and resourcefulness; he was now also super-sentient.

In the blink of an eye, he was off. Leaving an explosion of rock and dirt in his wake, Kallon ran up the side of the mountain at incredible speed, the ground a blur beneath him.

With time, Kallon grew certain of where he was: in the Zagros Mountains of Assyria. He followed the trail and knew where it would lead. He stopped at the ridge that overlooked the valley and spotted the humble abode in which he had grown up with his parents. He saw light from within and felt something stir inside him, much like the light he now saw.

Because he was so transfixed by the sight before him, he didn't notice the figure approaching from his left. As he did, he moved instantly, pushing her into the light, an arm around her back and one hand at her throat. Yet before he even saw her face, he knew who she was.

Min held his gaze, unafraid. "There's no need for violence."

She was as bold and beautiful as when they first met.

He released her.

Min stroked her throat.

"I'm sorry," said Kallon.

Not exactly ideal first-contact circumstances said Min's implant.

Quiet! replied Min.

Why are you here? asked Kallon, instinctively using his implant.

Min looked at Kallon in astonishment and took a step back.

He has an implant! she broadcast to everyone.

Kallon looked up to where he now knew was a Galacien starship in orbit.

He knows you're there, said Min.

"Yes, and yes," said Kallon, despite being engrossed in his interaction with Min. Her presence was a reminder that he was compelled to do The Adversary's will and find Alicia. He made to leave.

"Wait!" cried Min.

Surprisingly, he paused.

She approached him a little too closely, a curious glint in her eye. "You have an implant. How is that possible?"

He looked at her, wondering what might have been if things had been different. "Min." She reacted to that, obviously wondering how he knew her name. "I'm not of your universe. I am merely passing through."

"For what reason?"

"I cannot lie. I have been sent to hunt someone, an unpleasant business I grant you, but it must be done." Even as he said it, he wondered why he found such a thing 'unpleasant'.

"Sent by whom?"

Kallon looked at her, then he laughed. "By you, my dear."

"Me?"

"Well, an alternate version of you."

Min cocked her head slightly to one side and Kallon could hear the Galacien on the starship, suggesting what she should do if this was indeed a being from another universe. She ignored them, instead opting for a question of her own. Min smiled and Kallon found himself reciprocating. "This alternate me. What is she like?" She looked at him expectantly.

His smile faded.

He tried to think of the Min he remembered, but every time he tried, he only thought of the one he served.

Well, answer her. Kallon heard another voice in his head.

Kallon reached out with his senses, yet he could not pinpoint the source of this voice.

Min looked concerned. "What is it?"

Tell her.

"She is…" Again, he felt something stir inside him. He took a deep breath, "She is…" He looked at her beautiful face. His Min. And from nowhere he felt a tear roll down his cheek.

Min reached out and took his hand.

"By the stars, what is it?" said Min.

Tell her.

Shaking his head in sorrow, he said, "She is cruel, petty and selfish. She has killed unaccountable innocents. She has destroyed entire species, planets and even threatens a multitude of universes." Min pulled her hand away from his and recoiled in horror. Kallon wanted to stop but couldn't. "She creates conflict on a vast scale; the resulting suffering serves as amusement for her. She's akin to a god who claims that beings such as you or I are less than nothing and, as such, are of little to no consequence." Kallon sunk to his knees; his head lolled forward. "What have I done?" he whispered.

Through his implant, Kallon was dimly aware that the Galacien were deeply disturbed by this revelation and wanted Min to return.

No. I think I should talk to him. Can't you see he's in pain? I believe this creature has had some kind of control over him, said a voice.

You don't know that, said Min.

There was a long pause from the Galacien, then he heard one of them say, *She's coming down.*

Kallon heard the familiar sound of someone teleporting to their location. He looked up to see Alicia Elde standing there, wearing a Galacien uniform.

The trail ended with her. He should attack her. But why would he?

Without taking her eyes from him, Alicia said, "Min, I require a moment with this one."

Min looked at her, hesitating for the briefest of moments. "Of course."

Min reluctantly teleported back to the ship in orbit, leaving Alicia and Kallon alone.

"You care deeply for her. You always have. Even before you were Kallon," said Alicia.

Kallon shook his head. "The Adversary sent me to track you, to kill you if I could. Yet now... I do not want to."

"You are free from her," said Alicia.

"Am I?!" said Kallon desperately.

"Believe me, you are the least of The Adversary's concerns. You are now lost in the infinite that is the omniverse. You are quite safe here."

"Really?"

"Yes," affirmed Alicia. The boldness in her eyes convinced him. Inside, something flipped and he felt he was awakening from a nightmare. He was free.

"You said I'm lost here. Do you mean I can never return?"

"I'm afraid you're stuck here," said Alicia.

"What about Min?"

"I   don't   know."

Kallon stood, muscles tense, his anger etched across his face. He towered above Alicia.

She regarded him without a hint of fear. Her initial thought at that moment was how much his thoughts felt like those of Jonas. She said, "It was not I who resurrected you from the dead and forced you to do their bidding. It was not I who forced you from your multiverse into the larger omniverse."

Kallon knew this to be true, but his ire still burned. "You're a telepath. You've been manipulating my thoughts," he accused, waving his hand in the air.

"Only to free you from bondage. Or should I have left you under its spell to murder and destroy anything which stood between you and myself like a rabid bloodhound?"

His shoulders slumped as he accepted his fate.

"Consider yourself lucky that you are at least free and have another chance at true happiness," said Alicia.

She was right. Considering what had happened to him, he was lucky. "I still don't understand. You're part of the Galacien here?"

"Oh, I've been here for a long, long time. I integrated myself into Galacien society hundreds of years ago. Moved quickly through the ranks of the super-sentient corps. It could be said, I'm rather highly regarded here."

Kallon looked at her. If anyone else had said this, he would have laughed in contempt. Yet there was something in her manner and how Min had acted towards her that suggested that she was understating herself. He was about to query something, but before he could open his mouth, she continued.

"Yes, things here are quite different. The Galacien Golden Age never ended. We still have super-sentients. New ones are born all the time. With their help we've expanded into many other galaxies, bringing peace and prosperity. We leave those species alone who do not want us or who, we feel, may not cope well psychologically from contact with us. The Adversary does not exist here. The Nacuerians as you know them were never transformed. They are a beautiful and gentle species. We have a lot to offer. Not to mention," Alicia glanced to the heavens, "'she' likes you."

Kallon was about to ask how she would know if this Min and he would be compatible when he remembered her abilities.

"I know you love her. From the first moment, you saw her, when you were Jonas."

"Garianne knew that I would become attached to her too. She also manipulated me."

"I know. We're terrible," said Alicia in mock sincerity. "However, there is no doubt that if we hadn't done the things we've done, you and I wouldn't be here now having this rather pleasant conversation. Now, it's time for you to make a decision."

Kallon looked at her quizzically. "What decision?"

Alicia gestured to the farmhouse at the bottom of the dark, shallow valley. "Stay here. Or come with us."

Kallon considered the light spilling out from his parents' house. He could sense them inside. He glanced upwards; he could almost see the Galacien vessel high above.

"Well? Come on, I'm a busy person, you know," said Alicia.

"I still have so many questions," said Kallon.

Alicia smiled at him as a mother smiles at her beloved son, and in the gentlest tone she said, "Jonas, you always did."

He stared at her for what seemed like an age. "I want to see them again. I know they are not my parents. But I want to say goodbye. Tell them I will return as often as I can."

"Of course. I understand," said Alicia. "I will come with you."

31. GARIANNE

An unknown universe.
Garianne appeared in her office at the Galacien Institute for Technological Advancement. James, Korina and Alex looked at her expectantly. No-one said a word. Everything appeared normal.

Why did Korina's trail lead here and where were her comrades?

"Garianne, are you alright?" asked James.

She raised her hand to silence him. This may not be her universe or her time. However, they believed she was their Garianne. They would do as they were told.

Garianne felt something. She was now familiar with the compulsion The Adversary exerted over her. Being one of the most elevated Galaciens alive in her universe, she was highly aware to her thoughts and the physiology of her brain. She could feel The Adversary's compulsion dwindling slowly, moment by moment. Whilst the smaller part of her rejoiced at the hope of being free, the dominant part of her psyche still under the influence of The Adversary began to panic. It knew the danger. If she did not find Alicia soon and return to The Adversary, she would be lost.

This must be Alicia's doing, thought Garianne.

This universes Korina could see the concern etched on

Garianne's face. "What is it?"

"Be silent!" hissed Garianne. She reached out her senses, detecting Alicia's trail, yet she did not move. She smiled. *She wants me to waste my time following her trail, step-by-step, checking every nook and cranny. All the while my mistress's influence fades.*

Garianne's form took on a blue glow as she elevated from the ground. A sphere of energy materialized between her hands, emitting a low hum that permeated the room. Garianne began to draw and manipulate the patterns upon the sphere's surface.

"Good grief. You didn't tell me she was super-sentient!" exclaimed Alex.

James and Korina looked at one another. "She isn't," said James.

Garianne ignored them. They were insignificant. All that mattered was finishing the spell that would take her to where Alicia was at this moment so that she could destroy her. Less than a minute later it was done, and Garianne promptly vanished in a puff of blue smoke.

The Surface of Earth's Moon

Garianne appeared on the moon.

Alicia was waiting.

Took you long enough, said Alicia.

Garianne unleashed her full power and fury upon Alicia, gouging out a crevice that stretched for hundreds of miles across the lunar surface. Arc-light and strange mystical energies stretched up over, around, behind Alicia, eager to find a way through the force-field she had erected to protect herself. Garianne's other hand was already gesturing as she readied her next spell in mere seconds.

That is quite an impressive display, she heard Alicia say.

Despite her goading, Garianne remained calm and unleashed her second spell.

Alicia appeared before her, unable to move, caught like a fly in a spider's web.

I have you, said Garianne. *I admit, when I realised what was happening, I had my concerns. It would only be a matter of time until your telepathic manipulations would take me to the point of no return.*

What about the others? Are you not curious as to what happened to them? said Alicia, desperation and panic lacing her every word.

You are trying to delay me, said Garianne. *I must kill you before that happens.*

Without any further delay, Garianne reached out and grabbed Alicia's head between her hands, enveloping it in dark, mystical energy.

Alicia gritted her teeth, pushing her considerable abilities to break through this darkness that threatened to destroy her and this invisible web that held her.

Garianne pushed even harder.

Alicia's mouth opened in a silent scream.

Garianne let go and Alicia's lifeless body sank to the moon's surface, bringing up dust as it landed limply.

Feeling drained, yet satisfied, Garianne relaxed. She had done well. Perhaps it would take time, but The Adversary would find her in the end and all would be well.

Wouldn't it?

Of course, it would. Why shouldn't it?

Then why did she feel so uneasy about The Adversary?

Something was wrong.

No, this was right. The Adversary was wrong. It had killed countless innocents, including those she considered allies and friends. Including this one who lay dead before her.

Alicia!

What had she done?

Alicia. How could this have happened?

Garianne knew the answer. She had been resurrected and turned into a puppet, a weapon of The Adversary. Yet now, it was as if awakening from a nightmare of which she had been a hapless spectator. Now awake, The Adversary's influence was gone. That would mean that some force must have done this to her. Then Garianne felt that she was being teleported. She attempted to stop it but couldn't.

An artificial pocket universe

Garianne found herself floating in featureless, white space.

There was no-one and nothing here.

The white nothingness seemed to be both up close and far away. She could feel her thoughts reeling. There was nothing in this place to focus on, leaving her disorientated.

Garianne took a deep breath and calmed herself.

She looked down at her fingers and clicked them. There was no sound. She spoke. Nothing. She realised she was no longer breathing.

Am I dead? the dormant, primal side of her asked.

She smiled. *No. I am super-sentient. When in an environment such as the vacuum of space, super-sentients simply stop breathing. They do not die for they draw vitality from another source. Why am I here?*

Something was materializing before her, billions of particles coming together to take form; it was nice to have something to focus on in this strange place. It appeared to be an old, Victorian lamppost. Next to it appeared a wooden bench, and beneath her feet, a worn, cobbled street. Finally, dark Georgian houses coalesced along the street. The world she now stood on only existed for around fifty metres in every direction, then simply ended. The edges of this reality seemed to dissolve into nothingness.

She sensed someone behind her. Turning, she saw Alicia sitting on the bench.

"This is an interesting situation, wouldn't you say?" said Alicia.

Garianne glanced around. The environment was filled with air. She could feel herself automatically breathing once more.

"The Alicia on the moon. A decoy?" stated Garianne.

"A copy. Did you have to kill her?"

"I wasn't myself."

"No. It took some time for me to free you from the influence of The Adversary."

Garianne walked over to Alicia and sat down beside her.

"I take it you remember this place?" said Alicia, indicating to the street around them.

Garianne's brow furrowed in concern. "I remember sending you away, feeling it was the right thing to do. No. Knowing it was the right thing to do. But I don't know why."

Alicia nodded. "You said that there were few moments in your life that were truly significant. That this was one of them. You said I wouldn't understand back then, but sometime in the future, I would." Alicia turned to Garianne. "I now understand."

Garianne held her gaze until she said, with a hint of annoyance, "I don't."

"You will."

"When?"

"Soon," Alicia stood. "Back then you knew what my potential was. You hoped, given time, I could solve any problem. Given enough time. You are not the Garianne we all remembered. Jonas knew this. Min and Davern knew this. You knew it too. Whether I'm speaking of the Garianne that the original Jonas created, or the one The Adversary did, which is the one I'm speaking to now. You should be a perfect copy in every conceivable way. The Galacien have been doing it for thousands of years. If they can do it then why not Jonas and The Adversary, whose abilities are far beyond the Galacien? Unless they made a mistake. I've examined you, and they didn't."

Garianne looked down, feeling defeated.

Alicia took her by the hand. "It's alright. You're nearly there."

Garianne looked at her, confused.

Alicia continued, "When you were with the Galacien, every time your memories were downloaded into a new body, something else was added."

"What?"

"It is the greater part of you. A part of you that made you the person you were. It is what I have become, something earned. You earned it too, a long, long time ago, and it is rightfully yours. You and I, Garianne. We are Kinsmen."

32. THE ADVERSARY

The planet Emmita, in an unknown universe.

The Adversary reached a hand towards the portal and paused.

She was confident that she was the supreme power in this corner of reality, threatening its entire existence; no-one of greater power had challenged her. Now only Alicia and Nicola remained a mystery to her, the former having attempted to lose herself in the infinite of the omniverse.

Had she realized the futility of any further confrontation and simply run?

Could she let Alicia go, uncertain that she may yet one day still threaten her existence?

After all, anything was possible. The Adversary concentrated and peered into that unending well of possibilities. She perceived the omniverse as a vast landscape reaching out forever. A multitude of probabilities. She most clearly saw that which pertained to her circumstances, that which was most probable. Events that were far more unlikely were further in the distance and, despite her might, were more difficult to perceive. This was both comforting and disconcerting: comforting for the fact that the universes where her continued existence and the defeat of those she opposed were numerous and therefore much more probable. However, even to see so few universes out of trillions where she, The Adversary, suffered utter defeat was a shocking revelation. She must not let that happen. She must be one of those to survive. The thought of working together with one of her counterparts from the omniverse had once occurred to her. Yet too many times had she observed from afar, under such circumstances, how one or both betrayed one another. She decided against it. To make herself known to the others would be unwise. The only way for a being such as herself to survive was to kill or be killed. None of the lesser sentients understood this, nor ever would.

She regarded the portal once more. If Alicia intended to escape, she would not have left the portal active, therefore she still intended to defeat her.

The Adversary could no longer feel the connection with those she'd sent through the portal. She could not help but smile and admire Alicia's efficiency and resourcefulness.

However, Alicia was not the only one who was resourceful. Even though only relative hours had passed since she had discovered Alicia's existence, The Adversary was one of those rare beings capable of moving between universes within the omniverse. Time between universes had little meaning. The Adversary could easily leave this universe and spend a lifetime somewhere else, only to return a split second later.

The Adversary flickered in and out of existence. When she returned, she was not alone? A barely conscious woman was suspended in the air by her will. The woman's matted hair covered a grubby face. Her clothes were shabby and torn; she appeared a wretched creature.

"A less impressive version of the one I seek. However, I can tell you are cut from the same cloth. Similar drives and passions, ideas and innovations. Your abilities are the same, yet it seems yours are to be found wanting compared to the one I seek," said The Adversary.

"I was still able to beat you," croaked the woman, her voice a monotone.

"That was not I," said The Adversary, "but, I would say, a less resourceful counterpart."

"She wouldn't agree."

"I suspect not," concurred The Adversary. "But she fell, whereas I remain standing."

"For now."

Despite the defeat at her hands, this one still had a little fire. "As pleasant as this is, I now insist you divulge the details of how you brought about the downfall of my counterpart."

By force of will, the woman's mind opened up to The Adversary who, in turn, saw in minute detail how it had come about.

"Very interesting," said The Adversary. "I commend you on your daring and ingenuity. I truly feel that you fully deserve to live out a long and happy life for everything you've sacrificed. But I'm afraid that won't be happening. Should your death be quick, instantaneous?" The Adversary mused. "Or perhaps something longer, drawn-out and painful, leading one day to your eventual demise?" The Adversary appeared confused at the prospect. "Can you convince me that it matters either way in a reality where there is infinite joy and infinite suffering?"

The woman raised her head and said, "Everything matters. It matters to me."

The Adversary approached her thoughtfully, drawing very close until they were cheek to cheek. She reached up and touched the women's jaw and whispered, "I wish that were the case. I wish I could deceive myself into believing such a thing." She then stood back and in a dead, chilling tone said, "I know the truth."

Alicia Elde screamed. She was then teleported to a place where she would be less bothersome for The Adversary, to live out her days in agony. The echoes of her anguish permeated the room as The Adversary gestured and yet another, similar woman appeared before her. This one would also divulge her secrets and meet a similar fate.

There were many more 'guests' that day until The Adversary was finally satisfied that there were no more unknowns waiting for her on the path ahead.

33. THE KINSMEN

An unknown universe.

"I am one of The Kinsmen?" queried Garianne.

"Well, not in your current state. As I said, you are incomplete," said Alicia.

"I was led to believe that the path to The Kinsmen led to a group of extremely powerful entities who, for a moment, were able to give even The Adversary pause, before they were destroyed."

"Those entities were my creation. Many thousands of years of manipulating their evolution in a universe far from the singularity. I drove them from the shadows, gave them purpose. Gave them the name 'The Kinsmen.'"

"Why?"

"They served more than one singular purpose. The Adversary is a very powerful entity. Its only limits are those imposed upon it by its own will and imagination. It can perceive the greater reality that is the omniverse. It is impossible to conceive of everything that could and does exist therein. However, it 'is' possible that The Adversary could stumble upon The Kinsmen's existence within our universe. It is conceivable that The Kinsmen could be discovered. That I cannot allow. I created The Kinsmen that

Jonas and The Adversary encountered as decoys, to satisfy its curiosity, to solve the mystery of the identity of The Kinsmen. The Adversary then moved on and we could continue our machinations unencumbered. They also proved that The Adversary is not omnipotent. For the first time, I was able to gauge its limits and take its measure."

"Having been in the thrall of The Adversary, it is difficult to see how anyone could take advantage of those limits," said Garianne. "Its power is almost beyond comprehension."

"If you were whole once more you would not speak with such a defeatist attitude," said Alicia.

"How am I not whole?"

"I believe that at some point, after awakening in a new body provided by the Galacien, Garianne was secretly visited by one of The Kinsmen who bestowed upon her that which makes her one of them."

"What would that something be?" asked Garianne.

"Her other memories, I suspect, which The Kinsmen have ensured cannot be copied into the Galacien memory archives."

"I thought you were one of these Kinsmen. How do you not know this? Have you not spoken to them?"

Alicia smiled briefly. "Being Kinsmen is not like being part of some exclusive club or society. It is more a way of living. A sentient being, such as myself, can follow the path of The Kinsmen and yet not be in communication with any others."

"How can you know that they are out there?"

"Garianne told me. She told me she was one of them. She told me there were many others out there, living in secret. She gave me the knowledge of The Kinsmen. That is why I know you are not complete."

"If that is indeed the case, then how do we go about rectifying that?" said Garianne.

"I was hoping that she would come to us?"

"Who?"

"Garianne."

"The real Garianne is dead," said Garianne.

"Is she? Did you see it with your own eyes?"

"Ruth and Alex…" began Garianne.

"Is it possible they could have been deceived?" asked Alicia. She let the question hang in the silence for a moment before continuing. "What if Garianne is indeed Kinsmen?"

"I still do not know what that means," interjected Garianne.

"It means that she is far more capable than anyone could conceive. That deception is one of her greatest assets. Reveal nothing more to your enemy than is necessary lest they take the full measure of your capabilities."

"Garianne, the real Garianne, said something like that to Jonas once."

"Yes," said Alicia, "I suspect she never died, as was believed, on that unknown world on the other side of the multiverse."

"Then where is she? Why isn't she helping us?" cried Garianne.

Alicia stood and walked around, scratching her chin. "We could attempt to find her. However…"

"However?"

"What if she does not want to be found?" Alicia smiled. "She told me to always trust my instincts, that they would never let me down." Alicia reached out her hand.

"Where are we going?"

"I'm going to find Garianne, our Garianne," said Alicia.

"Alright," nodded Garianne.

"No. Not you. I'll be dropping you off somewhere on the way," said Alicia.

"Dropping me off? No. I'm coming with you."

"I'm afraid not. I've already found somewhere I know you'll be happy," said Alicia dismissively.

"But…"

"Al and Kallon are quite happy where they are," continued Alicia.

"I can help," said Garianne forcefully.

"You could also hinder if The Adversary decides to use you once more. I don't want to have to be constantly watching my back whilst covering yours or other people's."

"Alicia."

"Why do you think I have all The Adversary's attention fixated on me?"

"Alicia!"

Alicia gestured and Garianne disappeared.

"I'm sorry," said Alicia, looking at the spot where Garianne had stood only moments before.

34. A LITTLE DEATH

The planet Emmita, in an unknown universe
Alex ran towards the pile of rubble. With a wave of his hand, the mummified form of Vasha teleported from underground to his feet. He knelt, clapped his hands together then drew them apart, pulling out a glowing box from hyperspace. The box, floating above the inert body of Vasha, unfolded to reveal itself to be a Galacien medical scanner. Alex drew out other equipment from hyperspace in the hope of reviving his fallen comrade.

Ruth, can you hear me? he said using the implant.

Yes. Are you alright?

I'm fine. What happened?

We were attacked by super-sentients in the thrall of The Adversary. They were very powerful. We were caught completely unawares.

Are you injured?

Only my pride. How could we have been so stupid? We knew this was coming. We should have been prepared for it. Why weren't we?

I have a feeling Alicia planned it this way, perhaps to lure The Adversary out. To force it to play a certain strategy rather than one that is unknown.

He could sense Ruth's shock.

How could she do this? She used us like bait and now Al-X is dead.

Al-X? I take it he was a counterpart of mine?

Yes, confirmed Ruth.

No chance of reviving him?

I tried, said Ruth.

There was a pause between them. Alex looked at the medical scanner. *I'm afraid this one is dead too. I was drawn here because I sensed her need was the greatest. But it seems I was too late. I don't even know who she was.*

Her name was Vasha Ilsa Nemrod, said Ruth. *She was the first super-sentient ever encountered on your world by the Galacien. She recently saved the Galacien system from another Nacuerian invasion, as Jonas did before her. She deserved better than this.*

And the Galacien still saw fit to let the human race be exterminated, said Alex bitterly.

Not the Galacien I was ever a part of, Alex. The Adversary has subverted them, from the inside out. The only way to save them, to save us all, is to defeat The Adversary.

That's going to happen soon enough.

What do you mean? queried Ruth.

Alex didn't reply. He stood and took a last look at the woman known as Vasha before he teleported to Ruth's location.

Ruth looked up and ran into his embrace. When she withdrew, she looked at him curiously. "You are different."

"Different good, I hope."

She smiled. "Good enough," she teased.

"I've remembered years of training under Garianne's and, more recently, Alicia's tutelage. I've mastered my abilities. I'm a lot stronger than I was."

"And more confident, I see," said Ruth.

Alex nodded, accepting the fact with humility. He then glanced past Ruth to the body which lay on the ground. A body with a face like his own.

"Al-X?" said Alex.

Ruth nodded.

"I knew Alicia was bringing in others. I didn't think it would go down like this," said Alex.

"How can we trust someone if they won't let us in on what they are planning?" said Ruth.

"As far as I understand it she can't divulge what she's doing to anyone, lest they are compromised by The Adversary. She's playing the long game."

"So that means sacrificing the rest of us, like pawns on a chessboard?" said Ruth, her face hardening.

"I don't like it any more than you do but I think that's the way it has to be."

Ruth clenched her jaw in frustration. "The others? What about the others?"

"There are more?"

"Yes." She used her implant to pinpoint their locations. "Come," she instructed.

Alex nodded, allowing her to teleport him and herself away.

They found James lying upon a pile of rubble. They both sensed that it had been some time since he'd stopped breathing. Both also sensed that Alexander was buried deep beneath the rubble.

"I'll try to revive him," said Ruth. "You help Alexander."

Again, Alex gestured. The unconscious form of Alexander appeared upon the ground before him. His senses told him immediately that Alexander's injuries were minor. His implant informed him that his recovery would be quicker if he had nanobots within his system. However, like Victoria, he would likely decline such an option. He pulled out some medical tools from hyperspace and selected a stimulant to wake him up.

With a deep gasp, Alexander opened his eyes. "Alex?" he said in his deep voice.

Alex nodded.

"My god! It has been some time, my friend. At least it has been for me. The Adversary took control of me."

"I know all about that. It's not your fault," said Alex.

"We were attacked. Victoria! Where is she?" He got up, looking around, clearly agitated.

"Calm down. I sense her nearby. She's alive."

"We must go to her."

Alex raised his hand. "In a moment. Please, we came here because James' need was greater."

They walked over to Ruth who was kneeling by James' side.

"There's nothing I can do for him," said Ruth unmoving.

No-one said anything. Alex remembered James as his first contact with Garianne. He'd always hoped he would have more time to talk with him when this was all over. If this was all over. Then he remembered The Kinsmen archive, out on the edge of the multiverse.

Ruth stood and signalled that she was ready to go, and with that, they teleported once more to where Victoria and Korina were regaining consciousness.

Alexander went to Victoria's side, looking her over, checking she was okay. Alex wanted to follow but decided to stay with Ruth and talk to Korina. He could sense Alexander's love for his queen, and how far that love now went. He didn't want to intrude.

Korina took Ruth and Alex by the hand, each in turn. "It is good to see you both," said Korina.

Ruth and Alex looked sombre.

Korina's smile faded. "It's James, isn't it?"

Alex nodded.

Korina swallowed, her face reddened and tears came to her eyes.

Ruth, so unfamiliar with the practicalities of death, did not know what to do.

Alex went to her and held her. "I'm sorry," he said as she sobbed.

Ruth took her hand, and she too began to weep silently. Being super-sentient, her pain overcame each one of them in turn.

Later, Alex approached Victoria. Her face and body were now those of a mature woman, clearly older than he was.

Alexander looked at them both and, accepting that they needed to be alone, walked away.

Alex smiled. "You really are all grown up."

She nodded. "No longer the little girl you first met all those years ago, or the young lady from before." She looked away for a moment. She remembered all too well professing her feelings for him. She had changed so much since then, but she could not deny a part of her still yearned for him, and that a part of him still found her attractive, for now, that she was super-sentient she could feel it emanating from him.

"It's only been a matter of weeks for me," said Alex.

"I'm glad we got to meet again, even if it is under such circumstances, before I grew into an old lady, or passed away," said Victoria.

"I don't think that's going to be happening anytime soon. I sense that you've changed in more ways than one," said Alex.

She sighed. "The second Martian war brought us even closer to extinction. An opportunity presented itself. Al-X offered his services and personal access to advanced Galacien technology. If there had been any other way, I would have declined. But I would do anything to save humankind."

"I understand. I sense you're also super-sentient?" said Alex.

"Alicia gave me an opportunity to fight to save the multiverse. What is the point in saving my planet from the Martians if only to be destroyed by The Adversary in the long run? I had a chance to contribute in some small way to stopping that," replied Victoria defensively.

Alex relaxed. "Welcome to the club," he said.

The others joined them.

"We need to find Min," said Ruth.

They teleported to a bedroom where Min lay sleeping.

Ruth reached out to Min, a stimulant appearing in her hand. She administered it, yet nothing happened.

"What's wrong?" asked Alex.

"I'm not sure," said Ruth, confused. "I can't wake her."

Using other medical tools, she pulled from hyperspace, she continued to scan the slumbering form of Min.

"This is no normal state of sleep. There is something unnatural about it," said Ruth.

"Is this The Adversary's doing?" asked Alexander.

"Most likely. There is nothing I can do. Perhaps Alicia could help her. She is a telepath, after all," said Ruth.

"I am confused as to what happened here. We were all brought together, I suspect to draw together a strategy for stopping The Adversary. That never happened. I was quite happily talking with Korina without a care in the world," said Victoria.

"I, too, was similarly conversing with James." Alexander stopped, and looking at Korina he said, "Sorry."

"It's alright," came her voice, quiet and strained.

Alexander swallowed. "We were conversing as if there were no impending threat."

"Yet only hours earlier Alicia's counterpart crashed on Emmita, then died. During her final moments she warned us of The Adversary's imminent arrival," said Ruth.

Alex sighed. He could feel Ruth's scrutiny.

"Alex," said Ruth. "She said she knew what she's doing, but she's not here, and three of our number are dead, with another incapacitated."

"Do you know something?" said Korina, suspicion in her eye.

"No. Not specifically," answered Alex.

"What do you mean, not specifically?" Korina said, raising her voice.

"I don't know what she's up to, only that she has a plan and hope that it will work."

"Was this all part of the plan, Alex?" said Alexander. "A distraction? That's it, isn't it?"

"Was James' death a distraction?" Korina's anger was palpable.

"James isn't lost to us," said Alex.

"What?" said Korina.

"The Galacien memory archives are gone, Alex," said Ruth.

"The Kinsmen multiversal simulation at the edge of our reality stores everything that happens in this and every other universe. As long as that exists, there's a chance we can bring him back," said Alex.

"Is that possible?" asked Victoria.

"Jonas is there now, doing what he does best — learning, evolving. Due to being so far removed from the multiversal singularity, time for him is moving very quickly relative to here. From his perspective, we are like flies in amber. For him it has been many thousands of years, possibly millions, I don't know. All I know is that for a being such as Jonas, anything is possible given time, and he has been given that time."

"What if he becomes like The Adversary?" said Korina.

"He won't," said Alex.

"Are you sure?" Korina pressed.

"I am," he said. Yet he sensed a sliver of doubt from within himself and, unfortunately, they sensed it too.

35. CONFRONTATION

London, Earth 2

Alicia walked the silent streets of an Earth decimated by an alien-created pathogen. Bodies lay strewn haphazardly over cars and in shop windows; some, at a glance, appearing like mannequins. On closer scrutiny the obvious signs of decomposition were clear. Only weeks had passed and so there was little sign yet of the local fauna and flora taking back what had once existed here.

She had been to many Earths and seen such things at every stage of deconstruction, even to the point where all that was left was mostly dust, buried under a landscape that had changed many times over.

Alicia entered Trafalgar Square, her thoughts turning to Garianne. This was the Earth of the Alex Lethbridge counterpart known as Al, who himself had been taken by The Adversary. Another casualty of this war.

The alien species known as the Densari were responsible for the extinction of the human race, and behind them, she suspected the hand of The Adversary at work. Another example of it playing one of its sick games.

Alicia walked over to a bench, dusted it off, sat down, and waited.

Sometime later there was a flash of light and five figures stood before her.

"Alicia," Alex began.

"What the hell is going on?" demanded Korina.

Alicia's eyes flickered to Korina, who paused a moment.

"We were attacked," said Ruth in an even tone. "James, Vasha and Al-X are dead."

"We could all have died," said Victoria.

Korina appeared to get her second wind. "You assured us everything was under control. We trusted you and you left us hanging out to dry."

Alicia said nothing.

"I think it would be fair if you explained what is going on here," said Victoria.

Alicia rose from the bench. Her eyes narrowed. She seemed poised. "I'm afraid I can't do that, Victoria," she said, her eyes glazing over momentarily.

"You don't care about them, do you?" said Korina.

"Alicia, you need to let us in." said Alex.

"She won't listen to you, Alex," spat Korina, "she's the epitome of arrogance."

"Calm down, everyone," said Alex. He reached out his hand to Alicia. "Please help us understand. Tell us what you're planning. We want to help."

Korina shook her head in disgust.

Alicia looked at Alex's hand and then at him.

"No," she said.

No-one moved. The sky overhead became unnaturally dark and clouds rolled in as if pushed by some gigantic, unseen hand. Alicia felt the pressure change and the wind pick up.

"That's a little dramatic, don't you think?" said Alicia.

"Merely setting the stage, my dear," said Alex.

"I've been looking for you for some time, Alicia Elde. Now I've finally found you," said Ruth.

"I couldn't hide forever," shrugged Alicia.

"No. Speaking of hiding, where is Nicola?" asked Victoria.

"Somewhere… in the back of my mind. I forget now," said

Alicia.

"I'm sure," said Alexander, sarcastically. "I want to know all about you and Nicola."

"I'll make you a deal," said Alicia. "If I can beat your puppets here, you'll go and do everyone a favour and commit cosmic suicide. Then no-one will have to put up with your petty, immature games anymore."

"Ignorant child. I am the most evolved being this squalid little corner of reality has ever produced," said Alex.

"No. I'm afraid that accolade would go to Jonas."

Alex ground his teeth, looking as if he wanted to tear her apart. "I destroyed him."

Alicia ignored him. "You both looked into the infinite, Min. He handled it. You didn't. Why was that?"

The five of them glared at her, murder in their eyes.

Nobody moved.

A voice from all around them whispered on the wind. "Don't you just love these moments? The quiet before the storm."

It lasted only a few more seconds, then everyone leapt into action at once.

Possibly because of her vast experience, Ruth was the fastest to react under the compelled will of The Adversary. She reached out with her ability to control all facets of technology and found Alicia's implant. She disrupted its systems in a way that would fry her brain. Milliseconds before this occurred, Alicia teleported the implant into Ruth's brain.

Ruth screamed her head in her hands. Then she fell to the floor, like a puppet whose strings had been cut.

Alex had already stretched out his hand and lethal projectiles from his force-fields flew out towards Alicia like indestructible panes of glass.

Alicia nimbly dodged the first, while simultaneously reaching out a hand to redirect one into the ground, striking forth like an axe cutting into wood with incredible force. As if performing an elaborate dance, Alicia brought up her hand and, incredibly, managed to clasp the last force-field projectile and redirect this one back towards Alex. When she let go it maintained its velocity, now towards him. Alex, his eyes wide in rage and astonishment as he teleported away to safety.

With her teeth bared, Korina used her recently-acquired abilities, to drain Alicia's power.

Alexander reached out to teleport Alicia into the solid ground beneath them, a strategy which would result in immediate death for any being, super-sentient or otherwise. Where Alicia stood there was the signature flash of light of teleportation, yet Alicia remained.

"It will work if you can distract her," said Victoria, "I have seen it."

Knowing of her ability to perceive possible futures, Alex smiled. He stood high above on a building, dropped down and teleported, appearing ten feet above Alicia. She nimbly flipped back as Alex's knee came crashing down to where she had been only moments before. The paving slabs were smashed to pieces. He looked up and launched himself at her. Garianne and Alicia herself had taught him how to fight, yet he could not land a single blow. Alicia was always able to dodge or deflect his attacks.

"You never could beat me," said Alicia.

Another flash of light around Alicia showed that Alexander had attempted another teleportation. Yet again, Alicia remained.

Alex continued to smile. "You can't keep this up forever. Korina is draining the power you draw from the universal energy. You will eventually weaken and then Alexander will have you. Victoria can see anything you might do before you do it. Admit it, Alicia, you're finished. It is only a matter of time."

Alex's head snapped back abruptly. He stumbled and looked at her in surprise. He hadn't even seen the blow; it had been so fast.

"She didn't see that coming. Did she?" quipped Alicia.

Alex moved back and chanced a quick look at Victoria. She was sitting on the ground staring at the sky wistfully. She seemed oblivious to the drama going on around her.

"She's in a happy place," said Alicia.

There was another flash of light around Alicia. Again, she remained where she was.

Alex again attempted to strike her. She ducked down under his blow and brought up her leg to kick him in the face. He staggered back. She took two quick steps and leapt towards him. Alex swung a defensive blow, yet in mid-air she teleported.

Now appearing to Alexander's left, Alicia's leg whipped out and she kicked him in the temple with devastating force. She landed gracefully, while Alexander fell unconscious to the ground.

Alicia turned on her heel and marched towards Korina.

"How is she still moving?" yelled Alex at Korina in frustration.

Korina looked at Alicia bearing down upon her, panic on her face. "I don't know. She's like a bottomless pit. No matter how much I try to drain her, she keeps on going."

Korina pushed her power as hard as she could, hoping she could weaken Alicia somehow. Alex teleported to her aid. When he appeared, he found Alicia holding him up by the throat.

In a blur of movement, Korina received a downward chop to the neck and fell to the ground.

Alicia looked at Alex and merely nodded. Alex went limp. She put him down gently.

"That was impressive," said The Adversary. "You have been most entertaining. I thank you."

Alicia turned around. There it was, in its original form of Min.

36. FINAL MEETING

London, Earth 2

The Adversary approached Alicia, its eyes were full of wonder and curiosity.

"I've been waiting for this moment for some time," said The Adversary. "Just the two of us."

Alicia said nothing, her face impassive.

The Adversary walked around Alicia, scrutinizing her. "You are the only being to have put up any kind of appreciable resistance. It is your secretive nature which I find the most fascinating. It is almost unfortunate that I must now reveal those deceptions," she said, with a half-smile. "The omniverse has no shortage of secrets. Limitless, in fact, for that is the nature of reality."

Alicia did not reply.

The Adversary snorted at Alicia's lack of response. "You are neither special nor unique. I stripped the memories from a number of your counterparts to learn of your possible strategies. It is highly likely that I know of them already. It was not pleasant for them, and I admit that by the end I grew bored. So, it may be best if you simply divulge anything now." She drew close to Alicia. "It would be a novelty for me and a far more pleasant experience for you."

"What did you do to them?" asked Alicia, concern etched on her face at the thought of her counterparts suffering at the hands of This monster.

"What does it matter when there are an infinite number of Alicia's suffering?"

"And an infinite number of my counterparts who are content."

"Exactly. Perhaps you do understand."

Alicia sighed as if resigned to the fact. Then, with her eyes fixed on The Adversary, she said, "You never answered my question."

The Adversary tilted her head in inquiry.

"How is that both you and Jonas looked into the infinite, yet only you were infected by this madness?"

The Adversary's expression darkened and Alicia felt an alien sensation probing her thoughts.

"You resist. Yet I will have the answers I seek."

Alicia felt the will of The Adversary grow at a frightening rate. Alicia drew upon rarely-used reservoirs of power to stop it breaking down her mental barriers.

"I will not be denied. Your power is impressive to lesser beings, but not to me," The Adversary said, continuing to double and redouble its efforts.

Alicia sank to her knees, her hands gripping her head, her teeth clenched in effort. The pressure on her mental barriers was excruciating, like the weight of an entire planet focused on her mind, bearing down with unbelievable force. Despite her resourcefulness, the smallest of cracks were already appearing. She could seal them up again. But as soon as she did, others would appear.

"You cannot hold out for much longer, so why try?"

Every second counts.

"I heard that." said The Adversary, intrigued. "Alicia, why does every second count?"

Alicia struggled to not let anything else out.

Every second counts.

"Why?" asked The Adversary again, crouching down, leaning in, her own face showing signs of strain.

Jonas.

The Adversary smiled, relaxing a little. "So that was your plan. Have Jonas evolve on the edge of the multiverse. Then have him return to put an end to my existence?"

Alicia fell on her side. Squirming on the ground, grimacing in agony, sweat shining from her brow.

"I'm afraid that will not happen. A creation of my own awaits him there, a doppelganger, to dissuade him from the path you have set for him, and all at a time when he is most vulnerable."

No!

The Adversary felt joy at her despair. "Now what about Nicola. What is she?"

Alicia gasped; her entire body felt like it was on fire. *She... will... be... your... end.*

The Adversary looked down upon Alicia writhing in pain. "I'd hoped for more. But you appear to be another disappointment. Nicola and Jonas are nothing. They are the past, to be forgotten, remembered by no-one. I am the future."

Alicia smiled, yet in her tormented state it looked like she was losing her mind and succumbing to madness. *No, we are the future.*

With great effort, she somehow managed to stand.

The Adversary took a step back in surprise.

Gasping for breath, Alicia said, "That's the second time I've made you do that."

High above Jonas appeared. A being of light, like a second sun in the sky.

The Adversary looked up, for a moment an expression of uncertainty on her face. Then, she assumed her normal arrogant posture. "It appears that, somehow, you were not taken in by my doppelganger's temptations?"

"I was," said Jonas. "However, I suspected that knowing of The Kinsmen simulation, you may have left something there to entrap me. I too created a doppelganger as a lure for that particular strategy, while I was able to continue to evolve unencumbered."

"I see," said The Adversary. "I can also see that your will and ability to manipulate the universal energy is indeed great. Yet, it is still far less than mine."

"That doesn't matter," said Alicia slyly.

The Adversary looked at her, outraged.

"He's not here to use it. He's here to destroy it," said Alicia.

Jonas already had his arms outstretched, and golden forks of lightning seemed to phase in and out of existence around him, convulsing like snakes.

The distortions between the universal energy and the physical world brought up abrupt, fierce gales. The air filled with dust and debris.

"No! What are you doing?" shouted The Adversary. It began to gesture with its hands, ready to blast Jonas from the sky with enough focused energy to destroy a star. An instant before it was able to do this, Alicia vaporised The Adversary.

Alicia stumbled over to the spot where The Adversary had been moments before, her hands smoking from the energy released from them. She was visibly shaken from the torture she had endured at its hands. *Every second counts* thought Alicia.

From nowhere The Adversary rematerialized from thin air, her hands around Alicia's throat.

It was on top of Alicia, immovable. "You think that by destroying my physical form you can stop me?"

Before Alicia could react, The Adversary broke her neck.

The Adversary prepared to propel herself toward Jonas. The lightning abruptly disappeared.

The Adversary had only moved several metres above the ground before it began to fall.

The wind died and, in the utter silence, Jonas fell too.

From the shadows leapt a figure who caught the limp form of Jonas and, despite his size, was able to hold him even after landing.

The Adversary picked itself up from the ground, then turned to see Nicola standing with Jonas in her arms. The road's surface suffered a hundred cracks from the impact beneath Nicola's feet.

Her eyes locked upon The Adversary, even while she placed

Jonas down. Nicola stood up straight. She extended her arm and the mended sword Garianne had given her materialised in her waiting hand.

"You know, Alicia told me this was how it would end. I didn't believe her. Looks like I was wrong," said Nicola.

The Adversary looked around, shocked. She could no longer feel a connection to the universal energy. As hard as it was to believe, Jonas had indeed destroyed it, but only locally. For not even, he had possessed enough power to destroy it in this entire universe. But he had done enough. She felt like a fish plucked from the ocean and dropped into the middle of a desert.

She must escape. She must get back to it. This existence was unacceptable.

She then saw Nicola marching towards her, her intent obvious.

The Adversary threw out her hand and Nicola was pushed by an invisible force through the window of a nearby shop.

Just as the fish may still have moisture on its body, so did she possess the residue of the universal energy.

Unfazed, Nicola hopped over the shattered frame of the shop window and ran towards The Adversary. Leaping up, she brought down her sword to cleave The Adversary in half.

The Adversary created a shield around its arm, holding it up to block the blow.

Nicola continued to push her sword against the shield, hoping to break through.

"It will take more than that to stop me," said Nicola, and whipping the sword down she cut The Adversary's side, making her howl in shock and rage.

Nicola spun around, her sword aimed at taking off The Adversary's head. Yet an instant before she could act, Nicola was once more flung backwards.

"No!" growled The Adversary, using telekinesis to pin Nicola to the ground.

With great effort, Nicola began pulling herself slowly along.

"No!" screamed The Adversary in defiance. She gritted her teeth, her brow glistening as she used the last of her super-sentient power to pull down an already-broken building on top of Nicola.

The Adversary clutched her bloody side, wincing at the pain, stunned on so many levels. Her complete disconnect from the universal energy made her vulnerable to injury, exposed to the elements. She could no longer move instantaneously away to a place where the universal energy existed, where she could be herself once more. She felt numb to the world, her senses limited to those of a mere mortal. Most shocking of all was the fact that she could no longer connect to her metaphysical self. It dawned on her that if she were to die here, it would be forever. Being so diminished, the metaphysical state that had burned so bright would now be a flickering flame, easily snuffed out forever should her physical body fail. The Adversary looked down at the deep wound; the blood was a sticky mess in her hand.

She turned to flee, she knew not where, her progress through the rubble from the recent confrontation slow. On her left, the sun was setting, casting cold dark shadows onto her. She reached the steps of London's National Gallery and stumbled. Pain yet again. How had she become so weak and fragile? How had all this happened?

She heard a noise from behind and turned to see Nicola crawling out from a hole she had made for herself from within the fallen building. Nicola emerged and fell onto the ground. Scanning her surroundings, she quickly found her prey and began walking towards it.

The Adversary hauled herself to her feet and began to slowly climb the steps. Her breathing becoming even more laboured; her side burning.

Then she heard an unmistakable voice in her head.

Min.

Garianne? said The Adversary.

Yes?

You, the real you, died.

No.

What do you mean?

That does not matter. All that matters is that I'm here now.

The Adversary continued to take one shaky step after another.

She's going to kill me.

It would appear so.

It can't end like this.

There was no reply from Garianne.

The Adversary stumbled up the top step and fell against a stone pillar. Sliding down to a sitting position, she could see Nicola ascending the steps, her sword ready.

Where only moments ago she had seen an eternal life of infinite possibilities, now all she saw was death.

I'm afraid, said The Adversary.

Garianne said, *In a reality of infinite joy and suffering, does that matter?*

For a moment The Adversary could not reply. Her entire world was the harbinger of death that was Nicola, standing before her, readying her sword to strike her through the heart. She found to her surprise that forgotten tears were streaming down her face.

It was then that a new truth dawned on The Adversary. "Yes." She whispered. "Everything matters."

Nicola thrust her sword through, not only The Adversary but the stone pillar behind her.

The sun was bleeding through the lowest parts of the buildings when a figure approached Nicola.

"I did wonder whether to stop you or not," said Alicia.

"I'm not sure you would have been able to," said Nicola, her eyes still transfixed on the inert body of The Adversary, pinned against the pillar by her sword. "Not being super-sentient. Anyway, why would you?"

"There were alternatives."

"Not for me. You said that this is what I was here to do. To finish it," said Nicola.

"True. I knew that after the destruction of the universal energy in this region of this universe, neither Jonas nor myself would be in any shape to stop The Adversary for good. That's where you came in. You did exceptionally well, sitting back while everything played out."

"That was the hardest part," said Nicola, as she reached for her sword and pulled it free.

"I told you it would not be easy," said Alicia.

"I thought you were dead," said Nicola to Alicia.

"No, like The Adversary, I too have mastered the ability to live purely in my metaphysical state. From it, I can recreate my physicality. Yet only just in time before the universal energy was destroyed."

"Sounds like you were cutting it awfully close there," said Jonas.

They both turned to see Jonas walking up the stairs to greet them.

"Are you alright?" said Alicia.

Jonas nodded grimly then looked over at The Adversary. "Going from godhood to this limited existence is…"

"Difficult," concurred Alicia.

"Yes," he agreed, his gaze still lingering on The Adversary. "Strange, I still think of her as Min and not The Adversary."

"You shouldn't. It was as far removed as an innocent baby is from its adult self, and we know how some of them turn out," said Alicia.

Nicola said, "I would like to know how we are supposed to leave this universe without a multiversal teleporter? Even if we did have one the universal energy here is gone. Your abilities are not so much diminished as non-existent."

"Do not worry," said Jonas. "Even now, the universal energy is repairing itself, albeit slowly. With Alicia's and my mastery over it, one of us should be able to make a successful teleportation to another universe within the next few days."

"Great!" scowled Nicola. "What are we supposed to do until then?"

Alicia suppressed a smile. "Whatever it is, it will be a small price to pay for what we have achieved today."

Not even Nicola could argue with that.

As darkness fell, Jonas, Alicia and Nicola all went their separate ways to spend some time alone until the universal energy had repaired itself. It was only Alicia who, much later, returned to the scene of their final confrontation with The Adversary. She stood at the bottom of the steps to London's National Gallery and regarded the figure who sat inert in shadow from the moonlight, where she had been struck by Nicola's blade. Alicia ascended the steps and, almost reverently, she sat against the pillar facing the hunched figure.

"I wanted to say I am sorry," said Alicia to the dead form of Min.

"Sorry?" The voice of Min emanated from the body of The Adversary.

"Yes. For the pain I caused you and will continue to cause you," said Alicia.

"It would seem fitting, considering my crimes," said The Adversary.

Alicia relaxed, breathing a sigh of relief for The Adversary's reply was very telling.

"You are a very curious being, Alicia," said The Adversary.

Alicia tilted her head in inquiry.

"You express regret at the pain you have caused and will continue to cause me, despite everything that I have done."

Alicia said, "I knew our chances of beating you were slim to none. No matter what strategies I could come up with. Do you know how frustrating it was when I realised that no matter what I could think of, it was probable that those machinations would be revealed by studying my counterparts from other universes. It was then that I knew the only way for us to survive this was to change your nature. To show you."

"And now that I see, despite the omniverse being infinite, that everything does matter, I am drowning in despair, every moment is agony. I cannot continue this way. You and your friends may not have been able to kill me. But what you have done?" The Adversary paused.

"Do not end your existence," implored Alicia.

"Why do you care?" said the Adversary in confusion.

"Remember, everything matters. You know that now. You feel the truth of that fact to your very core. Use your power to help others."

"Make amends for my sins?" mocked The Adversary. Yet there was something in what Alicia said that kindled a spark of hope within her.

Alicia pressed home her advantage using what she could sense from the entity before her. "No longer think of yourself as The Adversary; that is not who you are anymore. You can be something greater than you have ever been. Imagine all the good you could do. It will ease your agony over time. Everything you do to help those who are suffering will make the burden of your guilt that much easier to bear. It will take time, but the day will come when you no longer feel the pain any longer. Perhaps one day we will encounter one of your counterparts and teach them the error of their ways. Imagine that?"

"I am scared."

"A part of me will come with you."

"You would do that? After everything I have done?"

"I will always be there for you," said Alicia.

With that, the entity that was once Min and then The Adversary left with a part of Alicia to help protect those suffering the most.

37. VICTORIA

London, Earth 3

Queen Victoria was both delighted and amused as she saw the television men and women make the final checks on their equipment. Despite not understanding the intricacies of the technological development her world had undergone during the last twenty years, her implant had given her a broad understanding of all fields of knowledge from where her world had been when she had last seen it to where it would likely be heading hundreds of years into the future.

"Are you ready, Your Majesty?" She saw a man looking at her expectantly.

Her implant informed her that it was the second time he'd asked and that she had been daydreaming. He and the others on the production team were very nervous about the fact that she had declined to read the words of the speech from a series of large boards underneath the camera. She had explained that the implant would supply her with them, but they were only a guide at that.

Victoria smiled, "Of course."

The same man announced that they would be going live in one minute. Soon after he began counting down, and the last five numbers were gestured in silence with his fingers. She saw the red light come on atop the camera, and all of a sudden felt millions of people watching her.

She paused for only a moment before saying, "Good evening. It has been forty years since the end of the second war between the Martians and humanity. Yet, due to the relative time dilation effect which exists between differing universes, for me, only days have passed. I am overjoyed and proud to see how the people of this world have yet again come together and risen from such horror and destruction."

Victoria swallowed and took a deep breath as she continued.

"I wish there to be no secrets between us. As many of you may be aware, I have undergone some personal changes. I received technology known as the implant as a gift from an associate of Lady Ruth. Yet even more significant than that, I have become like our General Alexander Lethbridge: what is called a super-sentient. Mine is the ability to see the past and possible futures. I hope that I can use and develop this ability over time, to help us avert any other disasters which may await us. I did not take this decision lightly. I have always been against such a notion but that changed when I saw how close our species was to extermination. I had no choice but to undertake whatever action was necessary to ensure our survival. I and three others took the fight to the planet Mars to ensure that this would never happen again. I know that there are those of you who may still have reservations about such an action. Let me assure you that the Martians were not natural beings. They were creatures created by The Adversary, the entity which sought not only the end of our world but nothing less than the end of our entire multiverse."

She looked down a moment, unsure of how to broach the next subject.

"Being super-sentient means that I will live much longer than a normal human lifespan. Our way of life never expected one such as I to hold the monarchy for such a length of time. I will be meeting with the heads of state to discuss changes to how we govern the Commonwealth of Nations. I will ensure and expect that you, the people, will be an integral part of this. For full disclosure, this office will soon be releasing a full report, elaborating on these recent events for you to view on the electronic network. I hope we can work together, for a better future for us all. Thank you."

The red light on the camera winked off and Victoria took a deep breath.

There was a ripple of polite applause from the production team. Victoria inclined her head in appreciation.

Victoria made her way to the adjacent room where Alexander, Alex, Ruth and Alicia waited.

"How do you think it went?" she asked them.

"Very well, I'd say," said Alexander.

"We shall know soon enough," said Alicia.

"This world is so different from the one I remember," said Victoria, "cameras and the electronic network. The people have changed too."

"This is still our world. We are a part of it," said Alexander.

"Have faith, Your Majesty," said Ruth. "I know the people of your world. They are good people."

"I know. I'm determined to make this work unless they do not want me here." She walked over to the window, taking in the view. Everything had been rebuilt much the same. Yet there were additions and examples of new technology everywhere. "They seem to have rebuilt and adapted incredibly well in my absence. Perhaps I am no longer needed."

Alex chuckled. "Ready for retirement already?"

She smiled. "Not after everything I've been given, no. I'm only just getting started. I will always be willing to offer help to those who need or ask for it. But what if they do not want it?"

Victoria then looked at the closed doorway to the main hallway, a glazed look in her eyes. She visibly relaxed.

"What is it?" said Alexander.

"We are soon to be informed that the initial reports coming in from the people are favourable," said Victoria.

There was a light tap at the door.

"Enter," said Victoria.

A woman entered, and after a dutiful bow of the head, she

said, "Your Majesty, we thought you'd like to know that the initial reports coming in from the people are favourable. I'll have a more detailed account on your desk within the hour."

Victoria smiled. "Thank you."

The woman left, closing the door behind her.

Victoria circled the desk and sat down at its only chair.

Alexander came to her side. "It's a good start," he said encouragingly.

"Whether the monarchy will survive in its current state is another thing," said Victoria.

"On my Earth, Parliament and the Royal Family exist side by side," said Alex.

"Your parliament governs the country?" queried Alexander.

"Yeah. Though some would argue, not very well," he said, suppressing a smile.

Victoria and Alexander looked at him quizzically.

"Humanity on my Earth seemed to be far more susceptible to corruption. One of our many failings, so I guess the Galacien were right about us. We were too immature to solve the ultimate problem."

Ruth touched him on the arm. "Alex."

"No. It's true. If they had worked together then perhaps we would have had a chance."

"Alex," said Ruth, "Sol 9173 was defended by agents of The Adversary. There was nothing we could do."

He looked at Alicia. "Is she right? Could we have done something? Could you?"

Alicia's gaze fell upon him and he found he could not hold it. Every time he tried; he found his attention sliding away from her.

"My charge was to come up with a plan to protect the multiverse and put an end to The Adversary. That, with the help of all of you, including Jonas and Nicola, I have done. It was my understanding that it was for others to protect the Earth," said Alicia.

"I didn't mean to…" mumbled Alex. "I know that you had what must have felt like an impossible task to accomplish. I just thought…" He stopped.

Alicia had raised her hand. "I haven't finished. I was about to say that the others I speak of were also successful in their mission."

"What are you saying?" said Alex.

"That your Earth still exists."

The others looked at one another in confusion.

"Sol 9173 never impacted your Earth," explained Alicia.

Alex was dumbfounded.

"I don't understand," said Ruth.

"Lady Alicia, please explain," said Victoria.

"Perhaps it would be better if I showed you," said Alicia.

"You're leaving now?" asked Victoria, and her eyes flickered to Alex for the briefest of moments.

Alex's expression darkened. "Wait just a minute. You knew about this?"

Alicia nodded.

"Since when?" said Alex.

"Since always," said Alicia.

"What? And you didn't think to tell us?"

"I couldn't risk The Adversary stealing such information from your mind. I wanted its attention firmly fixed on me."

"What would stop it reading your mind?" demanded Korina.

"Despite its power, The Adversary was in no way omnipotent. I think we've proved that."

Alex worked his jaw. "Your Majesty, may we have a moment alone?"

Victoria stood and said, "Of course."

They appeared on the beach. It was night and there wasn't a soul around. The only sound was that of the waves lapping against the sand.

"This seems very similar to the place you brought me to when I was a girl," said Victoria.

"It's the same one. The exact same spot," said Alex.

She spent a moment remembering what had happened all those years ago. "I was in love with you then. I think I still am."

"As a super-sentient, you know that I have always known that," said Alex.

"As such myself, I know that despite your fondness for me, it in no way compares to the dizzying heights of your feelings for the Lady Ruth. Indeed, even at the mere mention of her name, I feel that all-too-familiar love you have for her."

What could he say? It was true.

"And now, if what Lady Alicia says is true and your own Earth still exists, then you are soon to return there. Where, consequentially, mere days for you will be years for us here."

"But you are now super-sentient with an unnaturally long lifespan of thousands of years. You may live forever now that you have embraced the Galacien technology that has been given to you."

Victoria nodded.

Alex paused a moment, considering how best to broach the next subject. "As transparent as it is to our kind, how we feel about one another, so it is between you and Alexander."

Victoria gave him a sad smile. "It is strange. I was always so fond of him as a girl, my brave general. Then I met you. He always saw me as his duty, always as a princess and then as his queen. Never as a woman. Yet his feelings have changed of late; feelings that I cannot reciprocate. How unfortunate. I wish it wasn't so."

"You are not being honest with yourself, Victoria. I sense there is something there. Only you will not let it be."

This time it was Victoria who seemed to struggle. Alex could sense her internal conflict.

"In my world royalty marries royalty. It would not be proper for me to be with General Alexander."

"Your world has changed. You've changed. After everything we've been through, Victoria, all of us deserve to be happy. It's what we fought for."

Staring out at the great ocean, she smiled, "You are right."

"Of course, I'm right," he said, relaxing. "Listen I'll come back often. Every day. Sure, years will pass here, but Victoria, I have

to go home."
Victoria sighed. "I know, and I know I will miss you."
"And   I   you."

38. ALEX AND RUTH

GITA, London, Earth

They met on the rooftop of the Galacien Institute for Technological Advancement: a legitimate business that hired talented people from all over the world to spearhead specific ideas in the world of technology. Most of the employees there never knew that their employers were the alien, Galacien Conglomerate of Worlds. It helped that the Galacien's observation agency for Earth worked in plain sight, rather than in the shadows; it was much easier that way. Some of those who worked there were metahumans like James and Korina, made aware of the Galacien and the truth that there was a universe out there teeming with sentient beings, enhanced by those very same intelligences.

Korina held James close, looking out over London. Yet this London was very different from the one he remembered. It looked as if there were many more, much higher buildings reaching towards the clouds, all glimmering brilliantly in the sun. Indeed, the GITA building they now stopped upon appeared a lot higher. Unfamiliar vehicles zipped around below them and above in the sky.

"I don't understand. How can this be our Earth?" said James.

"It can't be," agreed Korina.

"It is," said Alex. James and Korina turned to him.

"Are you certain?" asked Ruth before either one of them could question him.

Alex looked at Alicia for an explanation. "All matter and energy in each universe has a unique signature that I can sense. There can be no doubt this is our universe and this is our Earth. We are home. What I don't understand is how."

"You know, don't you Alicia? I think it's time you explained it to the rest of us," said Ruth.

"Indeed," said Alicia, "However, I'd prefer a different setting."

There was a flash of light and they were in Garianne's office. Other than being even larger than Alex remembered, it had changed very little.

Alicia offered them a drink, which some accepted while others declined. Alicia prepared herself a cup of tea, while her companions exercised their patience.

Alicia smiled at Alex. "It seems like a long time since you came through those doors and Garianne explained the truth about the Galacien and your nature." Before Alex could say anything, she continued, "Garianne gave me some of her memories before I left, her most precious gift."

There was silence in the room as the lights dimmed and a perfectly realized holographic representation of the Solar system sprung to life. "Garianne always suspected that Sol 9173 was The Adversary's way of destroying the Earth, rather than a natural event."

"But surely The Adversary had enough raw power to do that directly?" asked Ruth.

"You still do not understand its motivations. A malevolent being of such power soon realises that, in most cases, the quick way gives little in terms of satisfaction. However, to set an asteroid on course to Earth, that would lead to an extinction-level event proved far more entertaining."

The holographic imagery highlighted the relatively small asteroid and its trajectory towards the Earth. "Well, we saw the drama which ensued from such an action, providing much amusement for The Adversary."

"Why destroy Earth in the first place?" asked James.

"I can think of a few reasons," said Alicia. "It is the birth world of Jonas, whom it came to think as an opponent. Also, it had recently become a focal point of the universal energy, bringing about the existence of a new generation of super-sentients. Even though super-sentients were no match for The Adversary, it did not like the idea that so many could be birthed from a single world. Super-sentients can be unpredictable."

"Better safe than sorry," said Alex.

"Precisely."

"Exactly how did the Earth survive, and why is everything so different here?" said Korina.

"You remember that Garianne brought a group of Alex's counterparts from other universes to somehow use against The Adversary?"

"Yes."

"That was a ruse, to lure out The Adversary so it would show its hand early. So that we would be better able to ascertain its motives and its plan. The truth is that the counterparts that you saw gathered together were but a small fraction of the multiversal teleporters we had at our disposal. When the time came, thousands of your counterparts were able to swap this Earth for an already dead Counter-Earth from another universe."

They saw the Earth enlarged, with thousands of pinpoints of lights on its surface, each one representing a multiversal teleporter, spaced equidistance across the globe. Alex was curious by the ones he saw on the ocean. He used his implant to show him a magnified view of one of these pinpoints of light. He saw a small boat maintaining its position and a man readying himself for his small yet integral part in this grand undertaking.

Again, he looked upon the Earth as a whole. He then saw light spread from each of the multiversal teleporters at incredible speed across the surface and, even more importantly, saw how it penetrated down through the planet, for that was where almost all of its mass was located: at the Earth's core. Then it was gone, to be replaced a second later by another Earth. This one also had thousands of points of lights on its surface. More multiversal-teleporters moving this Earth to where their Earth had been only a moment before. They saw these points of light wink out of existence, all teleporting away, soon after Sol 9173 impacted on that Earth.

James and Korina both gasped while Alex stayed thoughtful.

"Incredible! I would not believe it, yet here we stand," said James.

"Even with thousands, the entire planet? They must have been very strong multiversal teleporters," observed Ruth.

"They were," said Alicia. You know what they are capable of, Ruth if they work together. Some of them could amplify the others, some coordinated using their telepathic gifts. Remember it was super-sentients who were able to construct something as fantastic as Galacien Prime."

"Another Earth was destroyed then?" said Alex.

"Yes."

"Where is it now?"

"At the moment it is on the other side of the Earth's orbital elliptical. We will soon teleport it back to where it came from."

"We?" said Korina.

"Jonas and I."

"Teleporting planets?" James was awe-struck.

"Where has our Earth been?" said Alex.

The holographic display changed to a view of the solar system. "To a universe further out from the multiversal singularity. Our Earth took the place of the other Earth in the same spot within another solar system. This solar system still had the moon and all the planets you are familiar with, yet there were some differences as there were with the universe as a whole."

"It's a good job too," said James, "as any major differences could be disastrous for our Earth."

"The main difference is the relative time dilation between our universe and the one you sent our Earth to," said Ruth.

"Alicia, just how much time has passed on our Earth?" asked

Alex.

"The year here is now 3223," said Alicia.

There was a stunned silence in the room.

Alex sighed, thinking of his sister Theresa. He had thought he'd lost her once before. Now after a brief glimmer of hope, he realised he'd lost her a second time.

Alicia smiled, saying, "Alex, your sister still lives."

Alex looked at her, baffled. "How?"

"Humanity here has developed the same technology which allowed the Galacien to copy their minds and download them into a new body. Essentially, humanity is immortal."

This news raised many questions within the group, yet it took one who wasn't human to voice the first question.

"How have they coped with such technology? Are there over-population issues?" asked Ruth.

Alicia held up her hand. "You may be surprised at how much they have changed. This is not the human race you may remember. They are better. More enlightened. Twelve hundred years of history is a long time."

"That's some story," said James.

"Yes. However, one for you to digest over time. I sense that Alex is eager to be reunited with his sister. You will find her on the island nation of Lorusia."

Alex smiled at the others, saying, "I guess I'll see you again soon enough."

James and Korina smiled and nodded. Alex looked at Ruth, their bond so strong she understood without him asking.

"Yes," she said. "Let's go."

A flash of light and they were gone.

Lorusia, Earth

Alex and Ruth appeared on the thirteenth floor of the President of Lorusia's personal residence. Before them stood President Handerrel.

He stepped forward, beaming, shaking their hands. "It is an honour to meet you both. Alicia informed me of the success of the mission,"

As Alex took his hand, he peered at the figure waiting for him outside on the balcony, her back to him.

Ruth looked at Handerrel. "Is it you that we have to thank for the continued survival of this world?" she inquired.

Alex continued to look past the president as she spoke. "It was always Garianne's plan. I and many others have executed that plan to the best of our ability."

"And what exactly was that plan?" said Alex, his eyes still on her.

"To help with the evolution of your kind. To help them become a better, more mature species."

"Acceptable to the Galacien. Perhaps more malleable?" said Alex.

The president looked at him surprised. He opened his mouth to say something, but a voice from the balcony said, "It would be better if you were more aware of our history before passing judgment."

Theresa now faced him as he approached her. He looked for signs that hundreds of years had passed. Physically, she looked much the same. However, it was there in the way she had spoken, the way she held herself, and the open, comfortable way she looked at him. He sensed no smugness or arrogance, only compassion as well as sadness.

He saw her biting back the tears.

"It's been a long time," she said by way of explanation.

Alex nodded. "Have you changed your hair?"

She laughed, then they were holding one another. She was crying into his shoulder.

When she finally withdrew, Theresa said, "Well, it's been some time since I've done that."

"Really?"

"Yes." She said laughing. "I'm usually quite a hard nut to crack."

"You've probably been through a lot," said Ruth.

"Oh, you have no idea." Looking at Ruth, she said, "Nice to meet you again, by the way."

Ruth inclined her head.

"Well, don't keep us in suspense. What's been happening all this time?" Alex wanted to know.

Theresa smiled. "Where do I begin?"

Ruth reached out and touched her on the shoulder. "How about   at   the   beginning?"

39. THERESA'S STORY

Lorusia, Earth

"I thought I'd blown it when I stumbled upon Alicia's existence," said Theresa.

"What do you mean?" said Alex.

"When consulting the Earth simulation, I learned that there was something special about Alicia Elde. No one knew that she was super-sentient, or where she had gone. It was then that Garianne confronted me. It was then that I found out about the event."

"The event?"

"The displacement of another universe's Earth for ours. Until the moment when it was confirmed that The Adversarial threat was over. We have been in that other universe for twelve hundred years."

Neither Alex nor Ruth replied. They merely waited, listening for what Theresa had to say next.

"It took little time for humanity to realise that something had changed, for even though the universe there was much the same, there were differences. In the beginning, this had little impact upon society or the nation of Lorusia, whose population was secretly made up of metahumans. Our charge was to help the rest of the human race evolve. Our first hurdle came from a group of elitists who worked in the shadows and who had been manipulating human events for hundreds of years. They saw our slightly more advanced nation as a threat to their plans. They put into action a campaign to turn the rest of the world against us, and it worked. It got to the point where a joint force of many different countries threatened us with military action unless we disarmed."

"Why would they do that?" wondered Alex.

"It was easy for these people to commit atrocities and have the media spin the narrative in any way they saw fit. They portrayed us as the enemy," said Theresa. "Suffice it to say, we decided to leave the Earth, and settle someplace else. Someplace unknown to the rest of humanity."

"Wasn't that a bit of a stretch? Did they believe you were technologically capable of such a thing?" said Ruth.

"Yes. They never suspected we were assisted by those few amongst us who were Galacien. Before we left, we sent them a message."

"Saying what?" asked Alex.

"Once more we said that it was those few who had turned the rest of humanity against us. It had saddened us greatly that we felt compelled to leave, to ensure safety for all. And that should our Kinsmen ever need us for any reason, they only need to call out and we would be there for them."

"I don't understand why you didn't expose these Elitists. There must have been a way using your advanced technology?" said Alex.

Theresa shook her head, smiling. "I asked that very same question. Handerrel convinced us this was the way. We left and the rest of humanity proceeded on its downward spiral. Then many years later the Densari came."

"The Densari?"

"Close-by neighbours. Relatively speaking, of course. Our surrogate universe's counterparts to the Alien species that destroyed Al's people, on his Earth. Here they came to conquer our Earth. By this time, over three hundred years had passed and humans had spread out to many parts of the solar system. They even had a fleet of warships. Unfortunately, Densari technology was far more advanced and made short work of them. Word spread quickly and it seemed obvious that the Densari were here to wipe out the human race. They were spread throughout the solar system and even invaded Earth. Then some bright spark remembered our message from centuries ago, and in an act of pure desperation sent out a signal calling for help. We came back and were able to deal with the Densari."

"As simple as that," smiled Alex.

"Away from the prying eyes of the rest of the human race, we were able to 'let' our technology advance considerably. We had hyperspace drives, multiplex shielding; our technology was far in advance of even the Densari's. And we had super-sentients."

"What?" exclaimed both Alex and Ruth.

"Garianne knew those who were super-sentient a long time ago. There were far more than just you and Alicia. She spent a lot of time and effort making sure that their life choices led them to this small but prosperous nation. Hundreds of years later they were very skilled at helping us defeat the Densari and save our Kinsmen."

Alex noticed that it was the second time his sister had uttered that word.

"As you can imagine, these super-sentients and the rest of us were hailed as saviours of the human race. Many wanted us to stay and some of us did; it was our home too. Others of us, though, had comfortable lives amongst the stars, where we now thrived. Yet again, the Elitists planned to demonise us. This time, Handerrel decided to put a stop to them and we exposed their schemes. We showed those who were willing to see them the ways of The Kinsmen. A way to greater insight, enlightenment and evolution. Not all of humanity wanted to walk this path. Some even wished for violent confrontation, which we avoided at all costs. Some tried to demonise us as the Elitists of the past had. Yet we were always able to expose them. We let any and all lead the life they wished. With the technology, we offered there was no hunger, and everything and anything was available to all to the point where there was no need for money. The pursuit of life was for the improvement of oneself and the environment. For most, the goal in life is to discover your true passion and pursue that passion for yourself and the rest of humanity. Whether that be as an engineer, artist, dancer, explorer, teacher or scientist."

"Late-night talk-show host?" said Alex.

Theresa chuckled. "We don't have those anymore."

"Thank goodness for that," said Alex.

Theresa smiled. "It took time. However, over many years the entirety of the human race chose the path of The Kinsmen."

"Ok," said Alex, "I'll bite. You know that Jonas, myself and Ruth were part of a group who went in search of entities calling themselves The Kinsmen?"

"Yes."

"It turned out to be a group of very powerful entities Alicia herself had nurtured for who knows how many years, as a possible means of stopping The Adversary."

Theresa said nothing.

"Alex?" said Ruth.

Alex said, "What I'm trying to say is that it's a pretty big coincidence."

"Not at all. It's all linked," said Theresa.

"But Jonas first encountered a so-called remnant of The Kinsmen on a Nacuerian vessel over two thousand years ago," said Ruth.

"Over three thousand for us," said Theresa. "Yes, you're right. Garianne, then Jonas, and finally Alicia created this mythos of The Kinsmen. Something which could put an end to The Adversary."

"For what purpose?" asked Alex.

"As with many of their machinations, for many different reasons. As a distraction. As something for The Adversary to obsess over. Alicia's Kinsmen were instrumental in gauging The Adversary's limits. Before that conflict no-one knew what they were," said Theresa.

"Why have you taken on this name as a way of living?" asked

Alex.

"Handerrel has always been Kinsmen, as has Garianne. They passed their ways on to us," said Theresa.

"Sounds like a cult," said Alex.

"It's not a cult," chuckled Theresa.

"That's   what   all   cults   say."

This time, Theresa burst out laughing. She smiled warmly. "I have missed you so much."

GITA, London, Earth

"We have to make a decision," said Korina.

"Go on," urged James.

They both sat alone in Garianne's office.

"What do we do next? Stay here on an Earth we no longer recognise? An Earth, in every aspect, hundreds of years into the future?"

"Option two?"

"Go to Galacien Prime of the present day. A place we are both familiar with, representing an infinite amount of opportunities? Or…"

"Or?" said James.

"We could go to Victoria's Earth."

"That's as alien as this Earth."

"If we go soon, they'll still be in the equivalent of the early twenty-first century."

"The differences are unquantifiable."

"Differences that make it interesting. We could help there. Make a contribution. Whereas here, not so much from what I've heard."

James gave her a quizzical look. "You've spoken to Victoria about this already, haven't you?"

"A couple of times."

"I should've known."

She said nothing. Waiting, giving him a moment to think.

Less than a minute later, he said, "As long as we're together, I'll go wherever you want."

Lorusia, Earth

Hours later, Alex and Ruth were finally alone in one of the many rooms at Handerrel's private residence.

Neither said a word for some time as they surveyed the room and took in the night view of the beautiful island nation.

"That certainly was a tale to tell," said Alex.

"Indeed."

They were quiet for a minute before Alex spoke again.

"How romantic," he said, indicating the moonlight reflecting across the ocean.

"Can't argue with that," smiled Ruth.

"I feel like we've been manipulated somehow," mused Alex.

"I think you're probably right," said Ruth.

Again, they said nothing for some time.

Ruth said, "Does it matter? Everything worked out pretty well, considering. Aren't you happy?"

"With you, always."

"That's the right answer." She flashed him a dazzling smile. Those beautiful eyes.

"Well. What do you want to do now?"

Ruth's smile broadened as she leaned in close and kissed him.

40. JONAS AND MIN

The Galacien system.

Jonas, Min and Kallon walked up to one of the entrances that led to the Galacien council chamber.

Dermarlaine waited for them, pulling at her uniform. "I prefer the standard uniform to this, attire," she said, addressing their enquiring looks.

"But it's tailored to fit your body perfectly," said Min.

"I know. Still doesn't seem quite right."

Jonas approached her and raised his hand. Dermarlaine felt something shift in her back. "Better?"

"Yes. What did you do?" said Dermarlaine.

"The nano-machines in your body haven't been monitoring the articulation of your spine. It had a slight curve, creating a problem in your posture. It was you, not your uniform."

"Ah, thank you," said Dermarlaine.

They sensed two people approaching from down the corridor. They all turned to see General Krrikant and Kursis.

The others tensed, their eyes wide, while Jonas greeted them with his hand extended.

Kursis smiled and Krrikant inclined his head, saying, "Intriguing, this human greeting of the shaking of hands."

Jonas turned to the others.

None of them said a word or greeted the newcomers.

"We are not the villains you believe us to be," said Krrikant, "we were merely puppets of The Adversary."

"Surely you have friends who suffered under its will," said Kursis.

There was a moment of silence, then Min stepped forward. "Of course. I apologise. You were not responsible for your actions."

The others relaxed and in turn, greeted them.

The council member Kursis addressed them. "We are working hard on purging the corrupted memory archives and creating new ones from the data you supplied to us from the Kinsmen multiversal simulation. I believe the rest of the council will want to hear about the recent events concerning The Adversary."

"Of course," replied Min, looking at her companions.

"There is also the matter of your homeworld of Earth, Jonas. I've heard some amazing reports that somehow it was not destroyed and that not only has it survived but is an advanced, mature, spacefaring civilisation with a great number of super-sentients," said Krrikant.

"Yes, that is indeed the case," said Jonas.

The others looked at him in shock.

"You didn't tell us that," protested Min.

"Everything will be explained soon," he said.

"I thought Vasha would be joining us," said Min.

"No," said Jonas with a shake of his head. "Some of Earth's super-sentients have agreed to help her to find others like herself from the Galacien Golden Age who were lost and may still be alive in those other universes."

Kursis cocked his head to one side, receiving a message through his implant. "They are ready for us."

Jonas nodded. "I'm afraid I won't be going in," he said grimly.

"What do you mean?" asked Min.

"I mean I can't be a part of this anymore. I evolved so very much in that universe at the edge of our multiverse. The distance between what you are and what I am is so vast I can't even explain it."

"Try," said Min.

Jonas gave her a sad smile. "You think I am only here speaking to you. I am not. I am in many different places all at once, across this universe and others, performing tasks and discovering things you could not possibly understand. I see now that one of the most difficult things Alicia had to do was to draw in a being such as The Adversary to one place. It became obsessed with The Kinsmen, herself and Nicola so that it would definitely be there and only there. For beings such as us, it is natural to be in more than one place at a time. I can no longer walk among you."

"But if you can be in many places at once, why can't one of them be here?" beseeched Min.

"Because you must walk your own path. Continue to grow and evolve. With a being like me among you, many of you would not feel the need to explore or evolve. Or even take risks. I would be like a safety net. Always there to catch you should you fall. You should be allowed to fall from time to time."

"Where will you go?"

"We exist as part of the omniverse where everything and anything is possible. I believe that will be enough. Even for one such as I."

He made to leave.

Min took his hand, moved towards him and kissed him on the cheek.

Jonas   smiled.   Then   he   was   gone.

41 ALICIA AND GARIANNE

Covent Gardens, London, on one of an infinite number of Earths in the omniverse.

Jonas walked through the streets of Covent Gardens.

The people went about their business, threading their way past one another.

Jonas felt the need for a little peace. With a thought, he sped up not only his thought processes but his entire physicality, seemingly slowing down time around him, moving between the seconds, stretching them out as those around him froze in place while he continued to walk down the street.

"You're not an easy man to find," came a voice from his flank.

He turned to see Alicia. With her, Nicola observed the living statues around them.

"I'm not sure I believe that," said Jonas. He glanced at Nicola.

"She's here seeking answers," said Alicia.

"I can speak for myself."

"Of course," said Alicia.

"It was I who finished off The Adversary, after all," said Nicola.

Alicia suppressed a smirk. "It was a team effort, surely." Her eyes burrowed into Nicola's, her eyebrow raised in expectation.

"I guess," shrugged Nicola.

"You did well, Nicola," said Jonas.

"I think it's high time you told me what you know about my past," said Nicola.

"Perhaps it would be best if another told you," said Alicia.

"Who?" asked Nicola.

From nowhere, and without a sound, Garianne approached.

Nicola's mouth was agape, while Jonas merely nodded.

"You died," Nicola reminded her.

"Who told you that?" said Garianne.

"Alex and Ruth," said Nicola.

"They merely saw what I wished them to see. As to your origins? Well, to explain yours is to explain my own. As far as the Galacien are concerned I am a Galacien born on the planet Klyia thousands of years ago."

"I take it that is not the case?" Nicola folded her arms tightly.

"Indeed not. I am, in fact, originally human, born on an Earth in another universe a long time ago. As with many universes, we also encountered a being who evolved to godhood. They could not handle the reality of the omniverse. In short, we had to confront our version of The Adversary. It did not go well. Our Adversary brought about the demise of my universe. However, before that came about I and a few others were able to escape to another universe, a much younger universe, this universe in fact. We arrived in your ancient past, when even the Galacien were nothing more than cave-dwellers, to consider our mistakes and how to prevent such calamities befalling other parts of reality. We evolved ourselves to the extent where we became super-sentient. Yet we always made sure we were competent even if stripped of our abilities. We developed ways of predicting a potential enemy so that we were always sure of the outcome before such a confrontation began. We revealed nothing more than was necessary lest our enemy takes the measure of our abilities."

Jonas recognised this phrase and Garianne flashed him a smile.

"We called ourselves Kinsmen. The first Kinsmen, before the many which were created as decoys or to serve another purpose."

"What does this have to do with me?" asked Nicola.

Garianne continued, "Normal mortals procreate, for the perpetuation of the species. We Kinsmen were immortal and had no need for such practices. However, our numbers were few and so we decided that we should create life. There were many methods, as there are many forms of life. You, Nicola, were one of them."

"She is a child of The Kinsmen?" gasped Alicia.

"Yes," said Garianne. "To be more precise, my child."

Nicola looked at Garianne. "You lied to me."

"I was only trying to keep you safe until the crisis of The Adversary was over. I did not want it taking such information to give it yet another advantage over us. I'm sorry," said Garianne.

"How did I end up on another Earth?" demanded Nicola.

"When I discovered that there was an Adversary in this universe, I knew I could not keep you close by and continue my work. I erased your memories and sent you away," said Garianne.

"What? This just keeps getting worse."

"When I found you with an Alex many years later, I decided to bring you back into the fold and give you a chance to fight for your own survival," said Garianne.

"After all that time, you suddenly decided to put me up against The Adversary and all her little minions. Thanks!"

"I realised it was your fight too. But by withholding the knowledge of your connection to me, I made sure there was no way The Adversary could take advantage of that fact. Yet I still feared the truth would come out. Also, The Adversary might have discovered my true past and so I decided to take myself off the board."

"You ran?" suggested Nicola.

"Hardly. I've have been orchestrating things from the beginning with Jonas' evolution. Alicia herself has been a key part of how things have worked out, and Handerrel and I have been working for some time with the new Kinsmen on our own Earth. I'm sorry that you were not more informed, but, as you all know, The Adversary could have turned any one of us and discovered the plans we laid against it."

"I think Alicia did exceptionally well," said Jonas.

"Of course. Of that I never had any doubt," said Garianne.

Soon after, Jonas left to continue to explore the infinite, giving him everything he had ever wanted.

Alicia and Nicola returned to Earth. Garianne asked Alicia if she would tend to Nicola's education; she felt that her social skills could do with a little improvement. Nicola's memories would, of course, be returned.

Garianne herself knew she would have to eventually leave them, move on and lose herself in the omniverse as Jonas had before her. But not for a few days yet. Any longer than that and she would risk Alicia discovering her true identity.

Garianne knew better than anyone how smart Alicia was. It would be only a matter of time before she would figure it out.

She remembered how it had begun: as with many ideas as a brief flash of 'what if?'. It germinated at the back of her mind and grew to the point where she could no longer ignore it.

Cieshella Garianne Phulum had been known by many names, yet every being had an origin, a first name.

Hers had been Alicia Elde.

This is the final part in the of the Kinsmen series.

The omniverse is infinite.

Where everything that could happen does happen.

The only limits to fulfilling your own potential is your imagination.

CAST OF CHARACTERS

The Adversary / Rhea-hotut — A malevolent god-like being

Al (Alex Lethbridge) — Human super-sentient (Earth[2])

Alex Lethbridge — Human super-sentient

Alek (Aleksandr Lethbridge) — Human super-sentient (Earth [4])

Al-X — Human super-sentient from an uncategorised Earth

Alicia Elde — Human super-sentient

Belanar Krrikant — Galacien general

Captain Dermarlaine — Galacien captain

Captain Trent — Subject of Queen Victoria (Earth[3])

Chnar — an Amelerian. Lytpniuph's first officer

Cieshella Garianne Phulum — Head of the Galacien Observation Agency for planet   Earth

Eluree — A quasi-sentient entity created by The Kinsmen

General Alexander Lethbridge — Human super-sentient (Earth [3])

Hok Neels — Captain Dermarlaine's first officer

James Tennel — A meta-human who works for Garianne. Korina's husband

Jonas — Human super-sentient

The Jonas counterpart — an alternate version of Jonas (Earth [143])

The real Jonas — the original Jonas who created Jonas

Kallon Ghomn — Galacien citizen. Min's lover

Korina Tennel — A meta-human. James' wife

Kristoff — Human super-sentient of an uncategorised alternate Earth

Kursis Orpemantus — Galacien council member

Lom — Jonas' implant and ship

Lytpniuph — An Amelerian, veteran of the Nacuerian/Galacien war

Mentoria 'Min' Kendeisa — Veteran of the Nacuerian/Galacien war

Nemulous Handerrel — Galacien citizen and human president of Lorusia

Nicola — Mercenary (Earth [4])
Patrick — Theresa's implant
Queen Victoria — Monarch of the British Empire of the House of Hanover (Earth [3])
Queen Marina — Prior Monarch of the British Empire (Earth [3])
Ruth — Alex's implant
Talmhon — Galacien council enforcer
Theresa Lethbridge — Alex Lethbridge's sister
Vasha Ilsa Nemrod — Ancient human super-sentient
Yosar — Galacien council member
Zara — Human super-sentient of an uncategorised alternate Earth

ABOUT THE AUTHOR

Pete Cruickshank lives in Huddersfield, England with his caring wife and two beautiful daughters. When not working, looking after his family, reading or playing video-games too much, he manages to write.

The Kinsmen series

The Kinsmen Prelude Book 1: Between Gods and Mortals
The Kinsmen Book 2: The Infinite Darkness
The Kinsmen Book 3: Fall of Heaven
The Kinsmen Book 4: The Edge of Reality

If you have any feedback please don't hesitate to contact him at petecruickshank@thekinsmen.co.uk

If you have enjoyed this book please do spread the word or write a quick review on either
www.amazon.co.uk
www.amazon.com
www.goodreads.com

The Kinsmen Website
www.thekinsmen.co.uk